The Gift of the INN

The Gift of the Inn

GOLDEN KEYES PARSONS

WhiteFire
Publishing

This is a work of fiction. All characters and events portrayed in this novel are either fictitious or used fictitiously.

THE GIFT OF THE INN

WhiteFire Publishing
13607 Bedford Rd NE
Cumberland, MD 21502

ISBN: 978-1-939023-88-9 (digital)
          978-1-939023-87-2 (print)

A Note from the Editor

On February 16, 2017, I thought I was going about a normal Thursday. Organizing edits, designing covers, and e-mailing authors. That day, I was working with Golden, assuring her that her first round of edits would be coming from our editor by the following Monday—the same day I was supposed to Skype with Golden and her book club, who had just read one of my books.

But when I got up the next day, it was to a heartbreaking message from another of our authors—the evening before, hours after we'd e-mailed, the beautiful Golden Keyes Parsons had been killed in a tragic automobile accident.

While her family reeled from the sudden loss and celebrated the life and legacy their matriarch had left, we at WhiteFire waited to see what they'd want to do with this last book Golden would ever write...and dedicated ourselves to making it the best it could be for her.

Golden was a woman of deep convictions, breathtaking passion for our Lord, and a heart as big as Texas. We're honored to have worked with her and pray that we produced a book she'd have been proud of. Special thanks go out to her friend and critique partner, Linda LaRoque, who assisted us in revising the manuscript, and to Golden's eldest daughter, Amanda Garcia, who served as the contact for us and her family.

May the light of our Lord shine through Golden's story and the love put into it by her family, friends, and the staff of WhiteFire Publishing. It's our prayer that this book brings the hope of Christmas into your heart.

Cheers,

Roseanna White
Senior Editor

In loving memory of Golden Keyes Parsons

ONE

Christmas Eve, 1944
Colorado Springs, Colorado

Some of my men will come home in a body bag. So, I don't want to hear it. This topic is no longer up for discussion." Quenton's tone reflected his annoyance at the too-familiar argument. Bending his lanky form in front of the mirror atop the ornately carved oak dresser to knot the tie of his uniform, he continued. "My men deserve to be at home on Christmas Eve. They may never spend another Christmas with their families." A mingled expression of passion and sadness flitted across his face as he turned to his wife. "Hitler's evil and he's cunning. The madman actually wants to conquer the whole continent, and who knows what he will set his sights on next. We have to stop him."

Naomi's stomach churned. She didn't have an adequate answer to his argument. Her husband's hazel eyes, which always won her over in a disagreement, held hers in a direct gaze. He was not likely to be sent overseas. The Army Air Corps needed flight instructors to train men for combat, so he was safely stateside for the time being.

"What about *our* family? Every year I hope you'll be at home with us on Christmas Eve. You know how much I need you with me—especially on Christmas Eve." Chewing on the inside of her cheek to keep from crying, she looked up at Quenton.

He traced his thumb along her jawline, as his eyes softened. Naomi patted the scarf tied around her hair. Always rushed, busy, and disheveled, she rarely made the extra effort anymore to look glamorous. With the workload she carried when the inn was full of tourists in town for the holidays, who had time for makeup or hairstyling? A quick brush through her thick brunette hair, which she kept covered with a scarf when she was working, and a swipe of bright red lipstick was the extent of the grooming session each morning. Her eyelashes were still long and thick, so she never bothered with mascara. She brushed a hand over the skirt of her too-tight housedress.

The familiar dread of Christmas Eve washed over her. Peculiar how the anniversary of any traumatic event spun its twenty-four-hour journey tugging at buried memories—memories that popped their unwelcome heads around corners then withdrew into the shadowy crevices of the mind. Certain she was fine one moment, Naomi would find herself gripped the next in a vise of unbidden emotions. Her frazzled nerves bristled with accusatory thoughts—that her husband really didn't *have* to go to the base but simply wanted an escape from her annual Christmas grief.

Quenton put on his cap and took a final look in the mirror. He gathered the coins from the dresser top and dropped them in his pocket. "Tell you what I may be able to do. I'll try to get home before it gets too late. Sergeant Miller's family didn't come in for the holidays. He volunteered to man the office for me."

"Then why not—"

"I said I'll try to get home before it gets too late." Quenton thrust his arms through his jacket. "Wait up for me?" Reaching around her, he picked up his briefcase lying on the bed. "C'mon, walk me to the car." Clasping her hand, he pulled her up beside him.

They made their way quietly down the hall, past their sleeping daughters' bedrooms to the large laundry room adjoining their apartment in the back of the inn. The bottom of the outside door to the parking lot dragged along the faded green linoleum as Quenton pulled it open.

Before zipping up his jacket, he tied a wool scarf around his neck. "Looks like we're in for more snow."

Naomi blinked threatening tears away and joined him at the doorway. She picked a piece of lint off his epaulet with the new oak leaf cluster. "I'm proud of you, Major Lockhart."

"Humph." He jerked his head toward the insignia. "All this means is that I'm headed for a desk job. I'd rather have captain's bars on my shirt and remain a flight instructor than get a promotion. They're moving the younger guys in to train pilots for air combat—captains and first lieutenants— moving us older guys out."

"You're only thirty-nine. And your experience is invaluable." She touched his temple. "You haven't a gray hair, unlike some of us." She smiled and swiped her bangs to the side with her fingertips.

"Comes with being a redhead, I suppose. You'll remember my dad didn't either. His hair was as red as mine the day he died." He moved her scarf back and squinted. "Where? I don't see one gray hair."

"That's because I pluck them out." She stepped back from him and reset the headscarf. "Actually, I wouldn't mind if you got a desk job. It's time, Q."

"I'm not ready." His curt reply cut her off as he pulled on his gloves.

Naomi clung to his arm. "Please get home as soon as you can tonight."

A frown creased his brow. "I already said that I'd try. You'll be fine. You've got the girls and your dad to help with the guests—and Robby and Gracie are just across the street if you need some extra help." He knelt and looked at the gouge in the floor. "Gotta fix that before it gets worse." He stood and moved the door back and forth. "Don't let the girls sleep too late. There's a lot of work to be done with the inn being full."

"I know. But it's vacation for them. We can let them sleep a little later." She shoved a pile of dirty sheets aside with her foot. "We'll get it done. I just want you home for Christmas. No, I need you here with us—around the fireplace and the Christmas tree, with the girls in the morning as they open their gifts." She hugged her arms around her chest. "Go on. It's snowing harder and we're letting cold air in."

He gave her a mock salute. "Yes, ma'am." His smile dissolved. "Come here." He gathered her in his arms. Her heart still skipped a beat when Quenton held her. "Honey, I know this is always a difficult day for you, but…it's been seventeen years, plenty long enough to get on with our lives. After all, "Tis the season to be jolly,' 'Peace and goodwill to men,' and so on." He chucked her beneath her chin.

She hated it when he attempted to cheer her up. "If God meant this to be a season of peace and goodwill to men, I guess we slipped through the cracks somewhere." She felt her eyes start to burn. "I try, Q, I really do. But all of this"—she waved her hand toward their apartment—"the trappings of Christmas, all of the decorations and parties, even the smells, weigh me down. I feel like I go through the season with bricks on my shoulders and chains around my ankles. All I seem to be able to do is put one foot in front of the other. I feel like an empty shell moving through the days until it's over. I'm simply numb." She took his hand and nuzzled it against her cheek.

Quenton sighed and embraced her tightly, holding her as several moments ticked by, both of them silent except for Naomi's sniffling. Then giving her a light kiss, he whispered in her ear, "I love you, Naomi."

"I know. You'd better go on."

He turned and went out the door, picking his way across the slick sidewalk to their Oldsmobile station wagon. Throwing his briefcase across to the passenger side, he started the car and reached underneath the front seat for the ice scraper. He could hardly brush the increasing snowflakes away from one side of the windshield before the other side was covered. After several minutes of scraping and letting the car run, he lifted his gloved hand in a slight wave, got into the car, and inched his way past all the slumbering cars in the lot to the rhythmic whap-whap of the windshield wipers.

Naomi closed the door on the brittle cold and, after clicking on the radio, addressed the Bendix. "Well, time to empty you of your load and put in another one." She pulled tangled sheets from the washing machine and laid them on the folding table. Then added new detergent and began refilling the machine. Steam rose from the tub, giving her an unwanted facial. She lifted the pile of dirty sheets from the floor and stuffed them into the foaming water, taking care not to fill it too full. It was tempting to try to do fewer, fuller loads, but if she did, the sheets wouldn't get clean and would wind themselves into a knotted ball.

The lid banged shut. The chug-a, chug-a, chug-a offered friendly assurance that the work day was underway. Bing Crosby crooned "White Christmas" over the airwaves, keeping rhythm with the churning water. Humming along with the popular tune, Naomi patted the top of the undulating machine, grateful her parents had purchased the Bendix before the war started. The government had suspended manufacture of the machines for the war effort. The work was hard enough, but if they'd had to put sheets and towels through a wringer washer, the task would be backbreaking.

She plucked several clothespins from a cloth bag dangling on the small rope Quenton had crisscrossed in the laundry room and clipped them to the edge of her apron. She pinned the corner of a wet sheet, stretched it tight, anchored the middle edge of the sheet, then on to the end. Getting the sheets dry in the freezing winter was one of the biggest challenges in running the inn. She'd taken to ironing them dry.

She glanced at the ironing board in the corner of the laundry room. It looked as if it were standing at attention awaiting the next batch of sheets. *Not today.*

"Good morning, Mama." Cynthia, their teenaged daughter, stood in the doorway between the laundry room and their bedroom. She stretched her arms in the air then bent over to touch her toes. She tightened the belt on her chenille robe. "Brr. It's cold in here."

"Won't be for long once the washing gets going."

"Did Daddy have to go to the base?"

"Yes. But he promised he'd try to be home early this evening."

"Mama. It's Christmas Eve. Why did he have to go in?" Cynthia folded her arms and leaned against the doorjamb. "I wanted us to be together today."

"I know. I did too." Naomi ushered her daughter back into the bedroom and closed the door to the laundry room. "C'mon, Christmas Eve or not, we have work to do. May as well get it done early. Maybe Daddy will be home by suppertime."

Two

As darkness increased so did the snow. Naomi struck a match and lit the red candles nestled among branches of fresh cedar on the mantel. A familiar muffled calm crept into the apartment on downy wings.

She walked to the door and stared through the frosted window panes hoping to see the headlights of their car poking through the storm and into the parking lot. No cars at all on the road. She could hardly see the lights in the restaurant across the road from their inn. With her nail, she scratched a zigzag in the ice crystals forming delicate frosty etchings on the inside corners of the glass. She pulled her sweater from the coat rack and snuggled into it. The temperature must be below zero.

Splaying her hands in front of her, she stared at them as if they belonged to another. Red and chafed, her once smooth skin showed the effects of constant immersion in water, scrubbing floors, and doing laundry. At least all the chores were done for the day. She went into the kitchen to get some lotion and rubbed it into her palms, on the backs of her hands, and on her elbows. The mild almond aroma wafted up to her nose.

She opened the icebox and refitted the cover on the layered red and green Jell-O salad for the open house tomorrow evening. Yeast rolls sat on top of the stove, rising on schedule. She would cut up some apples and oranges for the buffet, heat green beans and sweet potatoes to go with the turkey and dressing, and that would have to do. She wished she could have gotten a ham, but she didn't have the ration cards. Christmas cookies and a fruit cake someone had given them would round out the menu. Not exactly the extravagant spread they'd enjoyed before the war, but everyone understood these days.

Opening a drawer, she picked out a spoon and stirred the last of the cocoa and sugar mixture into the hot milk simmering on the gas stove. She dipped the spoon into the smooth liquid and tasted it. Needed to be sweeter. She stared at the tin canister holding the precious rationed sugar. It was Christmas Eve. Splurge justified.

Measuring out another tablespoon, she swirled it into the mixture until it dissolved. Then she poured the steaming cocoa into a Santa Claus mug that winked a painted eye at her, went into the living room, and sat down to scrutinize the Christmas tree—alone.

Strips of shiny silver reflected a rainbow of colors from the multicolored lights on the tree. The girls always had fun tossing the icicles onto the prickly branches, giggling and racing to finish the task, but Naomi wanted the decorations to hang straight. Rather than fuss at them, she simply waited for her daughters to go to bed to rearrange the shiny threads to her own satisfaction.

The city had plowed the roads earlier in the day, but the evening snowfall had covered them again. *Come on, Quenton. Get home before you get snowed in at the base. Ah. Nice.* She set her cocoa on the coffee table and walked down the hall to check on the girls. The dim light spilled into Cynthia's room through the slit in the open door. Elise and Myrna, the six- and ten-year-olds who ordinarily slept in the bunks in the small bedroom across the hall, had crawled into their older sister's bed.

"I see you have company in your bed tonight, Cynthia."

The teenager rose from her vanity chair, holding her finger to her lips. "Shh. They just went to sleep." She pulled the quilt over the two sleeping girls. "I don't mind just for tonight."

Naomi stepped into the room and whispered, "I've hot chocolate on the stove if you'd like some. Reward for a hard day's work."

"Marshmallows too?"

"Of course."

"Are there any of those Christmas tree sugar cookies left?" Cynthia smiled and ran a brush through her long auburn curls. Then she pulled her hair back into a low pony tail and clipped a tortoise shell barrette around it.

"Sure, plenty."

"Be right there. I need to get these packages out of my closet. I hid them from the girls and almost forgot about them."

Naomi chuckled. "I've done that before, forgotten where I hid them, and then found them a month later. I'll get the stockings." She walked across the hall to her bedroom.

Opening the trunk at the foot of their bed, Naomi dug underneath the blankets and removed a cardboard box holding the precious velvet Christmas stockings her mother had labored over year after year at the arrival of each new member of the family. She clutched the box to her chest and let the lid of the trunk close with a thud. As she returned down the hall to the living room, the lights flickered. Once, twice…darkness.

"Arrgh." Pinned to the spot, Naomi stared at the light fixture in the hall, willing it to spring back to life, but it remained dark. She sighed and shifted the box, waiting for her eyes to adjust to the gloom. *Not tonight. Please, not tonight.* Her hands trembled the way they always did during a power outage.

Especially when it was snowing. *Just like that Christmas Eve.* She leaned against the wall. *Breathe in. Breathe out. One…inhale. Two…exhale. Three… inhale.* This was silly. Her emotions didn't need to skyrocket every time the lights went out. It was one of the hazards of living in the mountains. She grew up here. She should be used to it after all these years. But she wasn't— she didn't know if she ever would be.

Naomi felt her way into the living room and set the box on the sofa. The candles on the mantel flickered dimly. "Ouch! Shoot!" She groaned and rubbed the shin she'd hit on the corner of the coffee table. Limping into the kitchen, she went to the Hoosier cabinet and pulled down a glass kerosene lamp, sitting amongst her collection of old lanterns, from its perch on top of the cupboard. Thank goodness Quenton kept them filled and ready to be used at a moment's notice. She opened the cabinet door and found the match box. Fumbling with the carton, she broke the first match she tried but managed to coax a second to spark into a small flame. Her hands were barely shaking now. *Much better.* She lit the lamp and placed it on the corner of the cabinet. A soft glow spread through the small kitchen. She trailed her finger along the edge of the lamp's flue.

It was dirty. *Thought I washed that after our last blackout.* She made a mental note to do so when the lights came back on. Then she lit the brass lantern and carried it into the living room. *I might as well enjoy this until Quenton gets home. There's nothing I can do about it. And we're in no danger. No danger at all.*

She stoked the fire. "Keep the apartment warm with the fireplace," Quenton had admonished her that morning. "Radiator's not working right. I'll get it fixed right after Christmas."

She lifted a large round of oak from the copper tub and put on the back of the grate. "That should last for a while." The flames licked around the logs and provided light for the room as well as warmth.

Naomi opened the box she'd left on the sofa and unwrapped the stockings. All six of them had their names sewn in sequins on the cuffs—Quenton, Naomi, Cynthia, Myrna, Elise—and Julia. Each stocking was a different jewel-toned color—Quenton's a forest green, hers a rich cherry red, Cynthia's a royal blue, Myrna's gold, Elise's deep pink—and Julia's royal purple.

A large, hand-sewn sequined Christmas tree sparkled on the toe of each one, plus a wreath and a candle decorated the middle. Some of them had snowmen. In addition, her mother had personalized them with handmade emblems or figures to designate each family member's personal interests. Quenton's, of course, had an airplane and pilot's wings. Sequined musical notes twinkled on Naomi's for her interest in music—piano—although she didn't play much anymore. The piano she played as a child sat in their dining room, but it simply served as a piece of furniture these days, holding family pictures on its shiny polished top. The girls' stockings sported dolls and angels and school pennants, and Elise's had a dog for the puppy she got for Christmas two years ago.

Naomi stopped at Julia's stocking and traced her finger along the name on the cuff. Only the tree, a wreath, and a candle adorned this stocking. Naomi didn't know what Julia's interests were. Was she musical? Did she love sports? Perhaps she was a cheerleader like Cynthia. If she was still…

The night bristled with the cold. And her heart bristled with the still-raw wound of a missing child. Naomi had almost reconciled herself to the fact they would never find their oldest daughter—almost. But somewhere deep in her soul, she had to admit a faint glimmer of hope still flickered. Although if she were honest with herself, that glimmer grew fainter with each passing season. And Christmas was the turning point every year.

Julia would be eighteen now. A young woman. They'd never found a trace of their child, but she could not bear to think that the unspeakable had happened. It was a thought she could never entertain. Julia was still alive. Even if they never found her. She knew in her mother's heart of hearts that their child still lived.

"Everything looks pretty." Cynthia came into the room. "This is really kind of swell, don't you think? Looks…I don't know…magical or something without the lights." She walked toward the kitchen. "Did you get the marshmallows out?"

"Oh, sweet pea, I forgot. They're in the pantry. A brand-new bag."

"I'll find them." Her daughter returned to the living room with a marshmallow floating atop the hot chocolate. Her cup was in the shape of an angel whose gold wings formed the handle. She went to the window and looked out. "Daddy's late. We're getting lots of snow tonight, huh?"

"Yes, 'fraid so. Would you please hang the stockings for me? I need to go check on Grandpa and our guests."

"Sure thing." Cynthia inspected her stocking in the candlelight. "My Christmas tree is looking pretty ragged. Some of the ornaments are coming unstitched." She cocked her head. "I suppose you will have to do it now that Grandma's gone?"

"I guess so. Not so sure I can measure up to her creativity, but surely I can manage re-stitching a few sequins here and there."

"I can help." Cynthia laid all of the stockings out on the sofa. "It's hard to tell in this dim light, but it looks like all of them could use some refreshing." She picked up the purple one. "Except Julia's. Hers hasn't been tossed around that much, I guess."

Thrum-thrum. The tiny heart-flutter every time she heard Julia's name let Naomi know it had not forgotten.

Naomi picked up one of the lanterns and went to the door to the parking lot. She opened it just enough to look for headlights coming down the street. Not that she could see a thing. The candles flickered as the cold air swept into the apartment. She closed the door quickly.

"I'm going to go check on Grandpa." She turned and went back through the kitchen to the private little suite in the rear. He'd gone to bed shortly after they'd trimmed the tree, saying the sooner they went to sleep, the sooner Santa would come.

He'd looked tired and seemed at loose ends without her mother. She knocked softly and listened. She pushed the door open, grimacing at the squeaky hinge. Her father was snoring softly, mouth open, in his easy chair in front of the fire. Glenn Miller's "String of Pearls" played too loudly on the radio. She tiptoed past him, clicked the radio off, and carefully removed his book and glasses out of his hands. She would come back later to see if he'd gotten into bed. The door creaked again as Naomi pulled it shut.

Returning to their own apartment, she passed Cynthia, who was busy hanging the stockings, and went to the foyer.

She glanced out the window of the front door and noted the streetlamps on their side of the street were off, but they were still burning across the street, as were the lights in the restaurant. The heavy weight of the snow must have broken a power line on their side.

Every time a snowstorm descended from the mountains, Naomi wondered whether they had made the right decision to take over the inn in Colorado Springs from her parents, Ruth and Clarence Huddleston, when Quenton might be sent overseas any day. Snow had to be shoveled; logs cut for the fireplaces; broken pipes patched; the roof repaired; gardening done. Sometimes it seemed overwhelming even with Quenton there. But the girls loved their school and had made friends. At first she'd felt she could manage even if Quenton had to leave. Now she wasn't as confident. The war had rumbled on for four years. Surely it would end soon and she would never have to find out if she could run it by herself.

THREE

Winter 1942

My parents have hinted for years they wanted us to take over the inn, Quenton. This may be the answer to our prayers. We need the extra income, and we'll have living quarters as well. I could run it while you're stationed at Peterson Field. Besides that, Mom and Dad need our help now that they're getting older. We're going to end up having to run the place anyway, even if temporarily. We may as well invest in it, and—"

"Update it and run it the way we've always thought it should be run?" Quenton grinned and pulled her down beside him on the couch. It was one of the few pieces of furniture in their living room.

Naomi snuggled up against him. "You know it's a good idea. I'm tired of living in officer's housing. I'm ready for a place of our own. It's not like it was when it was still a boardinghouse. We won't have to serve meals. We won't have to rent out rooms unless we want to. I'd rather run an inn than go back to nursing." A plane buzzed overhead as it took off from the Fort Dix, New Jersey landing strip. "And you know I don't particularly care for the East Coast. I'd like to get back to the mountains where I grew up."

"Do you think you can adjust to living there—at the inn, I mean?" He rubbed the rust-colored stubble on his chin he always let grow on his days off.

"I grew up there."

"I know, but you don't think it would be too much for you to keep up? I know you don't want to live on base, but that's a lot of cleaning and housekeeping. And what about…you know. Won't there be too many painful memories around every corner?" Quenton put his arm around her.

"I can handle it. We may have to hire a housekeeper or two, but the girls are old enough to help, and…" She laid her head on his shoulder. "You can help in the evenings."

"With cleaning?"

"No, silly, I was thinking about things like cutting firewood and shoveling snow and light maintenance. You know, fixing a doorknob here and there."

"Light maintenance can turn into heavy maintenance pretty quickly—plumbing, roof repairing."

"We'd have to call a repairman for those kinds of things anyway, but I think we could manage. And as for being able to live in the inn after losing Julia, I don't know. Somehow it seems it may be comforting to be where we last had her. I think I've gotten over the trauma…for the most part."

"Let me think about it." Quenton got up and stretched. "What's for supper?"

It was late spring when Quenton secured a transfer and they took over the Golden Aspen Inn. Red geraniums in flower boxes at each window added color to the faded wood on the house. A terraced flowerbed in front teemed with pansies, cosmos, daisies, columbine, and delphiniums. The wooden steps, surrounded by the colorful flowers, leading to the wraparound porch, needed repair. Guests had to park down on the street, then maneuver the steep steps juggling their luggage. That would have to be remedied— probably an entrance around back from the side street, or a lot.

The first few months were busy, but the weather in Colorado Springs was perfect—warm, pleasant days, and cool, refreshing nights. The scent of the pine trees hovered in the air year round. After Quenton got home in the evenings from the base, they had a couple hours of daylight to work before the sun dipped behind the mountains. Professional painters coated the exterior of the inn a dusky blue and the shutters and railing on the wraparound porch and balcony a sparkling white. Naomi wanted to leave the original dark wood on the beautifully carved front double doors. She loved the contrast of the dark stain with the white trim and the prisms of color the sun produced flashing through the leaded glass in the doors into the foyer. The interior received new coats of paint as well. They stayed open as they worked, closing one suite at a time for renovations.

Quenton discovered the wood rotten in the steps, so a carpenter was contracted to install new ones. Then they put a small gravel parking lot and entrance to the side where guests could pull in easier. That necessitated building steps on the side of the porch. It seemed each new task required half a dozen smaller ones. But they eventually were able to set things in order.

When the weather wasn't too cool, the Lockharts spent evenings on the porch, lounging in the wicker rockers and gliding in the porch swing Naomi's parents had installed years ago. Naomi never grew weary of sitting with her husband in the crisp evening air, listening to the laughter and chatter of their daughters, gazing at the towering peaks of the snow-covered Rocky Mountains that lay to the west of the inn. The tat-tat-tat of woodpeckers and the screeches of blue jays echoed through the trees in the mornings when Naomi would bundle up in a quilt and take her coffee to the porch to read the newspaper. Only in the most inclement weather would she abandon her early morning ritual. It was a place her heart felt at peace.

Cynthia made friends right away with a handsome young man, Robby, from the Mexican restaurant across the street, Tres Hermanos, which his family owned. He seemed to be a nice enough kid, but Naomi wasn't about to encourage much togetherness there. Cynthia was too young to get involved with a serious boyfriend. Naomi had to admit, however, he was as cute as he could be, with a broad smile that creased his face constantly. Nice manners and courteous. Strong and tanned from skiing. *Gotta keep an eye on that boy.*

More recently, she'd befriended their new waitress, Gracie, who didn't seem to be much older than Cynthia but was pregnant. Her husband had been sent overseas. That was all they knew about the beautiful young woman. She didn't say much about her past or family except that she was from San Antonio, Texas and wasn't used to cold weather. On occasion, Naomi hired her by the hour to help with the laundry or housekeeping.

Myrna and Elise were content with each other's company. The whole family worked hard from sunup to sundown, but it was fun—for a season. Tourists came and went during the summer. When it began to snow in October, business slacked off, but the moment the winter holidays began at Thanksgiving, they were swamped. With Quenton's job at the base requiring more and more of his time, she hired Robby part-time to cut and stack firewood. Snow at night meant sidewalks to be shoveled the next morning. She could handle that herself if the girls would service the rooms. Sometimes the work overwhelmed her, and she didn't know if she could continue—especially at Christmas.

Four

March 1944
San Antonio, Texas

Surrounded by stacks of boxes in the dusty attic of the servants' quarters at her parents' large hacienda in San Antonio, Texas, Gracie wiped the perspiration from her forehead. Sweltering, humid weather already held the semi-tropical city in its grasp. She reclipped her shoulder-length page boy out of her eyes with a marquis-studded barrette. A black oscillating fan brought periodic relief as it rotated back and forth. High school graduation was around the corner, but that wasn't what occupied Gracie's thoughts.

If she didn't find what she was looking for here in the attic, she didn't know where else to look. Perhaps her mother's obsession for order would prove to be a blessing in this instance. Ordinarily the penchant for organizing everything to the "nth" degree annoyed Gracie, but now she had to admit the very thing that so irritated her might lead to the hidden treasure she sought. Surely the neatly marked boxes by date would produce the information she suspected was somewhere on their estate.

For as long as she could remember, people had commented that she looked nothing like her parents. "Oh my, goodness. She certainly doesn't look like you, Esperanza."

"Where'd she get those green eyes and red hair?"

"It's not red, it's mahogany, and it comes from the Castilian Spanish on my mother's side of the family," her mother would answer.

"That skin is like peaches and cream. Did she crawl out from under a woodpile when Jorge wasn't looking?" And they would slap their knees and laugh.

It wasn't funny to Gracie. Through the years the comments about her different appearance made her feel isolated and set apart from the rest of the family. The explanation was always the same. "It's the Castilian Spanish…." Then her mother would change the subject. Gracie was the oldest of three children—a sister two years younger than she and a brother three years younger than that. Both of them had dark brown hair and brown eyes and were short of stature and small boned. She was tall and large boned.

Although the comments irritated her, Gracie brushed them off and didn't really take them seriously in her younger years. Not until the day she took a pitcher of iced tea to her *abuela*'s quarters. The open windows allowed the air to circulate, and brilliant magenta oleander blossoms lilted in the gentle breeze. The elderly woman suffered from loss of memory but retained her stature as the matriarch of the family. Esperanza sat in a large rocking chair beside her mother's bed and fanned herself with a black lace fan. A servant stood behind her grandmother, stirring the air with a large palm frond.

"I thought you might like some iced tea, Abuela." Gracie set the tray of tea and *biscochitos* on a small table beside the bed and nodded to the servant to pour the tea.

"Thank you, dear." The elderly woman's voice had grown thin and shaky.

She stared at Gracie. "What a beautiful young lady." She took Gracie's hand. "Is she the child you and Jorge adopted?"

Esperanza snapped her fan shut and stood, shoving the tray of cookies toward her mother. "Why, Mamacita, it's Gracie. What in the world are you talking about? Would you like one of these delicious little biscochitos? Rosa made them because she knows you love them."

Gracie's world spun into another dimension that day. She sat in her grandmother's room listening but not really hearing the chitchat in Spanish. Conversation between the mirror images of the two older women lobbed back and forth like well-played tennis volleys. All the remarks through the years about her different appearance clicked into place. Adopted. She must be adopted.

Presently, Esperanza rose. She kissed the bronze skin of her mother's forehead. "You rest now, Mamacita. I'll see you later this evening at supper." She turned to the servant. "Take the tray down to the kitchen, please."

"Sí, señora."

Gracie looked at the contrast of her white skin against the olive tone of her mother's as Esperanza took hold of her arm and walked her out onto the veranda. How could she have been so blind all these years? It was blatantly obvious to her now.

As they walked through the courtyard to the main quarters, Gracie stepped in front of Esperanza and turned toward her. "Mama. Stop." She searched her mother's dark eyes. "I am adopted? Why have you lied to me all these years?"

"What are you talking about? You are not adopted. You are my firstborn child."

"But Abuela. She said—"

"Pfft!" Esperanza flicked her fan open and fluttered it back and forth.

"Mama is an old woman who has lost her memory. Don't pay any attention to her. She was just confused."

"Confused about what? Why would she say that? We don't even know anyone who has been adopted, do we?"

"Not that I know of. And you are not adopted. I am insulted you would think that. You are Graciela Esperanza Gonzales, our firstborn, much loved daughter. Why would we lie to you about such a thing?" Esperanza's voice rose and her eyes flashed a warning. She pointed a jeweled finger in her daughter's face. "Do not bring this up to your father. It would break his heart. We will not discuss this ever again. Do you understand?" Her voice trembled as did her hands, flicking her fan open and shut, open and shut.

"Tell me the truth, Mama. I deserve to know the truth. Why are you lying to me?"

Gracie's head snapped to the side before she even realized Esperanza had raised her hand. She stared at her mother and touched her smarting cheek with the tips of her fingers. Tears sprang to her eyes. "M…Mama…" She mouthed the word but no sound came out.

Esperanza stepped toward Gracie and took hold of her wrist. Through clenched teeth she spoke—low, soft, and menacing. "We have given you everything you could ever want, young lady. Don't you ever question me about this again, and never accuse me again of lying. Never!" She spun on her heel and left Gracie blinking at the outburst. Something Gracie saw in her mother's eyes frightened her. Something dark.

Gracie never spoke of it again. But neither did she forget it, and she vowed one day she would search out the truth.

Now here she was searching for that truth. She pushed aside the more recently dated boxes and formed a little aisle as she worked her way to the back wall. Most of the boxes were labeled by the year. Some were labeled by subject matter. She looked for anything with her name or "Family" or the year of her birth, 1926. Spotting a stack of boxes against the wall labeled "Children's Records" and "Keepsakes," she pulled the top one down. She sat it on the floor and tore off the brittle tape. Dolls and stuffed animals.

The next box held a filing system of doctor's visits, vaccination records, report cards, school papers, birth certificates, and a passport her parents had secured for her when they took a trip to Spain the year she turned twelve. Her heart thudded as she yanked the birth certificate folder from its musty resting place and rifled through it.

Serafina Maria Gonzales, born June 19, 1928, signed by Dr. Silverio Sandoval. Jorge Ramon Gonzales, Jr. named after their father, born May 12, 1929. Her brother's certificate was also signed by Dr. Sandoval, and both of her siblings were born at their residence. She ran her fingers through the papers. Where was her birth certificate?

She went back through the folder but knew with an increasing sense of dread that she wouldn't find it. She found vaccination records for herself, school papers scrawled with houses with blue skies and bright smiley suns that floated at the top of the manila paper, but no birth certificate. It was as if she simply suddenly appeared with no paper trail. If she wasn't really Gracie Gonzales, who was she and where had she come from?

A raggedy stuffed dog of soft chenille her grandmother had made for her hung limply over the edge of the box labeled "Keepsakes." One button eye dangled at the end of a loop of thread. She remembered that doggie so well. She'd slept with it every night until she started school. Gracie tugged on the forgotten friend, but it refused to come out of the box. Something had wrapped itself around the hind legs. Gracie dug to the bottom of the box and pulled out a cloth bag whose strap proved to be the culprit.

Extracting both items, she unraveled the strap of the gray bag from the legs of the dog. She sniffed the stuffed animal, once pink but now a barely blush color. Smelled the same. Smiling, she repacked the dog in the box. Gracie opened the flap of the gray bag with faded red piping around. She didn't remember ever seeing the bag.

Inside were old, worn diapers, diaper pins, and a little bunting-in-a-bag outfit. She felt along the inside and detected something flat and hard like a large folder or envelope. There was a side pocket, but the object seemed to be in the lining of the bag. She sat cross-legged, put the bag in her lap, and pulled on the stitching along the inside edge. It gave way easily, and some of the fabric tore. Gracie gasped and looked over her shoulder. *I'm just looking through my childhood memories. Nothing wrong with that, right?*

She maneuvered a large envelope out of the lining. There was something stiff inside. Raising the flap, she pulled out a piece of cardboard—rather two pieces of cardboard taped together with something in the middle. She released the tape and extracted a photograph of a smiling baby, who appeared to be around nine or ten months old, sitting on a blanket with a Christmas tree in the background. A Christmas stocking with the name *Julia* sewn on the cuff laid across her lap. In the bottom right hand corner of the picture glinted gold script writing. *William Wyler, Photographer, Colorado Springs, Colorado.*

Gracie could not quit staring at the baby with the laughing face—the baby whose face was the same one she had seen in picture after picture in the Gonzales' family albums. Her own face laughed at her from the photograph.

FIVE

Christmas Eve, 1944

The toddler's wide smile, forever etched in Naomi's mind, beamed at her from the faded, gold-framed picture lying in the bottom of the box. Hidden away, the velvet stockings protected the precious memento all year long. She had other pictures of Julia, which she kept in photo albums, but this Christmas photo made an appearance only once a year. The child's stocking lay across the laughing baby's lap, her name visible on the cuff.

She had kept several different shots of that photo session in an album, but this one was her favorite. Julia had laughed out loud at two months old and seemed to have an ever-present smile on her face. She'd awakened happy every morning and went to bed happy. Naomi wiped the dust from the picture with the edge of her apron and set it on the end of the mantel above where Julia's stocking hung. Naomi hesitated and sat down in the recliner across from her second daughter.

"Do you still miss her?" Cynthia pulled her legs up on the couch and covered them with an afghan her grandmother had crocheted for her twelfth birthday.

"I…I guess the wound created in a mother's heart when a child goes missing never totally heals." She touched her heart as she spoke and blinked back the tears gathering in her eyes. "The raw pain and shock have diminished with the passing of time, but the hurt is still there…aroused by simply a word, or a gesture, or…" She looked toward the mantel and flicked a tear aside.

"Or a picture…or a stocking?" Cynthia set her cup of hot chocolate on the coffee table and reclipped the barrette around her hair.

"Yes, a picture." Naomi moved a coaster underneath the cup and wiped her eyes with a napkin.

"So why do you torture yourself every year by hanging the stocking and putting the Christmas picture on the mantel? If it makes you so sad, why do it?" The girl stared at the picture of her older sister who would forever remain an infant.

Naomi touched her daughter's arm. "Does it bother you?"

Cynthia shrugged. "Not really. What bothers me is for you to always be sad on Christmas. It seems every year from the moment that picture goes up, the mood goes down. I want us to have a happy Christmas without the cloud of Julia hanging over us. I just wish we were enough for you." She stood and folded the afghan, draping it on the back of the couch.

Naomi jumped to her feet and caught Cynthia by the arm, pulling her into an embrace. "Oh, sweet pea. You are, you are. You are more than enough. Please don't think you aren't."

Cynthia wrapped her arms around her mother's waist and laid her head on her shoulder. "I'm sorry, Mama. It just seems sometimes like…I don't know…like you spend more time at Christmas crying about Julia than you do sharing the good things with us."

Naomi's heart clenched as she held Cynthia at arm's length and searched her eyes. "You're right. Please forgive me for when I've…when I've made you feel shoved aside." She brushed a curly auburn tendril from Cynthia's forehead.

"It's okay." Cynthia pulled away from her mother and looked at the empty boxes waiting to be put in the store room. "Where's the nativity?"

Naomi took out a handkerchief and blew her nose. "Still in the box, I guess."

"Don't you want to put it up? May I?"

"Sure. If you want to." Naomi opened a small box marked "Manger Scene" and unwrapped a stable made of cardboard painted to look like wood, and tiny, carved ivory figures—Mary, Joseph, wise men, shepherds, animals, and the Baby Jesus in a manger. She set them out on the coffee table. "Put them wherever you'd like."

"On the mantel?"

"You'll need to move the candles." Naomi gathered the newspaper wrapping and stuffed it back into the box.

"How about we put the candles on the coffee table? I think the manger scene would be pretty with the cedar boughs around it."

"That's fine." Naomi picked up the empty boxes and started through the kitchen. "Get that silver tray out of the buffet to put the candles on. Be careful moving them while they are lighted. Why don't you leave a couple on the mantel while the lights are still out?" She set the boxes down on the kitchen table and picked up a flashlight. "I'm going to wait until the lights come back on to put these boxes up. I need to go check on our guests."

Cynthia stood back and observed her arrangement. "See? Doesn't this look nice?" She turned to her mother. "Do you think Daddy will be home soon?"

"I hope so, sweet pea."

Cynthia took her cup. "I'm going to get some more hot chocolate and wait for him. Do you want me to help you check on our guests?"

"No, thanks. I'll do it," Naomi said over her shoulder as she walked toward the foyer, the flashlight providing a faint beam in front of her feet. "I won't be long."

She set the light on the large dark wooden bar they had salvaged from an old saloon to use as their check-in counter. The carved wood fit the Victorian décor of the inn and had proven to be quite a conversation piece for guests, especially if they were interested in antiques.

Fumbling through stacks of paper, she finally found the guest register. She knew who was in which of the four main rooms because she had made the reservations and checked them in. But Quenton had dealt with the young couple in the turret, the fifth room. And she couldn't remember their names. They'd called at the last minute. Naomi was still miffed at Quenton for relenting and giving the young couple the room. They very rarely rented it out, and certainly not at Christmastime. Too many memories. They offered the excuse that it was too difficult to heat. But Quenton said the couple was desperate for a getaway before the young husband was shipped overseas. He said he didn't know they had a baby when he rented the room.

Naomi started up the creaky wooden steps of the winding staircase. She gripped the banister as she trudged upward, the dull pain in her shin reminding her of the collision with the coffee table. The wood on the banister felt slick. She needed to tell Cynthia not to use so much lemon oil. She wiped her hand on her apron and straightened a bough of cedar that was hanging crooked.

Topping the landing, she went to the credenza against the wall and lit a pair of antique milk glass oil lamps. She loved those lamps. They had been wedding gifts to her parents when they married in the late 1890s.

She probably should keep them in the safety of their apartment, but they fit the décor up here so well. And she wanted to keep the upstairs just like it was when her parents had run the inn. Maybe someday she would do some redecorating…someday.

The soft light reflected off the dark wood of the landing area, illuminating her way to the first room. She knocked on the door to the Victorian corner room on the right-hand side of the credenza where the elderly Thomases had stayed every Christmas for the last twenty years. They had been boarders in the inn that fateful Christmas Eve. They were almost like family. The elderly couple loved the view of both the mountains to the side and then the activity in the street from the front window. "Mr. Thomas? Are you all okay?"

Mr. Thomas flung the door open, holding one of the kerosene lanterns the Lockharts made sure were in every room for occasions such as this. His bright smile and white beard always reminded Naomi of Santa Claus.

"Yes, we are fine. Won't you come in? We had just heated water on the hot plate when the electricity went out. Come and join us for a cup of tea?"

Naomi shook her head but stepped into the room and closed the door. A fire crackled brightly in the fireplace, and one lone candle shimmered on a small wicker desk. "I see you have your fire going. The radiators aren't working all that well, so keep it burning through the night if you can." She glanced at the firewood rack, in which logs had been stacked. "You have plenty of wood. What about candles?"

"You always have plenty stocked in the desk for us, just like your parents did. You know they always treated us well whenever we came." He indicated the wicker desk. "We just kind of like it dim…and romantic." He chuckled and puffed on his pipe.

Mrs. Thomas smiled at Naomi from the wicker rocker beside the fire. She struggled to get up. "Come in. Come in. Please sit and visit a spell."

Her white bun, loosely wound on top of her head, bounced as she walked toward Naomi. She touched her on the arm, and Naomi noticed that the elderly woman had developed a tremor as her head bobbed slightly.

"Thank you, but I need to check on my other guests. Do you need anything? Hopefully this blackout won't last long." She nodded toward the front window. "The lights are on across the street, so it can't be too bad."

Mr. Thomas shook his head. "Don't need a thing."

Mrs. Thomas shuffled back toward the rocker. "I have some fudge for you—I saved my sugar rations for months so I could make enough of it. I know how Captain Lockhart loves it. I was going to give it to you tomorrow, but since you are here now..." She held out a box wrapped in aluminum foil and tied with a big red bow.

Naomi took the box that held the Thomases' annual gift to her family. "Oh, it's heavy. Thank you. Quenton and the girls always look forward to your fudge." She ran her hand over the wrapping. "Where did you get enough foil to wrap this? The girls and I have been saving every bit we can find and rolling it into a ball to sell."

"Oh, I have my ways." Mrs. Thomas chuckled. "My neighbors and I trade our ration cards. They know I like to wrap my fudge in foil, so they save those cards for me." She tapped the top of the box. "There's the usual fudge, and I put a batch of toffee from a new recipe I found this year. I think you will enjoy it too."

"I know we will. Oh—and it's *Major* Lockhart now."

Mr. Thomas beamed as if he'd heard good news about his own son. "Splendid. He deserves it. Glad to hear it." He clapped Naomi on the shoulder as he repeated, "Splendid."

"Roy, don't beat the girl to death." She eased herself back into the rocking chair and covered her legs with a quilt.

Naomi moved toward the door. "Well, keep warm tonight. Remember, you're on your own for breakfast in the morning, but don't forget the open house tomorrow evening from four o'clock to six. Merry Christmas."

"Say, I noticed that the..." Mr. Thomas stepped out in the hall with Naomi and nodded toward the end room. "That you all have rented out the turret room this year."

She sighed. "Quenton felt sorry for the young couple. He's being sent overseas next week. New baby."

"And that was all right with you?"

Naomi set the box of fudge on the credenza. She looked into the wrinkled, kind eyes of the old man. "Not really. But it's Christmas and..." One of those telltale clutches in her throat gripped Naomi, and she had to stop and swallow before she could continue. "I'm fine...really. Merry Christmas."

Mr. Thomas smiled and patted her on her shoulder. "Merry Christmas, dear one. You know this is the season of hope." He smiled and put his pipe in his mouth. "Yes, indeed, the season of hope."

Six

Naomi looked at the box of fudge on the credenza as Mr. Thomas returned to his room and closed the door. She wondered how much longer Mrs. Thomas would be able to stand at the stove and cook batches and batches of the chocolate treat for family and friends at Christmastime.

The Rocky Mountain room on the other side of the credenza was next. It was a small suite with two bedrooms and an efficiency kitchen. A couple and their two grown children had rented the suite for the holidays to be with their daughter, who was in nursing training at Camp Carson.

She listened for a minute at the door and heard gales of laughter. Smiling, she knocked once. The laughter and stomping of feet continued. She knocked again, and the son, a college senior, answered the door, out of breath.

"Hello, Mrs. Lockhart." He bent over with his hands on his knees. "We were...I was..." He threw back his head and laughed again. "We were showing our parents how to do the swing." He stepped back. "Come on in."

Naomi stepped into the rustic room decorated like a mountain cabin. Deer and elk trophies lined the walls. The rough log furniture had been pushed back against the edge of the room, and a bear rug lay rolled up in the corner. They too had a fire blazing in the stone fireplace. "Without the radio?"

"Well, Dad is trumpeting 'In the Mood' for us."

She looked at the balding Mr. Garrison as he sheepishly pursed his lips and emitted a pretty good imitation of a horn. Naomi chuckled. "I see."

Mrs. Garrison straightened her plaid wool skirt. "Were we disturbing you? I'm afraid we were getting a little loud. I told Natalie to tone it down." She glared at her daughter.

"No, not at all. These walls are pretty well insulated. I just wanted to check and see if you needed anything."

Natalie put her arm around her mother. "I don't think so. Only instruction on how to do the flip-over in the dance."

"I told you girls not to try it with each other. You need one of us for that." Mr. Garrison indicated his son and then went to his wife's side. "We probably need to start settling down for the night. Do you have any idea how long the electricity will be out?"

"We never know. It could come back on at any minute, or it could be off all night. You should be fine with the lanterns and fireplace." She glanced around the room and backed out of the door. "Well, I'll leave you to your dance class." She smiled. "Merry Christmas. Don't forget—open house tomorrow evening at four o'clock."

"Merry Christmas to you. We'll be there." Mrs. Garrison watched Naomi walk out to the landing before closing the door.

A muffled baby's cry from the turret room startled Naomi. She backed into the credenza, the hardware on the front poking her in her backside. The glass chimney on the lantern rattled as her hand trembled. She set the lantern down and moved to the side, sinking to the floor, hugging her knees to her chest. The familiar roaring in her ears drowned out any other sounds. She covered her ears and rocked back and forth, waiting for the din to cease. *Please, not again. Not tonight.* She held her breath. Almost as if guided by an unseen hand, she turned her head and watched as the door to the end room slowly creaked opened.

Younger versions of herself and Quenton exited, quietly closing the door behind them. The baby no longer cried. Quenton stared at her, but seemed to look right through her.

Naomi closed her eyes and shook her head. As she reopened her eyes, the couple started down the stairs.

She jumped from her hiding place. "Wait! Don't go! Don't leave your baby alone in that room!" A blue haze hovered in the air like a sticky cobweb. She reached her hand toward the couple. A sob escaped from her throat. "Please, don't…"

The younger Naomi turned and took two steps back toward their room. She was wearing the smoky purple, drop-waist dress that her mother had made for her for the annual Christmas party. The jersey fabric hugged her then-slim frame and flared at the bottom in full gores. She carried a fox stole and a purple beaded bag.

Quenton caught her by the arm. "Julia's asleep. She'll be fine."

Young Naomi hesitated with her hand on the balustrade for just a moment—a quivering moment that forever connected the past and the future—then followed him down the stairs. Somebody was playing Christmas carols on the piano in the parlor. Off-key voices joined in. "Deck the halls with boughs of holly, fa-la-la-la…"

Naomi felt ill, like she needed to vomit. Sagging to the floor, she hugged her legs and put her head down on her knees. She had to stop these visions. With her eyes squeezed shut, she drew in a deep breath, then another. The world wasn't spinning…perhaps the flashback had stopped. She pulled herself up, holding on to the edge of the credenza, and hurried to the stairs. The couple was gone, but the singing of Christmas carols continued. She inched down the steps on legs that had turned to water and barely held her up. The banister was festooned with cedar boughs and red bows.

She stopped halfway down and peered through the blue haze out the front windows. The wind howled around the eaves of the house, and the snow seemed to be blowing almost horizontally. A blizzard, just like the night Julia disappeared. Was it then or now? She honestly couldn't tell. Inside, however, it was warm and cozy with a huge fire burning in the fireplace. Laughter and chatter floated up the stairs.

Naomi paused on the steps, gasped, and drew back. Her mother and father, younger and slenderer, elegantly clad—her mother, Ruth, in a navy blue evening frock, sat at the piano and her father, Clarence, in a tux, stood in the middle of the guests. He directed the housekeeping staff, dressed tonight as servants, as they served champagne from elegant silver trays.

There were the Thomases. Mrs. Thomas dressed in her Christmas red suit with the big raccoon collar that she wore every year. Mr. Thomas had a beard then, not yet white, and he was smoking his pipe. She watched Mrs. Thomas hand a package wrapped in foil to her mother. The fudge.

Three other couples were there that night: a couple from Texas who had been living at the boardinghouse while their own home was being remodeled; their attorney friend and his wife, visiting for the holidays; and a young couple, newly married, staying at the boardinghouse until they found a more permanent residence. There were no children. Only Julia. Naomi remembered every detail of that night, of that party. What each person wore; what they said; where they stood or sat; the sounds of the tinkling glasses.

Naomi followed the group into the dining room, and…she was there, in the moment as she had been that night. She looked down at her skirt, the swirly, purple skirt. Quenton pulled her chair out for her as she draped the fox stole over its back. She patted the finger waves in her hair—no scarf. As she sat, she looked up at her husband and stammered a soft, "Wh… wha…" Oblivious to her confusion, he sat beside her and grabbed her hand underneath the table.

A large, lighted silver candelabra, with its outspread arms, stood in the center of the dining room table like a regal queen receiving her subjects. Boughs of pine, cedar, and red holly berries surrounded the tall, curved piece, which sat hidden away the rest of the year in the china cabinet. Garlands of red berries interspersed with a garland of silver beads hung from the crystal chandelier.

Her mother had outdone herself this year with the china and silver settings. She'd been to an event at the Broadmoor Hotel and decided she could reproduce some of the elegance she'd seen there, if on a smaller scale. Silver napkin rings with a sprig of holly surrounded freshly starched and ironed linen napkins that matched the tablecloth. Embroidered poinsettias dotted with sequins winked at the guests from the edge of the cloth. A silver rimmed set of china shimmered in the candlelight.

Quenton turned to the attorney and his wife on the other side of her and nodded.

The attorney leaned forward and introduced himself. "I'm Charles Maldonado from Houston, Texas, and this is my wife, Carmen." He didn't offer his hand.

His wife glanced briefly at Naomi, looked at Quenton, and a small smile tugged at the corner of her mouth. Gray. Everything about her was nondescript gray—her eyes, her hair, her dress. Even her skin held a slight grayish tint.

Naomi nodded. Quenton stuck out his hand. Mr. Maldonado rose slightly and shook it. The man was medium height with a jowly face and pudgy hands. His lips pulled downward, even when he tried to smile. A grimace seemed a more apt description.

Soup was being served. The pungent scent of onions floated into the room as the servants placed the thin white china soup bowls in front of the guests. Naomi stared around the table at the young couple, the Texans, her parents. "Do you live here with your parents?" She could barely hear Mr. Maldonado between his slurps of the onion consommé.

"What? Oh, no, we are just visiting for the holidays. We live in Denver."

"So you are used to the snow and cold weather?"

"One never gets used to storms like this—or I don't, anyway—especially if you have to travel in it."

"Yes, I'm rather concerned about tomorrow. We had planned to leave early. I hope we can get out. We came by train." He coughed into his napkin.

"That should be fine then." Quenton leaned over and chuckled. "If we can get you to the train station, that is."

The lights flickered off and on for a pregnant moment. Then darkness wrapped around the room except for the candles on the table.

Her father stood. "I was afraid this was going to happen. Everyone remain calm. This is a common occurrence here in the mountains. We have the fire to keep us warm and plenty of candles. A true dinner by candlelight. What could be more festive?" He smiled. "Keep your seats and enjoy the evening." Beckoning to the servants, he instructed, "Bring more candles and continue serving the meal."

The head server shook her head as she set the main course, a ham, down on the sideboard. "The girl I hired to help us out tonight has disappeared. Only Della and I are left."

Clarence huddled with his employee, their words barely making it to Naomi. "Where could she have gone in this storm?"

"I don't know but I can't find her. Should have known she was undependable. What kind of name is Cookie? Probably got scared about the storm and had someone come and get her." She stood with her doubled-up fists on her ample hips. "We can handle it. Everything is already cooked. It's only a matter of serving it up. It'll just take us longer."

She started taking the soup bowls to the kitchen. Ruth pushed back from her place at the table and helped them. Clarence sat, motioning for everybody to remain seated.

Naomi's heart thudded, and she jumped up.

Quenton caught the chair and grabbed her arm. "Sit, sweetheart. Everything's fine." He patted her hand. "Don't worry. The electricity will come back on shortly."

"No. The baby. You don't understand. The baby. Danger."

"The baby is in no danger. Keep your seat. I'll go check on her."

"No, I'll go. We'll both go." She pulled Quenton away from the dining room, through the foyer and up the stairs, sprinting over the landing to the room. She pushed open the door to the dark room, the fireplace providing the only light. Julia lay sleeping quietly in her bassinet, her Christmas stocking hanging on the mantel for its inaugural Christmas, alongside Quenton's and Naomi's.

She went to the bassinet and stared in wonder at her child.

Quenton put another log on the fire and stoked it as it popped. "See, she's fine. It's no more dangerous than when we leave her alone in our bedroom at home. This is your parents' home, and we are eating dinner. Come on, now. No more worrying. Let's go eat."

Naomi looked around the room and shook her head. "No. I'm not leaving her alone. You go on—"

The roaring in her ears returned, and she was once again an observer and not a participant.

She watched helplessly as the young couple descended the stairs, leaving their infant daughter defenseless in the upstairs bedroom. Why had she allowed Quenton to talk her into going back down to dinner, leaving their daughter all alone in that room?

That was the last time they ever saw their firstborn child.

SEVEN

"I'm home." The bell jingle-jangled, and the front door of the inn banged shut as a blast of frigid air burst in with Quenton. He stomped his feet on the welcome mat and threw his gloves on the check-in counter. "Where is everybody? Meeeerrrrrry Christmas!"

Naomi peered over the railing and rushed down the stairs into her husband's arms. "Oh, I'm so glad you're finally home. Were the roads bad? Did you have much trouble? The lights are out. Did you notice if they're out all over town?"

"Whoa, whoa. Slow down." He hugged her briefly, shook the snow off of his hat, and unbuttoned his jacket. "Yes, the roads are awful, but I was determined to get home." He looked at the darkened overhead light fixture and pulled on the chain of the banker's lamp on the counter to no avail. "And no, the lights are not out all over town, just on this side of the street, fortunately. If all of the streetlights had been out, I don't know that I could have made it. It was hard enough to see the highway markings as it was."

Cynthia came into the foyer and launched into Quenton's arms, nearly knocking him over. "Daddy, you're home."

Laughing, he kissed her on the cheek. "Take it easy, sweet pea. Yes, I'm home, safe and sound and ready to enjoy my girls. Where are Myrna and Elise?"

"Daddy, it's way past their bedtime. They're already asleep so Santa will come." She smiled and winked at him.

"Of course." He turned to Naomi. "What were you doing upstairs?"

"I...I was checking on our guests. Quenton, I—"

"C'mon, Daddy. I'll get you some hot chocolate."

"That sounds good."

"Wait a minute, Quenton. Could you come upstairs with me for a minute? Cynthia, go ahead and take Daddy's things and get his hot chocolate ready. We'll only be a moment."

He handed Cynthia his hat and jacket. She grabbed his gloves and disappeared into the apartment.

Naomi picked up her lantern, took her husband's hand, and led him up the stairs. "Your hands are like ice."

"Yeah, so are my feet. It's freezing out there tonight, and I think the temperature is still falling."

Naomi stopped about halfway up the big staircase and turned toward him. Her lips quivered ever so slightly. "It happened again."

He frowned and stared at her. He shook his head slowly. "Naomi..."

"I know." She continued to the landing. "But everything is déjà vu tonight—the storm, the electricity out, Christmas Eve." She chewed on her lip. "I went back there again...to that night."

He sighed and shoved his hands in his pockets. His eyebrows knitted together. "Can't we simply have Christmas for once without all the drama?"

She blinked away the tears burning in her eyes. Nodding, she pointed to the box of fudge on the credenza. "You're right. I...there's your annual Christmas fudge from Mrs. Thomas."

"That's my girl. Ahh…been thinking about sinking my teeth into that gooey sweet stuff all day." He pulled the red ribbon off and lifted the lid from the box. "I knew she wouldn't let me down." Grinning, he unwrapped the chocolate, closed his eyes, and yummed his way through one piece and then another.

Naomi put the lid back on the box. "Slow down, soldier. You'll make yourself sick. Have you had supper?"

"They had soup in the mess hall for us. It was pretty good." He snuck his hand back into the treasure trove of goodies. "What's this? Something new?"

"She said she tried a new recipe this year and hoped we would like it. It's toffee, I think."

Quenton popped a small piece into his mouth and crunched the brittle piece of candy. "Wow, that's wonderful. Tastes like a Heath bar, only better."

"I know you like Heath bars."

"It's the one bright spot in the ration kits. No comparison to this, however."

"Will you go with me to check on the other rooms?"

"Sure. Still mad at me for renting out the turret room?" He leaned against the credenza, pulled her to him, and nuzzled her neck.

"Stop it. Somebody might see us."

"So what? It's Christmas Eve, our house, and you're my wife." He tried to kiss her, but she broke the embrace.

"Later, dear. We have things to do yet tonight."

Quenton playfully patted her rear. "Well, let's get on with it then."

She swatted at him. "Leave the candy on the credenza, and let's check on these rooms, so we can get downstairs with Cynthia. We have Santa yet to put out." She pointed to the turret room. "You do that one."

Shaking his head, Quenton knocked on the door. Naomi hung back from the room where memories of the worst night of her life lingered in every corner, from every beam. The young husband answered, and behind him Naomi could see his wife rocking a baby beside the fireplace. The infant was wrapped in a large, pink knitted blanket and appeared to be sleeping. The husband, a pilot in training at Peterson Field, was one of Quenton's men. When he saw his commanding officer, he stood at attention and saluted, although not in uniform.

"At ease, son. You're not on duty nor am I. While you're here, I'm Mr. Lockhart…or Quenton, and you are…David, isn't it?"

"Yes, sir. Very good, sir, Major…uh, Mr. Lockhart." He didn't look very at ease to Naomi.

His wife, a tiny little thing with a halo of blond hair cascading around her shoulders, walked up behind him, still holding the baby. She wore a green velvet robe made with white embroidery on one shoulder.

"We love the room. It's so cozy. And the bed is so…so…uh…comfort… able." The girl stumbled over her words and blushed. "I mean…"

"Gloria." He put his arm around her shoulders. "What she means is that we are very comfortable here. It's very nice. Thank you, sir, for making it possible for us to spend Christmas together."

"No problem, son. It is our pleasure, right, Naomi?" He pulled her close to his side.

She nodded and realized she was staring at the infant. The mother held the baby out to Naomi. "Would you like to hold her?"

"Oh, oh no. But isn't she beautiful?" Her breath quickened and she backed up. The child made little sucking movements with her rosebud mouth, but her eyes remained closed. Still keeping her distance and with her arms folded, Naomi asked the polite questions. "How old is she?"

"Nine months. She's getting so big. I don't want her to grow up."

Naomi uncrossed her arms and gently touched the edge of the blanket. "She's fast asleep, isn't she? They do grow up quickly. Enjoy every moment you have with her." Unbidden tears sprang to her eyes. She blinked them away.

The young mother kissed the baby on the cheek. "We intend to. We pray every day that God will keep her healthy and strong…and protect her."

Naomi turned to leave. *We prayed for our Julia, and still…*

"I'm sorry. Did I say something wrong?"

Quenton shook his head. "No, no, nothing at all. She has a lot on her mind. Don't forget the open house tomorrow evening. Merry Christmas."

"Yes, Merry Christmas to you as well. Good night, sir."

"Quenton, please."

"Yes, sir, Quenton, Mr. Lockhart, sir."

Quenton smiled as they closed the door. "He's a good soldier. Gonna be a good pilot too. My guess is he'll be shipping out pretty quickly."

They moved to the other two rooms. The Gold Mining room, a smaller unit, had two brothers from back east who were stationed at Camp Carson and couldn't go home for Christmas, and lastly there was a honeymoon couple from Louisiana in the bridal suite. Hadn't seen much of them.

Naomi went to the credenza. "I'm going to leave these lamps burning until the electricity comes back on." She motioned to Quenton to pick up the box of fudge. "I…I need to tell you something, but I don't know quite how to say it."

"Just say it." He opened the box and ate another piece of the candy.

Naomi shook her head. "Your stomach is going to be a mess if you don't quit."

"It's Christmas." Quenton started down the stairs.

"Wait. I want…need to tell you what happened." She sat on the top step, still holding the lantern. Her hands started to shake again, rattling the glass chimney. She set the lantern down and buried her face in her hands.

"Sweetheart…aw…don't do this." He sat beside her and put his hand on her knee. "Are you all right? You're trembling."

She shook her head. "Yes. No." She looked at him through misty tears. "I don't know." She chewed her lip to keep from bursting into tears. She took off her scarf and wiped her eyes with it. "I saw us. I had just checked on the Garrisons, and we…we came out of the turret room. The two of us together…it was us. It frightened me so badly that I hid behind the credenza. You turned and looked at me, but it was like you didn't see me. Everything happened just as it did that night."

Quenton ran his hands through his hair. "Naomi, this has got to stop. It's crazy." He leaned forward with his elbows on his knees and clasped his hands, turning his head to look intently into his wife's face.

"Believe me, I know how crazy it sounds, but Q, I was there. I had on my purple dress. We walked down the stairs together. I heard the Christmas carols they were singing that night." A lone tear hung in the corner of her right eye then slid down her cheek.

Quenton brushed it away with his thumb. "Don't cry, sweetheart. It's okay."

"But you don't understand. It was as real as you are to me right now. I could even taste the onion soup we had that night. I could smell the smoke from the fire."

He hung his head. "When did the dream end?"

"It wasn't a dream. It was real." She sniffled. "After we checked on Julia following the power outage and went downstairs to dinner. Left her all alone in that room."

His eyes went misty. "You still blame me for making you go back downstairs and leaving the baby, don't you?"

Naomi looked down and barely shook her head. "No, but if I'd stayed or if we'd taken her downstairs with us, we'd still have her. What kind of mother leaves her baby alone in a room in a boardinghouse?" She pounded her fist on her leg. "What kind of mother? If we just hadn't left her alone, we'd…still…have…her." A hiccupping sob interrupted her.

Her husband put his arm around her. "Maybe, maybe not. Honey, we were in your parents' home. Everybody leaves their baby sleeping in their bedroom. We didn't do anything wrong. I think a plan had been set in motion, and whoever took her was watching for the first chance they had to whisk her away. It wouldn't have mattered what we did. Please, Naomi. Let's focus on the daughters who are here with us—alive, healthy and beautiful."

Cynthia approached the bottom of the staircase. "Are you coming? The hot chocolate is getting cold."

Quenton helped Naomi up. "We're on our way. Just enjoying some of Mrs. Thomas's annual fudge."

"Oooh, I want some." She started up the stairs but turned when she heard the bell jingle over the front door. A flurry of snow and blustery wind swirled in, and the door banged against the wall.

Two figures cloaked in snow and heavy coats blustered in. "Oh, my goodness. Sorry. Didn't mean to let the door get away from me like that," said a familiar female voice from behind a thick scarf wound around all but her eyes.

Naomi frowned. "Gracie?"

The second figure shoved back his hood, revealing Robby's grinning face. "We could hardly see to get across the road."

Naomi's throat went tight. Something must be wrong to bring the two young people here from the restaurant in this weather. "What is it? What brings you out in a storm like this?"

She braced herself for the worst.

EIGHT

Gracie held out a plate tied up with green and red ribbon. "We made tamales for Christmas, and Lupe wanted you to have some for your open house tomorrow. I volunteered to bring them over." Gracie had fallen in love with the Lockharts and felt at home with their family. Cynthia was nearly her age, and they had become good friends.

Naomi smiled—and there was a bit of relief in it, she thought. "Oh, how nice. I was wishing for something else to serve tomorrow evening. These will be perfect. But you shouldn't have gotten out in this weather. I thought maybe something was wrong with Lupe." She took the plate of still-warm tamales. "I'll need to get these in the icebox right away."

Quenton chuckled. "Did Lupe manage to make pralines too, even with the sugar rationing?"

"She did. I have them in my pocketbook." Gracie unwound the muffler from around her head and shook off the snow. "How did you know?"

"Because she always does…somehow." He held out his hand. "Here, let me take your things."

Gracie shrugged her coat off and handed it to him. She hadn't been able to button it over her bloated belly. Never needing a heavy coat in San Antonio, she'd purchased it after arriving in the Springs. She loved the tailored look of the camel hair wool and the tan color that blended so well with the fox collar, but she hadn't planned ahead for her swelling body. Hadn't really known that she would get as big as she had. She opened her purse, pulled out the small package of precious pralines, and handed them to Quenton.

"Can you stay and have some hot chocolate with us?"

Cynthia turned to Robby. "Oh, please do. It's really good."

He winked at Cynthia, and a charming broad smile lit up his handsome face. "Thought you'd never ask." He unbuttoned his jacket and hung it on the coat rack next to the front door. Folding his gloves, he stuffed them in a pocket, along with his toboggan. "Your lights are out? We've closed the restaurant. Nobody else will be coming in this storm, but we still have electricity." The young man pulled off his snow boots and left them on the rubber mat beside the front door. He straightened the legs of his pants over his thick woolen socks and avoided the puddles of melting snow on the floor.

"Surely it will be back on again soon." Quenton pulled on the lamp chain again. "Gracie, you need to be careful on these slick sidewalks. It would be so easy for you to slip and fall."

"I know. Robby helped me, but you're right. It's very slick. I'll be careful."

Naomi walked toward the apartment. "Come on in. I'll add more milk to the hot chocolate. Quenton, you may need to put some logs on the fire. And bring those pralines to the kitchen. You're already on sugar overload."

Cynthia wove her arm through Robby's and led him into the living room. "We were just finishing up decorating our tree and hanging our Christmas stockings. Your timing is perfect." She reached out and took Gracie's hand as well. "C'mon, slowpoke."

The lanterns and candles, together with the fire in the fireplace, gave the room a festive holiday ambience. On her way to the kitchen Naomi pointed to the couch. "Gracie, you sit and put your feet up."

"Oh, I'm fine. I don't need—"

"Let us pamper you. That baby will be here soon, and you won't get much pampering after that. Believe me." Naomi smiled and motioned to Robby. "Robby, pull that footstool over for her."

"Yes, ma'am." Robby gave a mock salute and positioned the footstool beneath Gracie's swollen ankles. "Do you want to take your shoes off?"

"No, thank you. I think I'll keep them on. My feet are cold."

Cynthia brought a tray of Mrs. Thomas's fudge, Lupe's pralines, and Christmas tree cookies from the kitchen and set them on the coffee table.

Naomi followed with mugs of steaming hot chocolate. "Here we go." She set the mugs on the table. "Oops, I forgot napkins." She hurried back into the kitchen and returned with a handful of cloth napkins of red fabric. "My mother made these Christmas napkins years ago. Seems fitting to use them this evening."

Quenton rummaged around in the copper wood holder and threw a couple of small logs onto the fire. "I'm going to go outside and get some bigger logs from the woodpile."

Robby stood. "I'll go with you."

"No need. I'll be right back." Quenton put on his gloves and went out the side door to the woodpile.

Cynthia sat cross-legged in front of Gracie on the floor. "I have an extra pair of slippers in my room. Would you like them?"

"No, thank you."

She looked at Gracie's saddle oxfords that were wet with the melting snow. "Don't you have any snow boots?"

Gracie felt her cheeks flush. "I'm afraid I wasn't very well prepared for a Colorado winter. I didn't think I needed boots." She laughed at herself. "We don't have many snowstorms in San Antonio."

Cynthia smiled. "I think we have a pair of boots in the lost and found—nice fur ones. I'll go get them. Maybe they'll fit you. Nobody claimed them, and we've had them for over a year. They're too small for me and too big for Myrna."

She got up but Robby stopped her. "I'll go get the lost and found box. I know where it is."

"Swell. Thanks, Robby." Cynthia stood in front of Gracie and chuckled, nodding her head toward Robby. "He can't sit still for a minute. You know, we'll have three or so more months of snow. You're going to need boots." She called over her shoulder as she left the room. "And I'm getting those slippers for you."

"Oh, all right. If you insist. Thank you." Gracie bent over to untie her shoes. She groaned as her belly hindered the simple task. A tightening in her abdomen took her breath away, and she sat up, rubbing her stomach. Oh! It went away after a few seconds. *Must have strained a muscle.* Placing her shoes beside the stool, she tugged off her wet socks as well. She leaned against the back of the couch and gazed around the room.

The decorations on the Christmas tree glistened in the reflected light from the streetlamps across the road. The illumination from the fireplace, candles, and lanterns gave enough light to make out the decorated mantel and beautiful stockings. In the darkened room, Gracie hadn't noticed the stockings until now. There was something strangely familiar about them that drew her attention. She read each name in sequence—Quenton, Naomi, Cynthia, Myrna, Elise and…and Julia.

She gasped and held her breath. *Julia?* Her eyes traveled from the stocking up to the photograph of a laughing baby resting on the mantel. She stood, knocking over the footstool.

Naomi paused in her duties as hostess and turned toward Gracie. "Are you all right?"

"Oh, I'm fine. Just clumsy these days." She righted the footstool then walked to the fireplace, the photo pulling her forward. She couldn't see it clearly in the dim light, but she could tell it was identical to the one she had. Taking hold of the stocking, she ran her fingers along the sequined name. She looked at the other stockings. "These…these are beautiful. Did you make them, Mrs. Lockhart?"

Not wanting to look at Naomi for fear the expression on her face would betray her angst, Gracie heard her say, "No, my mother made them. She made mine for me when I was a child and added Quenton's when we married. Each time we had a baby, she made another one."

"Oh." Gracie swallowed. All the sounds around her dimmed as if a blanket had fallen over the room. She reached out and touched Julia's stocking with trembling fingers. She could not speak above a hoarse whisper. "Who…who is Julia?"

Gracie finally turned around and faced the woman with the scarf on her head, sitting on the couch, sipping hot chocolate. Naomi stood and set her cup on the coffee table. She walked to the fireplace beside Gracie, so close she could smell the almond fragrance of Naomi's hand lotion. She picked up the photograph. It seemed to Gracie that an eternity was encased in that single moment.

Naomi traced her finger over the glass. "This is our oldest daughter, Julia, who was…" She took a deep breath. "…kidnapped on this very night seventeen years ago."

Quenton returned with an armload of wood. Robby walked to the couch with the lost and found box. Cynthia reappeared holding a pair of pink fuzzy slippers. And Gracie felt as if she was in a dizzying time warp.

She gulped. "I...I'm so sorry. I didn't know." She put her hand on the mantel to steady herself. "You never found her?" To her own ears, her voice sounded faraway, hoarse, choked with emotion. Naomi seemed not to notice.

"No. We have our suspicions but never could prove anything." Naomi replaced the picture and straightened the stocking.

Cynthia set the slippers at Gracie's bare feet. "Here. Put these on. Your feet must be freezing."

Gracie slid the slippers on, barely taking notice of the activity around her, and let her friend lead her back to the couch.

Things seemed to be moving in slow motion. Colors and shapes without meaning. Like a snow globe that had just been upturned, the disturbance settling around oblivious, inert figures.

She looked at Cynthia and reached for her hand. She whispered. "I didn't know you had an older sister. I didn't know about—"

"It's okay. There's no way you could have known. We don't talk about it much anymore except at Christmastime." She took Gracie's hand and sat beside her. "Mama never got over it. It's been a cloud over our Christmas every year. I wish..."

Gracie, still whispering, afraid of what Cynthia might say, asked her, "What do you wish?"

"That we could either find her or just forget about her altogether."

NINE

Quenton dropped the wood into the tub with a clang. Gracie jumped and gasped, her hand to her chest.

Naomi shushed him. "You scared Gracie to death, and you're going to wake up the girls."

"Too late. We're already awake." The two little girls, in their matching red flannel nightgowns trimmed in white lace, each holding a stuffed animal, stood at the door to the hallway. Elise, with a black and white teddy bear, ran and jumped into her daddy's lap. "Has Santa come?" Her short auburn curls bounced with every step.

Myrna held a stuffed dog by a torn ear, dragging it on the ground, rubbing her eyes. "Is it morning yet?"

Naomi went to the girls and knelt beside them. "No, it's not, and you're going right back to bed. Santa has not come yet and won't until you all are sound asleep."

"But we were and you woke us up. Now Santa may not come at all." She poked her bottom lip out and looked around at Gracie and Robby. Her pout turned to a smile as she sighted the hot chocolate. "Yummy. Can I have some? With a marshmallow?"

"'May I have some, please?'" Naomi stood and raised her eyebrows.

"May I have some, please?" Myrna repeated the proper phrase after her mother.

"Yes, you may. Come to the kitchen with me. We'll fix a plate of goodies for Santa while we're at it. We forgot to do it earlier."

"Oh, Mama, can we sing Christmas carols too?" The little girl's shining eyes beamed as she looked up at her mother. "Please?"

Naomi smiled and brushed the child's tousled hair out of her eyes. "Sure. Go tell everyone to gather around the piano, and I'll fix Santa's plate while you're doing that. Ask Daddy to put a lantern on the piano." Naomi heard Myrna's instructions and the scraping of chairs and bustling to the piano.

She worked quickly in the kitchen and hurried into the dining room. Quenton had lit the candles in the candelabra on the dining room table and set the lantern on the piano. Sitting on the piano stool, she thumbed through the hard-back book of carols she'd put on the piano as decoration. She loved the Currier & Ives images on the cover. "What do you all want to sing?"

"'White Christmas.'" Quenton's favorite. She'd have to play that one by ear.

"You lead out, sweetheart." She did a run to set the key, and Quenton, imitating the crooning style of Bing Crosby, started. "I'm dreaming of a white Christmas…ba-ba-ba-boom."

Robby stared at the man. "You sound just like Bing."

Quenton grinned and continued, "Just like the ones I used to know." They finished the popular song amidst giggles from the little girls and went on to "Jingle Bells."

Naomi modulated to a different key and pulled Elise to her side with her free hand. "Why don't you sing 'Away in a Manger' for us like you did in the Christmas program at school?" Elise ducked her head and stuck her thumb in her mouth. "Preferably without the thumb, please." She played the intro twice then started singing, nodding her head to urge Elise to join in. Finally Elise started the simple carol in a small voice, surprisingly right on pitch…all three verses. Applause erupted for her, and Naomi hugged her as she ended the song. "Good job."

Gracie brought a pillow from the couch and sat in a wingback chair to watch the family. For the first time, she noticed the similarity in the color of Cynthia and Elise's hair to her own as the burnt shades glistened in the candlelight during her song. Myrna was a blonde, but Cynthia and Elise had their daddy's dark auburn hair, which could be called…mahogany. She took hold of a lock of her own hair, brought it down over her shoulder, and looked at it glinting in the firelight. Auburn. Mahogany.

The group sang nearly every carol in the book, ending with "Silent Night." Naomi pushed back the stool and stretched. "That's enough. It's getting late. I'm played out, and you girls need to get back to bed."

Quenton picked up Elise and took Myrna by the hand. "I'll get these two wiggle-worms in bed. Santa's probably got his reindeer circling overhead, just waiting for you girls to go to sleep."

Bells jangled. Myrna looked up at her daddy, the whites showing all around her hazel eyes.

Quenton laughed. "I told you. C'mon, let's hurry and get you in bed." He scooted them through the apartment and down the hall.

Robby stood beside the Christmas tree as the group reentered the family room, grinning as he held up a string of bells.

Naomi laughed as she set the lantern on the table. "Good work, Robby. Did you guys set that up?"

"Yep. Just as we were singing the last verse of 'Silent Night.'"

Naomi stoked the fire and sat in the rocking chair. "They fell for it—and they will always remember it."

Gracie and Cynthia resettled themselves on the couch. Cynthia took a bite of a sugary brown praline. She closed her eyes and sighed. "Oh, yum. These are heavenly." She flicked a crumb of sugar off her lap. "What do you hear from your husband, Gracie? Gracie?"

TEN

G racie stared straight ahead, transfixed by the firelight. The moment Cynthia mentioned Jack, memories of her husband pushed the answer to her friend's question to the side. She didn't mean to be discourteous. Her thoughts and emotions were being shaken like one of those kaleidoscopes Jack had won for her at the carnival before he was sent overseas. But the pieces of colored glass wouldn't settle into a design that made any sense. She touched her distended abdomen lightly with the tips of her fingers.

She hadn't even noticed him the first time she and her best friend, Lou, went to the USO in downtown San Antonio. It was shortly after she'd rummaged in the attic and found the picture. She'd needed something get her mind off the startling finds, so she'd reluctantly agreed to go with Lou to the canteen where the soldiers from the air force base gathered on the weekends. She'd previously been drawn to the stereotypical tall, dark, and handsome guy, but Jack didn't fit that description.

Oh, he was handsome enough, that was obvious—with steely blue-gray eyes and blond hair. Something intrigued her about his good looks. She finally figured out it was his dark eyebrows and eyelashes, which didn't seem to correspond with his light hair, that made her take a second look.

When he first asked her to dance, she was surprised to find he was only a couple of inches taller than she. His broad shoulders and muscular build made him seem taller than he actually was. He was an excellent dancer. He knew the steps to each of the popular dances—swing, lindy hop, and the jitterbug—and swung her around with strength and expertise. But what she liked best of all was when he held her in his arms during the slow dances. His muscles rippled underneath his shirt.

She'd found herself picturing him in a swim suit, those bulging muscles visible. Her face heated, and she kept her head turned away from him. Understandably she became breathless when they danced the swing or the jitterbug. Those dances took a lot of energy. But she was a bit embarrassed at how breathless she was when they swayed to the slower tunes. Just being close to him made her pulse quicken and her palms go sweaty. "I'll Be Seeing You" became their song.

She'd had a couple of boyfriends in high school, but no one like him. Just a glance from Jack sent her emotions careening. They soon became known as a couple on the dance floor.

He told Gracie later he had noticed her immediately but didn't approach her that first night. He'd watched her from a distance. Watched her dance with several fellows. Watched her go to the refreshment table with her girlfriend. As he told the story, he'd nudged his buddy and asked, "Who's the tall drink of water with the long auburn page boy?"

Butch Waterston—from Georgia, while Jack was from Louisiana—hadn't known who she was either, of course. He'd encouraged Jack to introduce himself, but instead he'd lingered on the sidelines. He'd danced with a couple of girls, but according to him, he'd kept his eye on Gracie.

"Ew, that's creepy, Jack." Gracie had laughed—and perhaps exaggerated her concern over his attention when he told her about it.

"Not at all. I'm just discriminating about who I pursue." He'd smiled and put his hands in his pockets, shrugging. "These days are short lived. I don't want to waste my time."

She stared at this boy who spoke like a man. His sensitivity and maturity intrigued her. He didn't try to grope her like so many of the soldiers she danced with did. Never showed up with liquor on his breath. He was a gentleman. And she fell hard for him. Head over heels hard.

The only place they met for the first few weeks was at the USO.

March 1944

They'd danced, sat on the sidelines to talk, and now Gracie drew in a deep breath and Jack led her by the hand outside, into the shadows of the courtyard in the rear of the building. They found a concrete bench beneath a large magnolia tree in the courtyard, and Gracie sat, not objecting when Jack sat closer than the wide bench demanded. Water splashed in the three-tiered fountain in the center of a brick patio. Pigeons strutted back and forth, pecking at seeds or crumbs on the walkway.

Gracie tucked her skirt underneath her. "It's nice out tonight, isn't it?"

"Yeah, it sure is." He ran his finger around the inside of his shirt collar. Tiny beads of sweat had formed on his upper lip.

"The weather gets warm in Texas quickly. We hardly have a spring. It's winter, then all of a sudden, it's summer. Besides, it's late spring. Time to get hot."

"It's that way at home too."

"And home is Louisiana, you said?"

"Yeah, Lafayette, down on the Gulf. My family is of French descent." He chuckled. "Pretty obvious that I'm French with a name like Blauvelt. I'm only third generation. My parents still speak some French at home since my grandparents live with us."

She smiled. "Jack doesn't sound very French."

"It's actually Jacques, but that's way *too* French for this all-American boy." He punched his chest with his thumb. He'd taken off his army air corps hat and held it in his hands, folding and unfolding it. He was nervous.

She put her hand on his. She loved his hands. They were square and tan, masculine and strong, almost hairless. He kept his nails short and clean, not dirty and snagged like so many men did. Holding hands was the only physical contact they'd had, aside from dancing. She wondered when he was going to kiss her. A kiss like in the movies, like Scarlett O'Hara and Rhett Butler in *Gone with the Wind,* not like the pecks and dry, tight-lipped ones she'd received from the boys at school. She wanted to be swept away.

"Why are you so nervous and fidgety? Is something wrong?"

"No, not at all. In fact, something is very right." He turned to face her and laid his hat on the bench. He took both of her hands in his and searched her face, first her eyes then her mouth. He touched her hair, then traced his fingers along her jawline to her chin. A shiver shimmied down her spine, and her heart-flutters turned into thundering in her temples. She tried to swallow the lump that had formed in her throat but it only grew larger. She took a deep breath.

The reflection of the lights in the courtyard danced in his serious eyes. "You are so beautiful. I…I didn't intend for this to happen, but it almost seems as if we have been destined to meet and…" He paused. She waited.

He looked down at their hands. "Gracie, I have fallen hopelessly in love with you." He spoke so softly she wondered if she'd heard him correctly. He gazed into her eyes for what seemed an eternity. "I'm telling you that I love you." He softly kissed her fingers then pressed his cheek against them. He leaned toward her and took her face in his hands. "I love you." He tilted her chin up and kissed her tenderly, his lips soft and cool. He parted her lips gently with his and pulled her to him.

Gracie lost all contact with reality and swam in a rushing current of emotion. *So this is what it feels like to be swept away.* This kind of passion was new to her. She didn't want to push him away like she did the other boys who had tried to kiss her. She wanted to melt into his embrace and become entwined in him. Then the intensity of the emotion frightened her, and she broke away from the kiss. She touched her lips and stared at him.

"I'm sorry. Did I offend you?" His eyes grew wide. "I wouldn't ever want to offend you."

She went back into his arms, shaking her head. "Not at all. I just…I've never…." She didn't want to admit how inexperienced she was, but she needn't have been concerned about it.

"I've never felt this way either. Do you feel the same as I do? Could I possibly dare to hope that you love me too?" He brought her hand to his lips and kissed her fingers again, looking over the top of them into her eyes.

Just watching him look at her with such longing stirred physical responses within her she'd never experienced. Was this normal? Did other girls feel like this when they fell in love and were kissed by their boyfriends? Her mother had never talked to her about boys except to caution her: "Good girls get into trouble when they find themselves alone in the dark with a boy." That was the extent of her sex talk.

Her father was even less verbal. "Just wait until you get out of school to worry about boys."

Her girlfriends would giggle about how boys acted and what happened to…certain parts of their anatomy in passionate moments. But no one ever had talked about what happened to a girl's own body when in love.

She was finding it difficult to breathe, much less to answer his question about whether she loved him too. For a moment she could only smile and nod at this stranger who had become closer to her than anyone else in her life ever had with a single act and an "I love you."

She touched his lips, his chin, his forehead, then kissed each one. His face had grown hot. She whispered in his ear, "I love you too. I don't ever want to leave this place. Hold me tight, Jack. Don't ever let me go."

He kissed her again, deeply, the Rhett Butler and Scarlett O'Hara kiss she'd always dreamed about. More than she'd dreamed about. He nibbled on her lips and caressed her face. He ran his fingers through her hair and inhaled the fragrance of it. Taking a deep breath, he leaned away from her. "We need to stop. This could get out of hand."

"No, Jack, don't stop." She snuggled into his arms.

"Uh-uh. I don't want us to do anything we'd regret later. I love you too much for that." He took a deep breath and turned her face toward him. "We need to go back inside."

"What? What do we do with this? The way we feel about each other, I mean."

"I'm not sure, but I want you to understand this is not one of those wartime romances. One of those desperate lunges at love because it might be the last chance things."

"I didn't think that, but I'm glad you told me." She searched his eyes. "So where do we go from here?"

He caressed her hair again. "You're so beautiful…and so young. Give me some time to think."

Gracie chuckled. "I don't even know how old you are."

"I'm twenty-two. I'm concerned your parents might think there's a big gulf between a high school senior and a soldier."

"I'm eighteen, whether I've graduated or not. Let me take care of my parents."

He didn't mention marriage, but she was thinking about it. She wasn't as confident about her parents' reaction as she tried to make Jack think she was. She wasn't confident at all.

Eleven

racie invited Jack to her home the next weekend to meet her parents. He was to ride the bus to the USO and walk to the corner of Broadway and Nacogdoches to wait for Gracie and her father to pick him up. She spotted him right away, standing at the curb peering down the street, his hands stuffed in his pockets the way he did when he was nervous. Her father stopped the car, and she motioned for Jack to get in the back of the burgundy Cadillac.

Gracie introduced her father. "Jack, this is my father, Dr. Jorge Gonzales." The young man stuck his hand over the back of the front seat immediately and shook her father's hand. "Pleasure to meet you, sir."

"The pleasure is mine, young man."

She was proud of Jack's good manners and confidence. The two men discussed war issues, bombardier school, and Hitler during the short drive to her parents' house just outside the downtown area. Jack carried on an intelligent conversation. They pulled around the circular drive and stopped in front of the carved double doors. Jack released a long exhale as he stared at the house. Before Gracie could exit the car, he jumped out of the backseat and opened the passenger door for her. Dr. Gonzales opened the three-car garage door and parked the Cadillac next to the blue-grey Duesenberg.

The couple walked toward the house. "Why didn't you tell me?" His whisper wasn't very soft as they paused and waited for her father.

"Tell you what?"

"That your father is a doctor, you're rich, live in a mansion, have all those cars…and are Mexican."

"I…I'm not…rich."

"Compared to what I'm used to, you are."

Gracie faced him, disappointment clouding her heart. "Does that matter to you? That I'm Mexican? What kind of name did you think Gonzales was?"

"Of course it doesn't matter. And I never thought about the name. I'm just a little surprised, that's all. You don't look Mexican, with your red hair and green eyes. You don't have a Spanish accent."

"My hair isn't red, it's mahogany, from the Castilian Spanish side of the family." She tossed her head and tucked some locks behind her ear. "And I'm bilingual."

Jorge closed the garage door and joined them before they could continue the conversation. "Welcome to our home. Come in and meet the rest of the family. Dinner should be ready soon."

For the first time ever, Gracie was acutely aware of the opulence of their home as she brought Jack into the foyer. He stared at the surroundings. Serafina, just coming down the stairs, gave Jack a half-wave. "This is my sister, Serafina." The girl smiled and gave a low whistle.

"Serafina, mind your manners."

Her sister laughed and went on into the dining room.

Jorge Jr. came into the foyer and stuck out his hand.

"And this is my little brother, Jorge Jr. Watch out for him."

"Hey, I'm not so bad." He turned to Jack. "Nice to meet you, sir."

"No sir needed. I'm just Jack tonight."

"Well, to me you are a sir." Jorge Jr. peppered the poor guy with one question after another when he discovered Jack was a bombardier. "What does it feel like when you let a bomb go? Can you hear the boom in the airplane? Are you scared when you go up? Have you killed any Germans?"

"Jorge, that's enough." Her mother, Esperanza, stepped forward and nodded. "Pleased to meet you, young man. Please forgive our son's insensitive questions. His manners could stand some polishing."

Jack smiled. "The pleasure is all mine. And I don't mind the questions."

Gracie watched with appreciation as Jack maneuvered the potential minefield of impressing her family. His manners were impeccable during dinner except when his hand slipped while cutting his steak and beans splattered on her father's white linen shirt. They all stared as her father scraped the beans off with his knife. Jack was clearly mortified, but Jorge Jr. thought it was hilarious. He leaned his chair back and slapped his knees as he chortled.

"Junior, sit your chair up. You're going to break those legs if you don't stop doing that." Her mother swatted at the boy with her fan.

Gracie's father dismissed it with a pat on Jack's shoulder. "Don't give it a thought, son. I've done much worse in my time." He stood, excused himself, and went upstairs to change. "Please, please continue. I'll be back in just a moment."

Gracie's mother started to get up as well, but her father shook his head. "Nonsense, my dear. I can certainly handle changing my own shirt. You stay here with our guest."

He rejoined them quickly with a fresh white shirt on. Her mother was reasonably cordial during the evening, if a bit aloof. Rosa, their cook, served a delicious five-course meal, complete with flan as dessert.

Jack's face was a comical mask of bliss as he took his first bite. "Umm, what is this? It's delicious, Mrs. Gonzales."

"That's a typical Mexican dessert, Jack, called *flan*." The statement came across condescending. Gracie could tell her mother did not approve of him. They sat awkwardly around the living room after supper, making disjointed attempts at conversation.

Jack said his good-byes after about an hour. "Thank you, ma'am, for a wonderful evening. A home-cooked meal sure tasted good. I haven't had steak since I left the farm. And that flan stuff. I gotta tell my mama about it. We don't have anything in Louisiana like that."

"Hmm, yes. Rosa makes a delicious, creamy flan." Her mouth in a thin line, Gracie's mother excused herself and went into the parlor as Jorge fetched his jacket.

Her mother had already informed her that she wasn't to ride with her father when he took Jack back to the bus stop, but she walked him to the door.

He took her hand, squeezed it, and whispered, "See you next weekend?" with a light in his eyes that made her knees go weak. She nodded.

He followed her father out, glancing over his shoulder and winking at her.

Stepping out on the front tile walkway, she waved good-bye as the two men drove off. An unexpected emptiness came over her when he left.

Serafina stood behind her in the doorway watching the Cadillac leave. She flipped her skirt at Gracie as she twirled around and headed toward the stairs. "Very nice, sis. I approve." Gracie smiled and went into the parlor to join her mother. She sat on a large ottoman across from her mother and watched as she poured a glass of wine. A heavy silence hung in the room as she waited for her mother to speak. But the older woman only swirled her wine and stared out the window.

Finally Gracie asked, "Well? What did you think of Jack?"

"*Muy guapo.*" She took a sip and set the goblet on a side table. "Very handsome indeed." She leaned back, put her elbow on the arm of the sofa, and looked directly at Gracie, with her head cocked to one side. Uh-oh. Her mother's cocked head always meant trouble. "He's handsome, polite, and…"

"But what, Mother? I hear a *but* in your voice."

She tapped her painted fingernail on the side table next to the wine glass. "I can see why you are attracted to him, but he's beneath you, Gracie. He's not of our…our station, and he won't understand our culture. He's not Mexican." She took another sip of wine. "I thought you were smarter than this." She held the wine glass in her hand, swirling the burgundy liquid round and round, staring into the receptacle as if it were some kind of crystal ball, holding prophecies of the future. "Is he Catholic?"

Gracie stood. "Oh my gosh, Mother. Do you know how snobbish all of those comments sound?"

"Don't use common slang, Gracie. You have a better vocabulary than that."

Gracie hung her head and sighed. "I don't know what kind of social station Jack is from. We've never talked about it. Obviously, he's not Mexican. I didn't know that made a difference. Can't he learn about our culture?"

Jack's comments from earlier in the evening nagged at her. *You're rich… and you're Mexican.* Was her mother right? Would it make a difference? And they'd never discussed religion. Maybe he was Catholic? Dare she hope? There were a lot of Catholics from Louisiana.

"Give him a chance, Mama. I'm just getting to know him. I'll find out more about his background this weekend when we go to the USO again. You never know. Maybe he is Catholic." Her voice turned snarky.

Sliding her wine glass silently onto the end table, Gracie's mother stood and drew up every bit of her five-foot stature to face her. How could such a tiny little woman be so intimidating?

Her black eyes flashed. "You've gone your last time to the USO, young lady. I never thought it was a good idea in the first place. You're too young. And down there dancing with all of those common soldiers." She hit her ever-present closed fan in the palm of her hand. "You're too—"

"Too good to dance with boys who are sacrificing their lives for our country? Mama, some of those boys will never go to a dance again. Some of them—" She covered her mouth and wouldn't let herself think the unthinkable. "All of the girls at school go down to the canteen on the weekends."

"You're not all of the other girls. You're *mi hija*, and I say you'll not go anymore. Prom and graduation are around the corner. Then we'll be getting you ready to go to college. We don't need this complication." She snapped her fan open. "No more arguing about it. You will not see that young man again."

She crossed in front of Gracie and headed up the stairs, leaving a trail of Evening in Paris perfume in her wake to make Gracie's eyes sting all the more.

For the first time in her life, she determined to disobey her parents.

Twelve

Christmas Eve 1944

G racie?" Cynthia touched Gracie's knee. "Hello? Are you with us? You must be daydreaming about your handsome husband." She laughed and took a bite of a sugar cookie.

Gracie twisted the silver band on her ring finger. "I'm sorry. You're right, I was thinking about Jack. What did you ask me?"

"Have you heard from him lately?"

Gracie shook her head. "I haven't heard a word in over two months. I'm...worried."

Naomi and Myrna returned from the kitchen with the goodies for Santa. Naomi handed the plate to Myrna, and the little girl set it carefully on the coffee table along with the other sweets.

"Good job, honey." Naomi looked at Gracie. "They say 'No news is good news.' You'll hear from him soon."

"He's a bombardier, you know. It's a dangerous assignment."

Cynthia took a sip of her hot chocolate. "I can't even imagine flying in the skies like that, shooting at men in other planes, releasing bombs on towns below you—"

79

"Cynthia." Naomi frowned at her daughter. "I'm sure Gracie doesn't need a blow-by-blow description of what dangers her husband is encountering."

"It's not as if I don't think about it constantly, Mrs. Lockhart." Gracie held her hot chocolate atop her bloated belly. The baby hadn't moved much today. She hadn't said anything to anybody about it, but she wondered if it was okay.

Robby plopped down on the couch beside Cynthia, making hot chocolate slosh out of Gracie's cup onto her smock. "Oh, gee, Gracie. I'm sorry." He jumped up, causing her to spill the hot liquid again.

She laughed and held her cup away from her body. "Not to worry. It's fine." She struggled to get up, but Naomi waved her off. "I'll get a rag." She dashed into the kitchen.

Gracie's thoughts returned to the night Jack had splattered beans on her father's shirt. The night her mother had forbidden her to ever see him again. The night she designed her plan.

March 1944

She'd cornered Lou the next week at school and told her what had happened. Handing Lou a letter she'd written on blue monogrammed stationery, she pleaded with her friend to deliver it to Jack. The letter simply stated that she was not permitted to see him again. She chose not to go into detail. How could she even try to rationalize her mother's thinking?

The weekend passed painfully slowly. She pushed her food around on her plate during a silent, awkward Saturday evening supper with the family. She normally looked forward to dinner on Saturday evenings because her father always grilled burgers. Chatter about the golf game her brother and father had played at the country club kept the meal from being completely silent, but Gracie had little to contribute.

Her mother started to touch her hand but drew back. "You're not eating much this evening. You love hamburgers."

She attempted a smile but couldn't look her mother in the face. She'd decided she would not argue with her parents. But she would figure something out. "I'm fine. Just not very hungry." She excused herself and went to her room and listened to "Your Hit Parade" on the radio when she would ordinarily be at the USO with her friends. With Jack.

Sunday morning Lou called her. "Gracie, can you go on a picnic after mass this morning?"

"I…probably. Who all is going?"

"The senior prom committee. We're gonna make final plans for next weekend." Lou lowered her voice to a hoarse whisper. "I have a reply from Jack. Saw him last night, but he's on duty today…couldn't get away. He was a miserable man last night when you didn't show up."

"Hold on." Gracie called out to her mother, "May I go with Lou and the prom committee on a picnic after mass? We're putting the final touches on the dance."

"Just the committee? I thought the junior class did all of the planning for the prom."

"They do. Our class has to put together some awards and recognition scrolls though."

Her mother walked to the phone stand. "Who're you talking to?"

"Lou."

"Give it to me." Her mother yanked the phone out of her hands. "Lou?" Gracie could just make out Lou's "Yes, ma'am?"

"Oh, it is you."

"Yes, ma'am."

"Where is it the committee is going?"

"We're just going to pack some sandwiches and eat out at Brackenridge Park. We want to be sure we have all the details of the prom taken care of."

"Nobody else but the committee?"

"No, ma'am."

She handed the phone back to Gracie, nodded, and waved her hand. "That's fine. Come straight home after you're finished."

Gracie took the receiver and turned away from her mother. "Looks like I can go."

"Wow. The third degree, huh?"

"Yeah. I'll see you then."

"Okay, I'll drive. I've already fixed a lunch for us. See you at church."

Gracie sat with her parents, and Lou sat with hers, for the longest mass Gracie had ever endured. When it was over, her mother grabbed her by the elbow.

"I'm trusting you not to go anywhere else or see anyone else. Do you understand?"

"Of course."

"Can I go with you?" Serafina walked behind them down the aisle to shake hands with the priest.

"No, this is the senior prom committee."

Gracie's mother turned to her daughters on the steps of the church as her father and brother went to the car. "That's a good idea. Yes, you may go, Serafina."

"Mother! This is just seniors."

"Oh, they won't care. Serafina can learn a thing or two about planning a prom." Lou and her parents exited the church about that time. "You don't care, do you, Lou, if Serafina goes with you all?"

"Oh…oh well, I guess not." She looked at Gracie and raised her eyebrows. "Come with us to take my parents home, and we'll leave from there."

Lou went into the house to get the picnic basket when they dropped off her parents. She tossed the small basket into the backseat with Serafina, slid behind the driver's seat, and pulled away from the curb. "Everybody's probably already there. We're about twenty minutes late." She pointed to her purse between them on the bench seat. Gracie frowned and stared at her. Lou pushed it toward Gracie as she shifted gears and motioned to her to open it.

She spied a folded-up piece of paper beside Lou's wallet. Gracie glanced in the back at Serafina, who was looking in the mirror of a compact while powdering her nose and putting on bright red lipstick. Her mother wouldn't be happy about that. Gracie held the short note in her lap and read it quickly.

Gracie, I've found the love of my life, and I'm not letting you go. I'm being shipped overseas in three weeks. I must see you before I leave. Meet me somewhere. Tell me when and where, and I'll be there. I'll Be Seeing You … J. B.

Prom was next weekend. She'd planned on taking Jack as her guest. Out of the question now. She would simply go with her girlfriends who didn't have dates either. Maybe he could meet her there, and they could go somewhere.

She'd been excited about her dress—a seafoam-green satin gown, fitted in the bodice with a sweetheart neckline. Rosettes gathered up the little cap sleeves, and a long slender skirt floated around her feet as she walked. She loved the way it felt—cool, slick, and soft. Her dyed-to-match, three-inch-high sandals were uncomfortable, but she didn't care. They looked good.

The click of the compact from the backseat alerted her that Serafina had finished with her makeup. Gracie tucked Jack's note into her pocket as she swiveled around and stared at her little sister's pouty red lips.

"Oh, my gosh." She pulled a Kleenex from her purse and thrust it toward her sister. "Wipe that off right now. Where did you get that lipstick anyway?"

"I don't have to wipe it off. You can't make me. I'm nearly sixteen, and I can wear it if I want to."

"Where'd you get it? Mama will have a fit."

She showed Gracie the tiny white tube. "Margie's mother is an Avon lady now, and she gave us a whole bunch of samples, in all the colors." She shoved it back into her purse with a flourish and sat forward, leaning into Gracie's face. In her best sing-song sister voice she taunted, "And Mama's fit about lipstick will be nothing compared to her fit when she finds out you are making plans to see Jack again." She smiled. "You keep my secret, and I'll keep yours."

Gracie whirled around. "What do you mean?"

Serafina sat back and cocked her head making her look more than ever like their mother. "I know you haven't given up that easily on him. That note you just shoved into your pocket? I'm not as naïve as you think."

"Why, you little—"

"Hey, I'm for you in this. I think he's dreamy. And I won't squeal on you…as long as you don't squeal on me."

"Don't worry. I won't." Scowling, Gracie faced the front and crossed her arms. But how far could she trust her little sister?

Thirteen

racie stood on the sidelines watching couples bouncing in rhythm to "Boogie Woogie Bugle Boy." She looked for the fifth time in as many minutes at her watch. Jack was to meet her at the side door of the country club ballroom at eight o'clock. A walkway ran from the side door around to the patio and pool. Perhaps they could steal a few minutes by the pool unnoticed.

At ten minutes to eight Gracie walked to the refreshment table and motioned to Lou. "I'm going outside now."

Lou nodded. Her frizzy blonde hair sprang out from the headband she'd tied around her head in a vain effort to control the curls. She shoved a stray spiral away with a scowl. "Never again am I going to let my mom give me a perm."

"It looks fine." Gracie smiled.

Lou hugged her and squealed. "Oh, this is so romantic! Aren't you nervous? You look cool as a cucumber." She glanced over her shoulder.

"Are you kidding? My heart is jumping out of my chest." Gracie was already moving toward the foyer.

"Old Miss Turbeville is keeping watch by the door so nobody slips by her."

"I can get by her through the stage door. I'll be back before the dance is over." She ran toward the heavy curtain hiding the stage door and slipped through, then made for the French doors that lined the side wall and pushed one of them open. She looked both ways but didn't see Jack at first.

"Gracie, over here."

She whirled around as he stepped out from the shadows of a potted philodendron.

"Oh, you look nice. I didn't think about you wearing civvies." She'd never seen him dressed that way. She reached out to touch him but held back, suddenly shy. "How long have you been here?"

Jack laughed. "About thirty minutes. Come here." He pulled her into his arms and kissed her softly. Then he took her hand and twirled her around. "You look smashing. That dress, those shoes. Your hair! Oh, my gosh, your hair." He touched the bouffant up-swept hairdo lightly with his fingers. "You…you take my breath away." He held a white box in his hands. "Here, I got this for you."

Gracie stared at the box. "What is it?"

"I felt bad you didn't have a date for your senior prom, so I got you a corsage." He opened it and took out a small white orchid.

"Jack. You shouldn't have. Really. I didn't care I didn't have a date. If I couldn't go with you, I didn't care."

The flower petals shook as he held the delicate blossom. "Here, put it on." Gracie started to pin it on her dress, but Jack caught her hand. "No, put it in your hair." He took it from her and threaded it in her hair behind her ear. He stood back and looked at her. "Perfect."

Gracie motioned toward the lighted foyer. "C'mon. Let's get away from the building." She took him by the hand and led him around the pool behind the bath house. Benches and tables sat scattered beneath the trees, but no lights, except a few here and there lighting up the trees. They sat in a glider and pushed the seat into motion.

Jack put his arm around her and held her. Gracie sighed, pulled her legs up underneath her, and snuggled closer to him.

He cleared his throat. "I just had to see you before I'm shipped out." He lifted her face toward him and caressed it with the backs of his fingers. "I want to memorize every line of your face, the color of your eyes. I might not ever—"

"Shh." Gracie put her finger on his lips. "Don't even say it. You will come back."

Jack took her hand. "What happened with your parents? I thought they liked me well enough."

"It's not my parents, just my mother. My father likes you fine."

"Why doesn't she like me? Because of my bumbling manners?" He chuckled and rubbed his hand over the front of his shirt.

She laughed. "No. It's because…well…you're not Catholic by any chance, are you?"

"It so happens I am."

"Well, at least that's one thing in your favor. But you're not Mexican."

Jack's grin went lopsided. "Not much I can do about that, is there?"

They sat in silence for a few seconds. He stroked the back of Gracie's hand as the glider floated back and forth gently. The strains of "I'll Be Seeing You" wound its way outside.

"I can't let you go, Gracie. I don't want to cause problems in your family, but I can't leave thinking I'll never see you again." He pulled her out of the swing. "That's our song. Dance with me."

They stood. With her heels on, Gracie was as tall as he. She reached down and pulled them off. "These are killing my feet." He steadied her with his hand on her elbow then swept her into his arms. They swayed to the music.

"I'll be seeing you … in all the old, familiar places." Jack sang along.

"Mmm. You have a nice voice."

"School choir."

Their bodies molded together as Jack held her closer and tighter. He kissed her, still swaying to the music. She laced her fingers together in his hair and pulled herself closer. He snuggled into her neck, kissing her, and nibbled on her ear. His voice grew hoarse.

"Gracie, Gracie. I love you so much. I want you bad."

"Badly."

"In the worst way." Smiling, he broke away from their embrace and searched her eyes. "But I won't disrespect you. We'll wait until I get back to get married."

"Let's get married now."

"What do you mean? Right now?"

"No, but I've had an idea. Next week is our senior trip. I'll meet you, and we can elope. Can you get leave?"

"I don't know, Gracie. What about your parents?"

"They won't be happy, but they'll get over it."

"I will admit I've thought about it, but what if something happens to me and…and I don't come back?"

Gracie stared at this man whom she'd met only a few weeks ago but who had come to mean so much to her. "I'd rather be married to you for just a few days than never." She put her hand on his chest. "But you'll come back. God wouldn't bring us together to tear us apart, would He? He wouldn't be that cruel…right?"

He put his hand on hers, leaned over, and kissed her lips lightly. "God is not cruel, Gracie. But evil men are, and we are at war." He gathered her into his arms, not speaking, simply holding her.

She closed her eyes and molded her body into his embrace. She breathed in the spicy fragrance of his aftershave. It wasn't the overpowering, sweet scent like her father wore. The faint, lingering scent, while spicy, smelled woodsy and sweet. "What kind of aftershave do you use?"

Jack shook his head and chuckled. "We are talking about getting married, God, and the evil of war, and you want to know what kind of aftershave I use?"

"I just thought I should know my future husband's preferences." She snuggled against him again.

"Bay rum."

"I love it."

He kissed the top of her head. "I'll apply for leave next week. What day do you go on your trip?"

"Thursday. Are we going to do it? Get married?"

"I agree with you. I'd rather be married for a few days than never at all. And if I don't make it back—"

"But you will—"

He held up his hand. "If I don't, at least you would receive my veteran's benefits."

Gracie looked down. "I won't need them. My family is wealthy."

"What if they disown you?"

"Oh, they wouldn't do that." She paused. "At least, I don't think they would."

"Just in case…remember you would qualify to have them as my…widow."

"Don't say that."

He reached in his back pocket, took out his wallet, and looked at a calendar. "I may be able to wrangle four or five days leave before I'd have to get back. They're pretty generous with guys shipping overseas." He took Gracie by the shoulders. "I love you with everything that is within me. I can't find the words to express to you the depth of my feelings. I want to quote an eloquent poem or sing a beautiful song to you, but all I seem to be able to say is 'I love you.' And that falls miles short of what I'm feeling."

She touched his cheek with her fingertips. "You're doing a pretty good job, soldier." She kissed him, and he responded, taking charge of the moment. He explored her lips and mouth in ways she hadn't experienced before. She wanted more and more of him.

He pulled away and took a deep breath. His blue-gray eyes darkened. "Where shall I meet you? What time? I'm pretty sure I can borrow a car."

Gracie took a breath and sat back down to put on her shoes. "We're loading up at the high school at eight o'clock Thursday morning. Just meet me there."

"Won't your parents be there to see you off?"

"You're right, of course. I didn't think about that. Okay, we're stopping in Boerne to eat breakfast at an old inn in town. Wait for me there."

"What's the name of it?"

"Ye Kendall Inn. We'll be there by nine or so. It's tradition with the senior classes to eat breakfast at the inn on their trip." A ripple of excitement shot up her spine. "Are we really going to do this? Is there anything I need to do?"

"We'll need to get a marriage license. Don't worry about any of the details. I'll take care of everything." He took her hand. "I need to go, and you need to get back inside."

She knew he was right, but… "I don't want to leave you. And you got all dressed up for nothing."

"What do you mean for nothing? I got to be with the love of my life, dance with her, hold her, and kiss her. Thursday will be here before we know it." He took her in his arms again and touched his lips to hers. "It gets harder every time to leave you." He laughed at the flower that now dangled crookedly over her ear and straightened it. "Now go back to your prom. This time next week, you'll be Mrs. Jack Blauvelt."

"Gracie Blauvelt. I like the sound of that."

He grinned at her. "Me too. I'll see you at Ye Kendall Inn in Boerne, Thursday around nine o'clock."

She gave him another kiss on the cheek and walked to the corner of the bath house. When she turned to look at him before she opened the door, she could barely see him in the shadows.

"Gracie?"

"Mother!"

"Wha…what are you doing here?" She saw her father emerge from the cloak room down the hall.

Her mother drew her black lace shawl around her shoulders. "We decided to come have dinner in the restaurant and see all your friends in their prom attire. But the question is, what were you doing outside, and where did you get that lovely flower?"

FOURTEEN

Jack leaned against the hood of the borrowed gray Dodge and watched the school bus pull up in the parking lot of Ye Kendall Inn. Beads of sweat gathered on his forehead as heat rose from the damp parking lot in the early morning sunshine of south Texas. He took out a handkerchief and wiped his face. He'd worn his uniform today thinking it would be easier to persuade a justice of the peace to marry them if the official knew he was a soldier about to be shipped overseas.

The bus screeched to a lumbering stop. Students tumbled out, catcalling and laughing as they walked to the inn. Several glanced over at him, with no more than a passing acknowledgement.

Lou emerged and ran to him. "I don't know where Gracie is."

"What do you mean you don't know where she is?"

"I mean I can't find her. She's not at her house. Nobody's answering the phone. I went by there, and they're gone."

"They can't be."

"Well, they are." She reset the headband holding her wild curls away from her face. "Except…a guy on the bus this morning said that Serafina is staying with his little sister, so wherever they went, they left Serafina here."

"Do you have a phone number?"

"No…umm, wait here, and I can get it." Lou hurried inside. In just a few minutes, she returned with a phone number. "They'll be in school, so you'll have to wait until this afternoon."

Jack slapped his leg in frustration. "Can I go to the school and talk to Serafina?"

"Maybe." She tossed her curls out of her face. "It's worth a try."

He stuffed the small folded note into his pocket and gave the girl a hug. "Thanks, Lou. You're a good friend." He got in the car and started the ignition. "Wish me luck."

"Yeah, good luck. I think you're swell too."

He watched her waving at him as he drove back toward San Antonio. What was going on? Shaking his head, he recalled watching Gracie's parents approach her at the prom last week. He didn't like this game of cat and mouse. He liked things to be above board and honest, and this seemed sneaky and underhanded.

If he'd done what he felt was right last weekend, he would have approached her parents and told them right then what their plans were. But at the time he reasoned Gracie would not have wanted him to. So he stood helplessly by and watched them argue through the panes of the French doors.

He hit the steering wheel with the palm of his hand. He'd find her, that was all. Find her and make her his wife yet.

Jack cut his gaze over at Serafina, who was sitting in the passenger seat and smacking a big wad of gum. She looked nothing like Gracie, nor did she have the elegance and class of her big sister. But she exuded life and sparkle—and plenty of spunk. He liked her. After Jack told the front office at the high school he needed to speak to Serafina Gonzales, she appeared shortly, and they simply walked out of the building. The girl told the secretary he was her uncle, and there was a family emergency. Now they were speeding toward the Hill Country to the Gonzales' second home near Kerrville.

"Are you sure that's where they are?"

Nodding, she popped a bubble with her gum. "Yep. I guarantee that's where they are. Well, Mama and Gracie anyway, and Junior. He was glad to get out of school for a few days. He loves fishing on the river—goes early every morning when we're there. Pop probably had patients to see at his clinic. It's only about an hour away." She turned toward him and folded one bobby-socked foot underneath her. Grinning, she twirled a lock of her shiny black hair. "What are you going to do?"

"I'm going to get Gracie and we're eloping. Except now that everyone knows, I don't know if you call it eloping anymore. We're getting married, whatever it's called at this point."

"What if my mother won't let her?"

"Gracie's eighteen, right?"

"Yep. She sure is."

"Then there's nothing your parents can do if she's of age and chooses to leave."

"You don't know my mother. She's very possessive of Gracie." Serafina turned back around in her seat and continued to pop her gum as she stared out the window.

Except for music on the radio, they rode in silence for the next thirty minutes until they reached the outskirts of Kerrville.

Serafina pointed to a gravel road leading up into a large butte covered in cedar and mesquite trees. "Turn here."

White dust from the dry caliches clay churned behind them blending in with the gray color of the car. Turning right again at a fork in the road, they drove through a shallow stream then followed the road to a large white clapboard home with a screened-in porch facing the Guadalupe River.

Serafina indicated a clearance under a grove of mesquite trees where the Duesenberg was parked. "See. I was right. Pull up here."

Jack cut off the ignition and stepped out of the car. "This is beautiful. It's so quiet."

Variegated colors of wildflowers fluttered in a brisk morning breeze. It was a bit late for bluebonnets, but clumps of Indian paintbrush poked up through the soil. Cypress trees lined the bank of the river where the water burbled through knobby giant roots. It was noticeably cooler here than in San Antonio.

"Yeah, my parents love it here. Kinda boring, though." She tugged on his sleeve and started toward the front door. "C'mon. We may as well get this over with. Be prepared for explosions."

She opened the door to the porch and stepped in. Wicker furniture and potted plants sat on the left, and a porch swing hung on the right side. The rich aroma of coffee greeted them. "Hello? Are y'all up?"

Jack watched as the Gonazales' maid, Rosa, walked out holding a cooking fork with a piece of bacon dangling from it.

"Miss Serafina! What are you doing here? I thought you were at school."

"Oh, a friend brought me out." She motioned to Jack.

Rosa's eyes grew even wider. "¡Madra mía! Let me get Miss Esperanza. She's still in the bed."

Serafina caught Rosa by the arm. "Wait a minute. Where's Gracie?"

A tear glistened in Rosa's eye. She shook her head. "It's been bad, Miss

Serafina. Miss Esperanza kept Gracie locked in her room. All Miss Gracie does is cry."

Suddenly Serafina was all business. "Where's the key?" She picked up a napkin from the table and spit her gum into it.

"Miss Esperanza keeps it with her. I suppose it's in her room."

A surge of courage shot up Jack's spine. He'd never been surer of anything in his life. "I don't need a key. Where's her room?"

"Come with me." Serafina led Jack toward a large open room with rustic furniture and deer heads hanging on the walls. She walked to a staircase to their left. Pointing to a closed door on the ground floor of the other side of the stairs, she placed her index finger over her mouth. "Shh. That's Mama's bedroom there." She motioned for Jack to follow her up the stairs. "The stairs are gonna creak, but don't stop. Gracie's room is at the top of the stairs to the right. Go on."

She stepped aside to let him pass.

He took the stairs two at a time and quickly reached Gracie's room. He knocked softly. "Gracie? Gracie, it's Jack." He heard the scrape of bed springs then the shuffle of her footsteps.

"Jack? Oh, Jack, how did you find me?" She rattled the doorknob. "Get me out!"

"I will. Get dressed and gather your things. I'm coming in." He looked at the hinges on the door. The door opened inward. He heard movement downstairs.

"Serafina! What are you doing here?"

Jack looked over the banister as Esperanza emerged from her room, tying the belt of her robe. Serafina walked toward her mother as Esperanza spotted Jack.

She shook her finger up at him. "Young man, get out of this house!" She jerked her head toward Serafina. "How could you bring him here? How could you betray your family?"

"Because, Mama, this isn't right. You cannot force your will on someone by locking them in a room. I don't care whether it's your daughter or not. She's of age. She ought to be able to make her own decisions." She started around her mother toward the bedroom. "Where's the key to Gracie's room?"

"You wouldn't dare."

"Watch me. Where's the key?" Serafina went through the door of her mother's bedroom. Esperanza caught Serafina's arm, whirling her around, and slapped her. The crack resounded through the house. Jack rushed down the stairs to them. A stunned silence hovered over the room.

Serafina put her hand to her cheek. Her eyes sparking fire at her mother, she whispered, "You *cannot* force people to do what you want them to do. Where's the key?"

Jack stepped in front of Serafina. "Mrs. Gonzales, I mean no disrespect and don't want to interfere in family business, but this is between me and Gracie. I had hoped this would be a happy affair. I love your daughter with all of my heart and will be a good husband to her. I'm being shipped overseas next week, and we've decided we want to be married before I go. We would like your blessing and permission."

Esperanza's jaw worked as she replied through gritted teeth. "Over my dead body."

He sighed. "I guess we're going to have to do this the hard way. I will get into that room one way or another. If I have to break down the door, I will… and can…but I would rather you give us the key so we can be on our way."

Serafina darted to a bedside table, picked up the key, and threw it to him. "Here ya go."

He caught the key and ran up the stairs, unlocking Gracie's door before Esperanza could stop him. But it wasn't long before her footsteps came racing up after him—and in her hand she had a fireplace poker, which she waved in the air. "You'll not take my daughter away from us!"

"Mama!" Gracie backed away from her mother. "Watch out, Jack!"

He ducked as the woman, screaming like a banshee, swung the weapon back and forth. She missed on the first two swings, but the tip of the poker grazed his forehead on the third swipe.

He caught her by the wrist and removed the poker from her grip. "Mrs. Gonzales, there's no need for this."

The woman crumpled in a heap on the floor weeping, her hands over her face. "Please don't take my daughter away. You don't understand about her."

Gracie stepped around her mother and ran to Jack. "Are you hurt? Oh, Mama, what have you done?" She grabbed a towel from a washstand and blotted the trickle of blood that had started down his temple. He wadded the towel up in his hand and held it to his head. "It's not deep. It only grazed me."

Serafina, who had followed her mother up the stairs, stared with wide eyes. "Gee whiz, this looks like a scene from a movie."

"It's okay. Nothing really. Take your mother downstairs, Serafina. We're leaving now. We'll let you know where we are." He looked at the blood on the towel and threw it back onto the wash stand. "You know, I'm not taking your sister away from you."

"I know. I don't know why Mama is so possessive of Gracie."

Esperanza's quiet sobbing turned to wails as Jack and Gracie sped out the door. He bustled the trembling young woman into his car and hurried to his own door. A glance in the mirror showed that her mother had stumbled out the front door and onto the gravel driveway in her bare feet. He started the car and gunned it while she fell to her knees.

He glanced over at the beautiful profile of his sweet bride. Even with her eyes red-rimmed and her breath coming is gasps, she was the only girl in the world he could imagine loving. But he knew very well he'd just turned *her* world upside down.

FIFTEEN

Christmas Eve, 1944

Gracie's breath hitched as a band of steel clutched her abdomen and then subsided in the darkened living room of the Golden Aspen Inn.

"Are you okay?" Cynthia turned toward Gracie. "You are as pale as a ghost."

"I'm fine. Just not very comfortable." A tear, too proud to fall, hung in the corner of her eye. She exhaled, pressing the tear away with her knuckle. "I think the smoke from the fireplace is getting to me, and I'm worried about Jack."

Quenton stoked the fire to stir up the flames. "I'm sure everything's fine with him. Mail's got to be slow from overseas, and who knows when they have time to write."

Everyone nodded in agreement with him.

Why does everybody always say everything is fine, when they don't really know? Gracie traced circles on her belly with her fingers. That's what Jack had kept saying as they drove back to her house in San Antonio, patting her clenched hands in her lap.

March 1944

They skidded to a stop in front of the house, dust billowing. Gracie barely let the car come to a stop before she flew out of the car and rummaged under the sculpture of a frog in the flowerbed for the hidden key to the front door.

"Whoa there, girl. Wait for me." He followed behind her as she dashed up the stairs.

Pointing to a small door that led to the attic stairwell, she pulled him along behind her. She retrieved the old diaper bag with the picture and records of her childhood she had found and stuffed them into a box. "Here, help me with this." If she didn't take them now, she figured her mother would destroy them in her rage when it became apparent Gracie knew the truth.

They hurried back down the stairs. "Bring that box into my room."

She had to decide what would stay in the big, luxurious house of her childhood and what would be needed in her new life in a sparse apartment as a military wife. She started tossing toiletries in a train case and clothing into a larger suitcase she hauled from her closet.

"Hey, go easy there. I have to be able to lift all of this." He chuckled.

"I want to take all I can. I know I'll not be back for a long time."

"What do you mean? Once your mother cools down, I'm sure you can come home again while I'm overseas."

"I'm not coming back here. I'm going to Colorado Springs." She closed the train case with a thud and latched it.

"Colorado Springs? Why there? What about graduation? You can't just leave without graduating. You've only a few weeks to go." Jack's mood turned serious. He shook his head and took her by the shoulders. "Don't be foolish about this."

"No, I've thought the whole situation through. I decided if I ever got out of that locked room, I would never go back to my family." She sat on her bed. "Besides, they're not my real family. That's what I have to tell you." She looked up at him. "I don't have a birth certificate. I hope we can get a marriage license."

"I don't understand. That may prove to be a real problem." He put his hands in his pockets and stepped back.

"A few months ago, clues began to add up that I am adopted. Although my mother adamantly denies it, one day when my parents were gone, I decided to look for my birth certificate and any records I could find. I found this." She pulled the picture with the Christmas stocking out of the old diaper bag and handed it to Jack. "That's me. All of my baby pictures in our family albums look just like that. It's me. No mistake about it."

Jack traced the gold engraving of the photographer's name in Colorado Springs in the righthand corner of the picture. "So that's why you want to go to Colorado Springs." He paused. "Your real name is Julia? And you're not Mexican?"

"I suppose. I don't know for sure, of course, but I need to find out." She carefully replaced the picture into the envelope and into the diaper bag. "I'll stay with you until you ship out. Then I'll go to Colorado Springs, get a job, and try to trace my real family."

"Gracie, these people have loved you, given you a home, raised you in"—he looked around the beautiful pink and white bedroom with the four-poster canopied bed—"luxury and wealth. Are you sure you want to do this?"

"I need to know why my mother so viciously denies what seems to be more and more obvious as time goes by." She sat on top of the bulging suitcase and attempted to click it shut.

Jack waved her off. "Let me do this for you. We'd better get out of here before someone finds us." He pressed down on the edges of the suitcase and clicked the latches shut, grunting as he swung it off the bed. Gracie picked up the train case and started for the door.

She hesitated and turned to look around her childhood bedroom. Darting back to the bed, she knelt beside it and searched underneath with her hand. She withdrew the stuffed chenille dog she had found in the attic and hidden for the past few weeks. "I want to take this."

He smiled. "An old friend?"

"I suppose so." She stuffed the dog in the train case and set it on top of the toiletries. "Let's go."

They sped toward downtown. "Do you know where the courthouse is?"

She nodded. "It's in the middle of town. We can find it."

Jack looked at the gas gauge. "We'd better stop and fill up. My little unplanned side trip to the hill country has us on empty." He grinned and squeezed her hand as he started to pull into a Mobil station.

"No, not that one." Gracie yanked on his sleeve and caused the car to swerve.

"Wha…what's wrong with that one?"

"That's where our family always goes. We have an account there, and they would recognize me."

He shook his head and drove past the white station with the flying red horse emblem. "What would it matter? I'm sure the police are not out looking for you…yet."

"I don't want anything to keep us from getting to the courthouse."

He put his arm around her and pulled her toward him. "Don't worry.

Nothing's going to stop us now." After a couple of blocks, they spotted a Texaco station. "Does this one meet with your approval?"

She touched her cheek as her skin flushed hot, ducked her head, and nodded.

The attendant, an older man with deep creases in his leathery skin, emerged from the service bay, wiping his greasy hands on an equally greasy rag. He pushed his cap with the familiar red star back on his head and smiled. "What can I do for you, sir?"

Jack smiled at the guy. "Fill 'er up, please."

"Regular or ethyl?"

"Hmm, regular, I guess." As the attendant reached for the pump, Jack got out and moved to pop the hood.

The attendant stepped up. "I'll get that for you, sir."

"Just a habit. I worked at a service station my senior year in high school. I've borrowed this car for the day, but if it needs oil, let's take care of it."

The attendant looked at the clean dip stick and shook his head. "Nope, it looks fine. So does the water. You're good to go."

Jack paid, got back in the car, and started it. "Which direction?"

"We need to get on Main Street. That'll take us downtown and to the courthouse." Gracie rifled through her purse. "What if they won't give us a marriage license without my birth certificate?"

"Let's cross that bridge when we get to it. We'll keep going till we find someone who will." He stopped at a red light and gave her a long look. A pretty blush stained her cheeks, making him smile. "Don't worry. Things will work out."

Traffic picked up as they got into town. Gracie pointed to the Nix Hospital on the left as they drove by. "That's where my daddy's clinic is." She stared at the front entrance as if she expected him to emerge at any moment.

They found the courthouse after a wrong turn and a place to park right in front. Moist heat rose from the concrete sidewalk, wet from a sprinkler left too long on a flowerbed of sagging begonias. They ran up the steps hand in hand and burst through the big double doors into the cool interior of the austere foyer. They looked at each other, and Gracie giggled. "I wonder where we go now?"

Jack tugged her toward a small marquee with names of the many offices and their suite numbers by the elevator. Running his finger down the glass, he found the county clerk's office listed. "It's on the first floor."

The elevator dinged and the door slid open. An old man with a ring of fuzzy white hair around a bald crown and wearing a snappy brown uniform stuck his head out as he held the door. "Going up?"

Jack shook his head. "No, thanks. The office we're looking for seems to be down here."

The old gentleman looked at them and smiled. "Looking to get a marriage license?"

"Well, yes, sir, as a matter of fact we are." Jack pushed his cap back on his head and cleared his throat. "Is it that obvious?"

The kindly man chuckled. "I can always tell." He pointed down the hall. "Second door on the right. And good luck."

"Yes, sir. Thank you."

Jack opened the door to the county clerk's office and motioned Gracie to go in first. Several secretaries clacked away on their typewriters at desks set in rows behind a railing. They walked past the typing pool to a bank teller type window.

A woman who reminded Jack of an old maid got up from her desk and came to the window. She stuck a loose tendril of mousey brown hair with a few gray sprigs into her bun and looked through bottle-thick lenses at them. "Yes? What can I do for you?"

Gracie hung back.

Jack took off his hat. "Good morning, ma'am."

The woman looked at her watch. "It's been afternoon for a couple of hours now, young man." She repeated, "What can I do for you?"

"Right you are. Uh, we'd like to apply for a marriage license, please."

"I'll need your birth certificates."

Jack pulled a folded envelope out of his pocket and shoved it underneath the iron grid in front of the grim clerk. He put his arm around Gracie and brought her up to the edge of the counter then stooped down to talk to the woman behind the window. "We have a slight problem with my fiancée's birth certificate."

The woman raised her dark bushy eyebrows. "No birth certificate? I figured as much."

Gracie took a deep breath and squared her shoulders. "Ma'am, I'm adopted and have no valid birth certificate. I do, however, have immunization and school records. Will those suffice?"

"Your adoptive parents should have secured an official birth certificate for you after the adoption. I need that to issue you a marriage license." The woman leaned toward the window, and had it not been for the foreboding bars would have been only inches from Jack's face. "No birth certificate, no marriage license."

SIXTEEN

Tears burned in Gracie's eyes. "Oh, please. I guarantee I'm who I say I am."

Jack leaned in with his elbows on the counter. "Ma'am, I am being shipped, and we want to get married before I leave. Please…isn't there something you can do?"

"Well, there is a ten-day waiting period, and you have to get blood tests…"

"Blood tests?" Gracie's heart plunged like a canoe going over a waterfall. "I didn't know about that."

"Wait a minute. Ma'am, I have buddies who have gotten married overnight here in San Antonio. I know there is something you can do for us." Beads of sweat popped out on Jack's upper lip. He wiped them away with his thumb. "Please, ma'am? Something…?"

The clerk shook her head. A man in a suit, his tie loosened in the heat, stepped up to the window behind the clerk. He brushed a lock of straight hair back from his eyes. Gracie looked at the wrinkles around his eyes and the laugh creases around his mouth. He must be middle-aged but sure didn't look like it from a distance. He looked familiar.

"Is there a problem, Marge?" A badge on his lapel read "James Daughtry, County Clerk."

"Yes, sir. This couple wants a marriage license, but she has no birth certificate."

The man took a pair of glasses out of his coat pocket and scrutinized Jack and Gracie's papers in front of him. "Gracie Gonzales?" He peered over the reading glasses at her. "Aren't you Dr. Gonzales's daughter?"

She caught her breath. She recognized him now. This was the Mr. Daughtry her father occasionally played golf with. He had been in their home a few times through the years, but she didn't know he was now the county clerk. "Y...yes, sir." Her knees weakened and her stomach turned over.

The man took his glasses off and looked first at Jack, then at Gracie, then at his employee. "I'll take care of this. You may go back to work."

The woman huffed a breath through her nose. "Very well." She turned on her heel and walked away.

Mr. Daughtry motioned them to the end of the counter. "Come back here to my office." He walked with them toward the wall, opened a small swinging gate, and held out his hand toward Jack. They shook hands as Jack held on to Gracie's hand with his other one.

Jack's military shoes clicked on the wooden floor as they followed the man to a door with an opaque window, COUNTY CLERK, JAMES DAUGHTRY painted on it in bold black letters. He went around his desk and sat, tossing their papers on top of a desk calendar. Bookshelves on either side of the room were stuffed with law books.

"Sit." He leaned back in his chair and crossed his legs, ankle on his knee. "Now, tell me what's going on here, young lady. Do your parents know about this? And did I hear you say you're adopted? Who told you that?"

She licked her lips and swallowed. Her throat suddenly felt like sandpaper. "It's a long story." She cleared her throat.

"Would you like a glass of water?"

"Yes, that would be nice. Thank you."

Mr. Daughtry buzzed his secretary. A tall, attractive blonde stuck her head in the door. "Yes, Mr. Daughtry?"

"Would you bring us a pitcher of water, please?"

Gracie turned her face away, but not before the girl recognized her. "Hi, Gracie! What are you doing here?" The young woman had graduated from her school two years ago and was homecoming queen when Gracie was the sophomore princess.

Jack stood and acknowledged the young woman as Gracie spoke to her. "Hello, Delores. How have you been?"

"Wonderful." She stepped into the room and held out her left hand, her nails painted red and a small diamond sparkling atop a gold band. "I'm getting married this summer."

"Congratulations." Gracie looked at Jack and smiled. "Me too, but hopefully much sooner." She took Jack's hand. "This is Jack Blauvelt, my fiancé. Jack, this is Dolores Collins. Dotty and I were in the homecoming court together two years ago."

Delores batted her eyes at Jack. "Mmm. Handsome and a gentleman as well. Lucky girl." She fluffed her page boy.

"Delores, the water, please."

"Yes, of course."

Mr. Daughtry sat forward as the girl left the office. "You were saying, Gracie? It's a long story? Please, tell me." He leaned back in his chair again and folded his hands over his abdomen.

She took a deep breath and started her story. She went over the pertinent facts—how she began to wonder because of people's comments about her different appearance through the years, then her grandmother's slip of the tongue, and finding the picture in the diaper bag. "But there was no birth certificate, only immunizations, school records, and a passport."

Mr. Daughtry sat up. "Wait a minute. You have a passport?"

"Yes. From when we went to Spain four years ago."

"My dear, that will suffice to get you a marriage license. I don't know how you got it without a birth certificate, but be that as it may…with a passport you're legal."

Jack's eyes widened and he jumped out of his chair. "Jiminy, Gracie! Why didn't you tell me you had a passport?"

"Well, I…I didn't know it was important." She stood. "It's in the diaper bag."

He put his hat back on. "I'll go get it." He dashed out of the office door.

"Sit back down, Gracie. What about your parents?" The clerk tapped his fingers on his desk. "I think they don't know about this."

She gripped the arms of her chair as if they'd keep her stable. The wood felt smooth and cool unlike her sweaty palms. "You won't tell them, will you? I've just been through a nightmare with them."

He looked at his watch. "I have a tee time in Kerrville with your father at ten o'clock tomorrow. You'd better have a good reason for eloping. I don't want to have to lie to your father." He reached over by the telephone and picked up a pink slip of paper. "I have a message here to call him ASAP. My guess is he knows it would make sense for you to come here if you want to elope and wants to know if we've seen you. Why do you want to rob your parents of having a proper wedding for you?"

"My mother denies that I am adopted. Worse, she just kept me locked me up for a week to keep me from Jack. We got into an awful fight this morning when Jack came to get me. He's being sent overseas in three weeks, and we just want to get married." She leaned forward and put her hands on his desk. "Mr. Daughtry, she went ballistic. She's not thinking right. She even went after him with a fireplace poker. My father likes Jack and approves, but he won't stand up to Mama." She sighed and sat back. "Please help us."

Mr. Daughtry stood and walked to the window behind his desk. Looking out at the busy street, he took time to light a cigarette, inhaling deeply. He walked around his desk and sat on the edge facing Gracie.

Jack came back into the office, waving the passport in his hand. "I found it."

"Sit, young man." He set his cigarette in an already full ashtray on his desk. "I remember when your parents got you, Gracie. You were around nine or ten months old. They were so proud of you. It was a hard adjustment, as I remember. I recall your father telling me how much you cried for your mother, who, he said, had perished in a car accident. I can attest to the fact that you are indeed adopted." He picked up the cigarette and put it back in his mouth, inhaled, and then stubbed it out in the ashtray. "I disapproved of their decision not to tell you the truth. Information like that is bound to come out eventually." He shook his head. "But you know your mother. Once Esperanza gets her mind set on something, there's no persuading her otherwise."

He stood. "I sympathize with you, Gracie. But you need to talk to your parents before you do this. At least your father."

She lifted her chin. "I'm of age, Mr. Daughtry—and apparently have the legal requirements. If you don't give us the license here, we'll just drive to another country and get it *there*."

A battle flickered through his eyes for a moment. And then he sighed. "I believe you will. And I can hardly hold you here. Very well then, I'd rather be able to tell your father I saw you were well and happy. I'll tell Marge to issue you the marriage license, and I'll give you the name of a justice of the peace who's been performing quite a few ceremonies for soldiers about to ship out. He'll be sympathetic."

Gracie stood and offered her hand. "We can't thank you enough." Tears brimmed in her eyes. She pulled a tissue out of her purse and held it to the corner of her eye. "I'm sorry to be so emotional." She stood on tiptoe and gave Mr. Daughtry a kiss. "Thank you so much."

"I have a feeling your father won't be thanking me—but you've always had a good head on your shoulders." He embraced her and shook Jack's hand. "Young man, you treat this young lady well. She is a precious treasure."

Jack nodded and continued to shake Mr. Daughtry's hand. "I know that right well, sir."

Marriage license in hand, they found the justice of the peace in his office just on the edge of downtown. He was a slender man with a large Adam's apple and dark hair combed to the side, hunched over a desk.

Jack stepped toward him and held out the marriage license. "Sir, we'd like to be married. Can you perform a ceremony right away? I'm being shipped out soon."

The man looked at the young couple with lifted brows. "You must be the couple James Daughtry just called me about."

"Yes, sir."

"Come on in. I happen to be free at the moment. Let me get my secretary."

Gracie's knees shook so hard, she was sure the justice of the peace could see the fabric of her skirt rippling. A lone lamp sat on a small desk. A weary secretary with blond hair in finger waves, dressed in black and solid laced-up shoes, stood in as a witness. Reading the ceremony in a monotone voice, the justice of the peace went through it quickly and without comment.

In spite of the official's obvious disinterest, the familiar vows sounded strangely personal now. *For richer, for poorer.* She'd only known wealth and privilege. Would they be rich or would they be poor? She didn't care. *In sickness and in health.* What if Jack returned from the war wounded or injured? She would take care of him. *Till death do us part.* What if he didn't return at all?

Gracie clutched a bouquet of daisies Jack had purchased at a corner florist shop. The delicate white petals drooped in her fist. She hadn't changed clothing and still wore a light yellow blouse with a matching cardigan and her yellow plaid skirt. She looked down at her white flats and noticed scuff marks on the toes. Strange, what small insignificant details one noticed in the midst of the pivotal events of life.

Jack held her hand tightly and slipped a silver ring with small diamond chips onto her finger. She hadn't had the opportunity to get a ring for him. At the instruction from the dour justice of the peace, Jack took her face in his hands and kissed her tenderly. "I will love you forever…no matter how long or short our forever may be."

Out of the corner of her eye, Gracie noticed a small smile on the justice of the peace's mouth before she lost herself in her new husband's embrace.

Seventeen

The next few days passed in a blur. They found a small garage apartment an older couple was willing to rent them for a month. Jack had been able to obtain three more days' leave but had to go back to the base after that. His commanding officer let him go home at night. Gracie took care of small business items during the day. They were close to town, and she could walk to the grocery store to purchase a few things. She had gone to the bank and withdrawn all her money out of her account. She didn't dare go to school, lest her parents had someone watching the place. For the most part the newlyweds stayed sequestered in their room until Jack had to leave.

"What do you think brought us together?" Jack moved little green peas around on one of the stained white plates the garage apartment came equipped with. Gracie didn't know how to cook, but she had managed mashed potatoes and hamburger patties. Adding a can of English peas made them a decent meal.

"What? Do you mean like fate…or God…or something?"

"Do you think it's possible that God brought us together?"

She nodded and put down her fork. "I suppose so. I do think something brought us together. It couldn't have simply been coincidence. I cannot imagine being without you now." She covered his hand with her own. "Don't you like English peas?"

He smiled. "Not so much."

She moved onto his lap and nestled her head underneath his chin. "That's okay. I don't like them that much either."

He chuckled. His breath quickened, and he kissed her hand. His lips moved up her arm to her shoulder, then to her neck. Shivers rippled up and down her spine. Lifting her in his arms, he carried her to their bed. He took off her shoes and set them on the floor next to his, put her feet in his lap, and massaged them with his strong fingers.

"Mmm, I love when you do that." She giggled. "That tickles." Each time he kissed her, it produced a desire that startled her. Nothing had prepared her for the love she was experiencing for her husband.

She breathed deeply of his scent and responded to him. Why had her mother not told her how wonderful married love was? They spent each night of their honeymoon in each other's arms, fulfilling their dreams as husband and wife, almost afraid to waste any of their precious time sleeping. Was that normal? She didn't have anyone to ask.

The time came much too soon for Jack to leave. They took a taxi to the train station on a muggy morning. The mist was so thick it was almost raining, but the moisture had not formed into drops heavy enough to fall. They simply hung suspended in the hazy fog of early dawn. Gracie pushed her hair out of her eyes for the umpteenth time. When it got wet, all it did was fall flat and flop into her face. She dug in her purse for a scarf, twisted it into a headband, and tied it around her head.

Jack grinned and touched the makeshift headband. "That looks cute."

"You're biased."

"You bet I am."

"All aboard!"

How she had dreaded hearing those words. The steam from the iron monster of an engine whooshed and spit as the clanging of a bell pierced through the fog. Jack hoisted his duffle bag over his shoulder.

Pulling her up beside him, he embraced her with one arm around her waist. "Stay in here. It's too nasty outside for you to stand in the rain."

She felt the emotion rising into her throat and thought her heart was going to slam out of her chest. "I'm going with you as far as I can." Her chin began to quiver, and she bit her lip to stop it. "How am I going to go on without you?" Three weeks with her new husband, and she didn't feel she could continue living without him. She knew so much about him now—and yet so little.

"Shh." He put his finger on her lips. "It won't be forever. Everyone says this war can't go on much longer." The gray of his eyes grew dark, clouding the blue. "I'm concerned about you going to Colorado by yourself."

She shook her head. "I'll be fine. We went there on vacation a couple of years ago, and I'm kind of familiar with the town. I'll get a job and start poking around for information. The first place I'm going to try to find is the photography shop."

"What about money? I'll send you my first paycheck. Check in at Peterson Field when you get there so you can buy groceries and what you need at the PX. And if you have a medical emergency or anything, you can go to the hospital on base. Be sure you send me an address right away."

"I'll be fine. I will send you the address. Promise me you'll write every day. But I won't need any money. Keep your paycheck. I have plenty left, and money goes automatically into my account every month from the trust."

"I wouldn't count on that continuing."

She took him by his arm and walked him to the turnstile.

"Only ticketed passengers beyond this point, ma'am." An older gentleman in a dark blue railway uniform with gold trim put his hand on the steel bar. "Sorry."

Jack nodded. "We understand. I'd rather she stay inside anyway." With his hand cupping her elbow, he protectively led her away from the crowd. "Stand right here in front of this window, so I can see you as the train pulls away." He lowered his duffle bag to the ground and took her by the shoulders. "I will come home. Watch for me. Listen for me. Wait for me. I will return for you." He kissed her long and hard. Gracie hung onto him in a desperate clutch.

"All aboard!" The whistle blew and the conductor sounded his call again. "All aboard that's coming aboard!"

The blare of the train whistle, the wheezing and chugging of the engine, the conductor's warning, the acrid smell of metal grinding against metal pressed against her senses, but she saw only Jack's face, smelled only his scent, heard only his voice. He picked up his duffle bag, ran through the turnstile, shouldered his way through the crowd, and disappeared into the clouds of steam from the train like a scene from a movie—except this was raw reality.

He was gone. What would he face flying in bombing missions over Germany? She couldn't imagine, and she didn't even want to think about it.

EIGHTEEN

December 9, 1944
Over Stuttgart, Germany

German flak blasted around the lumbering B-17 bomber, threatening to bounce the plane out of formation. Black smoky explosions obscured the crewmen's vision. Mesmerized by their deceptively soft, cushiony appearance, Lieutenant Jack Blauvelt stared out the Plexiglass enclosure of the bombardier's perch. Captain Russell Thompson steadied the Flying Fortress and managed to keep the plane level.

Jack snapped back to the task at hand and crossed himself, grateful for their pilot's experience of over thirty bombing missions. One slight bobble could jeopardize the entire fleet. The target today—a railroad yard located in Stuttgart, Germany—should be a relatively short run.

"Oxygen masks on," Captain Thompson's voice crackled over the radio.

Jack pulled his mask over his face and glanced back at the navigator. Ernie had already donned his mask. He nodded at Jack and pointed toward the sky. The flak had ceased, meaning the German fighter planes would appear shortly as Jack's plane climbed higher. He checked for their "Little Friends," the Mustang P-51 fighter escorts. They had been put into service by the time he'd started his tour of duty. Before that, the German "Butcher Birds," the Focke Wulf 190s, had nearly devastated the Eighth Army Air Corps B-17s, especially during the Americans' daytime bombing raids. The British took care of the nighttime bombings, but their casualties were high as well.

Something caught his eye to his right. *Here they come.*

Painted on the side of their B-17, instead of a beautiful woman striking a sexy pose or a current cartoon figure spouting doom for the Germans, one of their crew had drawn a warrior angel in full medieval battle attire brandishing an intimidating sword. No sweet cherub, the angel's face reflected fury and rage, yet the stern eyes carried a look of compassion. His pose suggested he was swooping down on a sighted prey. And that he was. Just like the archangel Michael from the Bible battled for God's chosen people, their painted version battled for the bomber they'd dubbed *Heavenly Justice.*

Captain Thompson held his voice as steady as the airplane. "Approaching target."

Jack crouched over his post and checked the optical Norden bombsight. "Battle stations, Michael."

"German Butcher Birds approaching. Let's go down and let the Mustangs take care of them. Fire away, Scotty." The tail gunner never needed any encouragement to fire. The rat-a-tat-tat of the tail guns as the German fighters made their approach in the rear of the bomber kept the young sergeant busy.

The Birds swooped away, chased by the incoming Mustangs. The German fighter came so close to *Heavenly Justice* that Jack could see the pilot's face grimacing as he realized he was hit. Smoke billowed from the right engine of the attacker. He dropped below them and began spiraling to the earth.

He made sure the plug-in to his electric suit was making connection. The temperature outside at this altitude could get as low as seventy below—brutal. No, worse than that—deadly. Frostbite was a major factor to the flight crews if they found themselves at the wrong end of a German attack. If the bandits didn't get them, the weather would.

"Hold steady, men. We're staying our course." *Heavenly Justice* was leader of the formation, so Jack controlled the aircraft during the run. The other bombardiers were waiting to see the visual signal of *Heavenly Justice*'s red bombs as they released and then they would release their own. If he miscalculated the drift, they all would. Despite the frigid air in the plane, his forehead beaded with perspiration.

The ant-like structures below came into view. *Steady, steady. Now.* "Let 'em fly!" Jack hit the button. *Click, click, click.* He watched as the bombs filtered out and down toward the target.

In the beginning, he'd worried about the people who were killed or injured by the American bombs—families, women, and children as well as enemy soldiers. The memories harassed his thoughts by day and became nightmares as he lay on his cot at night. Tortured sleep became the norm.

After a dozen runs or so, he learned to compartmentalize his emotions. He was doing a job for his country. Hitler had to be stopped or he would take over the world. Innocent casualties were a byproduct of war. Unfortunate, unpreventable. And if the recent rumors they'd heard about concentration camps in Poland and Germany were true, thousands of Jews were being slaughtered daily. The Allies had to win this war.

So he patted Michael's wings every time he boarded the plane. "Battle stations, Michael." And when they landed, he'd touch them again. "Swell job, Michael." The angel just stared at him. Jack wondered if there really were guardian angels looking after them. If there were, they'd missed a few guys. He'd already lost too many buddies.

Jack turned to see a German Butcher Bird bearing down on them from his right. The plane rocked.

"We're hit! We're hit!" Scotty's raspy voice screamed over the radio.

Where were the Mustangs? One of the right engines flared up in smoke, and a piece of metal pierced the Plexiglass bubble.

"Captain, one of the right engines up in smoke, and the rest of the wing is torn off!" The plane began to career wildly. Cold wind slapped Jack in the face like a steely fist.

Captain Thompson's radio sputtered. "Are you…hit…Jack?"

"I…yeah, but I'm okay, I think. The Plexiglass has been punctured."

"Tail section damaged, but this baby can still fly." The captain's voice remained calm but intense. "Let's see if we can at least get over the border back to France. If we have to bail out, we'll have a better chance there."

Jack looked down to see blood dripping onto his flak jacket. Where was it coming from? He touched his face. His eye. It was his left eye. He couldn't see out of it. He wiped the blood away but still couldn't see.

"Get ready, men. I'm gonna take *Justice* as far as I can. Scotty? Scotty?" No answer. Jack fumbled, swiping at the blood blocking his vision. His hands, stiffened by the frigid wind despite his gloves, came away from his face bloody.

"Jack?"

"Yes, sir. I'm still here. I'm hit…my left eye."

"Boys, prepare to bail out." Static garbled the captain's orders. "We're going down!" More static. "Go, go, go!"

The plane careened into a spin. Ernie and Jack yanked their parachutes from the wall and clipped them onto their harnesses. Ernie pointed to their escape route from the bombardier bubble. "Let's go, buddy."

The Plexiglass exploded, and Jack was hurtled out of the bombardier bubble. Tumbling through the sky, he opened his chute and looked back at the plane as another engine exploded and caught fire.

He shouted into the clouds as if the crew could hear him. "Get out of there, guys! Jump! Jump!" He twisted around to look for Ernie. Below him he saw his buddy plunging toward the earth. "Open your chute, Ernie! Pull the cord! Pull it, pull it, pull it!" The passing seconds seemed like an eternity, but at long last, the billowy white chute flared open. The wind was carrying Jack far beyond where Ernie seemed headed.

Heavenly Justice veered to the left, then the right, losing altitude fast—Michael's defiant, silent pose helpless as the plane headed toward the earth. Jack watched the plane level as it flew out of sight. *Captain's still gonna try to make it to France.*

Jack's mind raced through his training instructions. No more guys jumping. He drifted toward the ground, the Black Forest in front of him, heavily wooded, and mountains behind him. If he could avoid getting hung up in the trees, the forest would provide good protection. Where was Ernie? Fighting to avoid the trees, he pulled the strings on the chute and swerved to the right, almost missing them entirely. But the edge of his chute caught on the branches of a tall pine tree about halfway down the trunk. Jack slammed against the tree, crushing his left arm, which was tangled in the parachute. He gritted his teeth and stifled his screams of pain. *Great, just what I need, a busted arm.*

Dangling akimbo from the chute, he looked down from his evergreen captor. The ground seemed to be only eight or ten feet below. He couldn't tell for sure because of the snowdrift around the base of the tree. However far down it was, he had to get out of his chute as quickly as he could. He'd heard too many stories of how trees proved to be a death trap for parachuting airmen. Enemy soldiers, spotting a parachuting soldier hung up in a tree, would simply pick them off like birds on a fence.

I don't intend to be on the receiving end of a Kraut's target practice. Not today anyway. An unnatural calm came over him as he mechanically went through procedure. A sharp stab like a hot poker shot through his left arm. He couldn't lift it, and his hand hung limp. He unclipped his knife from his belt, unsnapped it, pulled it out of the leather scabbard, and with some difficulty used his good hand to cut the strings of the chute, pitching himself into the snow. The fluffy white stuff broke his fall but buried him. He scrambled to find his footing and found himself thigh-deep in the drift.

The parachute flapped in the wintry breeze like a signal flag calling to all who would pass by that an American airman had just parachuted into their territory. And what territory was he in? Had he made it over the Rhein into France? He made a few vain attempts with his good arm to pull the chute down, but the stubborn silks wouldn't pull loose of the prickly needles. He would have to leave it.

Holding his arm against his side, Jack ran for the cover of the trees, hoping to see Ernie's parachute caught somewhere as well. A plain stone farmhouse sat on the other side of a clearing, but he opted for the forest. Stumbling into the underbrush, he fell against a tree, unshouldered his pack, caught his breath…and listened. Complete silence. He pursed his lips and whistled low, hoping Ernie would answer. Nothing. Where was he? Somehow, he'd have to find out.

A fallen log up ahead formed a shelter of sorts between two trees. Jack leaned his pack against the log and sat down to rest. Searching through the pack, he removed his canteen and the gray first aid kit. His arm throbbed with each movement. He pulled out the triangular bandage and, holding one end in his teeth, managed to tie a knot in it, fashioning a sling for his arm. Grunting in pain, he eased his arm into the sling. At least that eased the pressure.

The container of an injectable Syrette of morphine beckoned to him. *I can stand the pain for now. Better save it in case I need it later.* He rummaged through the kit looking for gauze and found the individually wrapped squares at the bottom under vials of ointment. Moistening a square with water from his canteen, he dabbed his injured eye, but the blood had dried. Without a mirror, he couldn't determine its condition.

Intermittent stabbing pains shot through his eye though. He needed to cover it. Holding the metal container between his knees, he pushed the roll of tape out with his good hand. He fished his knife out of his pocket once again. He never thought cutting a piece of tape could be so complicated. Each movement became increasingly difficult and painful to his injured arm, but at last he managed the task.

The pain and the cold settled in on him. He scooted over to allow the rays of the midafternoon sun to bathe him in warmth. Once the sun started to set below the crest of the mountains, it would get dark and cold fast. He closed his eyes and allowed himself now to think about Gracie. Would he ever see her again? And their baby? Gracie's letters were filled with her wonder at their coming little one. He couldn't leave her to raise their child alone. Somehow he had to get home.

God, I'm not the best at knowing how to pray, but please help me get out of this mess. I promise if you get me back to my wife and my baby, I'll...I'll be eternally grateful. I'll be the best husband and father a man can be. I...I promise. He drifted off to a troubled sleep.

Voices. He startled awake to three faces peering down at him, one of a young man holding his parachute.

Nineteen

Jack drew his pistol.

The young man stumbled backward with his hands raised, dropping the parachute. *"Nein, nein!"*

Jack waved the pistol at him and scrambled to his feet. Children's voices called out.

"Dieter!"

He whirled around to see a younger boy, about twelve years old, and a small girl, who looked to be about six.

Jack holstered his gun and raised his good hand. "I'm not going to hurt you. It's okay." He glanced around to see if there were any others. "Do you speak English?"

Dieter shook his head. *"Sprechen sie Deutsch?"*

Jack shook his head. "No. *Parlez-vous français?*"

The young man's eyes brightened. *"Oui, oui."* He continued in French. "You are a Frenchman? Your accent…"

"No…well, yes…French grandparents. I'm American, but we spoke French in our home." He motioned to the parachute. "I won't hurt you. Thank you for getting my chute out of the tree."

Dieter picked the chute up and handed it to Jack. "You are in danger.

Soldiers patrol the road with frequency. We are just down the road from the checkpoint at the Rhein Crossing."

"We are close to what town?"

"Baden-Baden." The two younger children came alongside the older boy. "Where is your plane?"

"I don't know. I think my crew was trying to make it to France."

"Good. Good. The soldiers won't be looking for a plane, then."

The little girl with blond pigtails stared at Jack, her pale blue eyes wide, reflecting a combination of fear and curiosity. His pain, forgotten in the moment, returned with a vengeance and his knees buckled.

He sat down on the log, the chute wadded up in his hands. "I need to get rid of this."

"We'll take it to the barn." Dieter pointed across the clearing where the late afternoon sun slanted its rays below the crest of the mountains, beginning the forest's plunge into darkness. The temperature was falling quickly. Could he trust these innocent-looking children? He hesitated and looked around.

Dieter held out his hand. "*Résistance*. We love the Americans. But we'd better hurry."

Jack shook the young man's hand. What luck. The Resistance—if they were telling the truth. Or it could be a trap. He stared at the children. Their faces looked like any other children's. He had no choice. He had to trust them.

He struggled to get to his feet. The young man took hold of his elbow and assisted him. Jack could feel the strength in Dieter's arms. "Merci." Good, salt-of-the-earth farm boy. No matter the nationality, country boys couldn't be beat for pure, physical strength and integrity. "What age are you, young man?"

"Fifteen years. Kurt, thirteen." Dieter put his arm around the little girl and pulled her to his side. "And Elsa, just six years."

"Your brother and sister, I suppose."

"Elsa is my sister. We, along with my mother, have been living with Kurt's family at their farm to escape the bombings." He turned to the two younger children and instructed them to go to the house. "Tell the adults we have come upon an American soldier who needs help. Kurt, get the wheelbarrow and come back."

The little girl offered no argument. She still appeared unsure and frightened of Jack, although the demeanor of the two boys relaxed. Jack pulled a chocolate bar out of his pack and gave pieces to the boys. Then he held a small square out toward the girl. She looked first at her big brother munching on his then back at Jack.

"What's your name again?" Jack asked.

Dieter spoke up. "She doesn't speak much French." He translated Jack's question to the child.

She ducked her head and held her fist up to her mouth. "Elsa." She spoke so softly Jack could hardly hear her.

He knelt down. "Elsa?"

She nodded and looked at Jack through thick eyelashes.

"That's a pretty name, Elsa. I am called Jack." Jack offered the candy to her again. She took it and stuck the whole piece in her mouth. Jack laughed then grabbed his arm as he stood. "Agh. Laughing hurts." He touched his eye and felt the crusted blood. "I guess I look pretty scary with this eye." He turned to Dieter. "Is it awfully bloody?"

"*Oui*, it is. We need to get you to safety, so *Mutter* can take a look at it." Turning to the others, he shooed them toward the barn. "Fast. Go on now. Run. It'll be dark soon. Kurt, come back here with the wheelbarrow as soon as you can. The soldiers will be changing shifts in thirty minutes or so. We need to get..." He lifted his brows. "Jack?"

"Lieutenant Jack Blauvelt. But please, call me Jack…and it's actually Jacques."

Dieter smiled. "Very good. Jacques it is."

Kurt and Elsa had already started running across the clearing hand in hand, Elsa's pigtails flying as she struggled to keep up.

Jack returned to his seat on the log and dug around in the first aid kit. He opened the container of aspirin with one hand and shook four out onto the log.

Dieter sat beside him. "Do you need help?"

He motioned to his canteen. "Yeah, could you open this for me?"

"Of course." Dieter unscrewed the lid and handed it to Jack. "Kurt will be back shortly. Let's get your gear back into your pack."

Jack gulped down the aspirin and closed the first aid kit, stuffing it into his pack.

Dieter set about picking evergreen boughs off the ground, stacking them in a pile. He removed a small hatchet he carried on his belt and hacked off some low-lying spruce branches. "We'll put you in the wheelbarrow and cover you with branches. If anyone stops us, we'll say we're gathering branches to decorate for Christmas."

Jack nodded. "Sounds like a plan. It also sounds like you've done this before."

"*Nein,* but we've discussed what we would do if this ever happened. Everyone has a task. Even Elsa."

"What is her assignment?"

"Get the scarecrow."

"Pardon me?"

Dieter laughed. "You'll see." He threw an armload of branches onto the growing stack. "You're our first American pilot to rescue. Baden-Baden has escaped the worst of the bombing since we have no industrial plants or airfields here."

"I'm not a pilot. I'm..." Jack cleared his throat. "I'm...the bombardier."

The young man maintained a stoic expression betrayed only by a flicker in his eyes. He threw another batch of branches on the pile. "It makes no matter. You're still an American soldier who needs help."

Jack stood. "Let me help you." He lurched sideways and caught hold of a branch.

"I think you'd best sit down and let me do this. You need a doctor."

He leaned back against the rough bark of the tree trunk, closing his eyes. "I think you're right. Give me a moment. I just need to get my balance."

Jack almost fell asleep while he listened to the swish of the evergreen branches, interrupted by an occasional whack of a branch. *Christmas. Our baby is due soon. Gracie, are you putting up decorations? Placing evergreen branches on a mantle somewhere?*

"Here comes Kurt. The guards will be changing shifts soon, we had better hurry."

Jack's head jerked up. "Shouldn't we wait until after dark?"

"When it gets dark the border guards patrol more closely with floodlights. They don't expect anything during the daylight."

Kurt guided the large wheelbarrow inside the edge of the trees.

"Come, quickly." Dieter helped Jack into the wheelbarrow then packed the parachute around him. "There is a small hole in the bottom where you can breathe."

Jack curled onto his side, lying on his good arm, trying to protect his broken one. The pungent fragrance of the freshly cut evergreen branches made his nose itch. It smelled like Christmas. Dieter nestled the prickly boughs around the broken arm to cushion it. He packed heavier branches around Jack's feet and legs, ending with another layer on top of evergreen branches. "We're ready. Kurt, check the road."

Jack peeked through an opening between the branches. The blue gray of dusk crept over the mountain crest. They had little time.

"Keep your head down, Jacques. Kurt, grab an armful of branches." The wheelbarrow tilted up as Dieter lifted the handles. Dieter lowered his voice. "Here we go."

Jack bounced against the sides of the wheelbarrow, gripping his broken arm and clenching his teeth to squelch the moans of pain. Should have taken that morphine.

"*Guten abend!*"

Dieter set the wheelbarrow down with a jolt. "*Guten abend.*" It sounded as though both he and Kurt left the wheelbarrow and walked away to the side of the road, which ran alongside the clearing. Jack's heart banged against his chest. German soldiers.

The brothers were carrying on what seemed to be a light-hearted conversation with the soldiers. Laughter. He'd been deceived. These boys weren't with the Resistance—they were conspiring with the Germans. What should he do? Remain quiet or make a run for it? That would be foolish. He'd get nowhere. He was trapped. Nausea swept over him, and vomit burbled into his mouth.

TWENTY

The swish of snow announced the approach of someone to the wheelbarrow. *"Was ist das? Schokolade?"*

Jack swore underneath his breath as he heard the crackle of paper. The wrapper from the chocolate bar! He steeled himself for his cover to be ripped off as a German rifle poked in his face.

Dieter's voice remained calm as he answered the soldier in German. Jack recognized some words like "chocolate" and "woods." He frowned. If the boys had betrayed him, they wouldn't be trying to cover for him now. The laughter at the road must have been them trying to act normal.

The soldier's footsteps crunched in the snow as he walked around the wheelbarrow. He said something about the cedar branches—that was easy—*zeder.* A bead of sweat fell from Jack's forehead into his eye. The branches rustled. Jack reached for his pistol.

"Nein, nein. Bitte. Dies ist nicht…"

The glint of a rifle barrel, the face of a German soldier, the flash of Jack's pistol all happened at once. Jack shot before he had time to think about it. The soldier flew back at the report of the pistol, and blood splattered in every direction. Jack heard grunts and shouts and sounds of a scuffle as he fought to throw off the branches. The hated German uniform blended with Dieter's dark woolen jacket as they collided.

Kurt shouted, "Dieter!"

"Please, God, no! No!" Jack pushed his way out of the wheelbarrow. Dieter lay squirming underneath the soldier. Kurt rushed to push the soldier off.

"I'm fine. I'm fine, just get him off me." Blood stained the front of the coat of the young man as Kurt pulled him up. "Are you hurt?" He tried to wipe the blood away with his sleeve.

Dieter shook his head. "That's his blood, not mine. Really, I'm fine."

Jack came alongside the two boys and stood over the body. Blood oozed from the single shot in the man's forehead. His unseeing eyes stared skyward. Silence enshrouded them as they gazed at the still body of another young man, one who had been conscripted to serve his country just as Jack had been. His helmet lay askew above the bloody bullet hole.

Jack looked into the panicked eyes of the boys. "I'm sorry, I had to do that."

Dieter wiped blood from his cheek. "It couldn't be helped. You did what you had to do. Nice shot." He glanced around. "We must hurry and do away with the body."

"The woods?"

"No, that'll be the first place they'll look. Let's put him in the wheelbarrow. Sorry, but you're going to have to lie on top of him. We'll disguise you as best we can with cedar boughs. Hurry."

Dieter picked up the soldier by his arms. "Get his legs." Kurt got one leg, and Jack helped with the other the best he could. They stuffed him in the bottom of the wheelbarrow, like loading a sack of potatoes.

The scream of two fighter planes overhead, punctuated by strafing bullets on the road, sent all three of them diving for cover in the snow bank. Jack looked up. The two planes rolled a salutation as they flew away. "It's okay. They're Americans. They must have been shooting at German soldiers on the road behind us."

Dieter stood, brushing snow from his trousers. "I don't care whose bullets they were. They all kill." His mouth set itself in a terse line.

"Americans wouldn't intentionally shoot down boys in a field, especially if an American soldier was with them."

"They can tell from the plane?"

"Oh, yeah. Did you see them wave at us? They saw us all right. They probably recognized my uniform." Jack's voice came across more confident than he felt.

Kurt sat in the snow bank, his head in his hands. "Whew, that was close." His emotions quivered in his chin.

"It's okay. It seemed closer than it really was. Everybody's going to be fine." Jack pointed to the ground where the soldier had fallen. "We need to cover up the blood somehow."

Dieter shook his head. "I don't have a shovel with me. We'll just have to put some branches and snow over it the best we can. If we're lucky, it'll snow again tonight and cover it up." All three of them scuffed snow over the blood and then laid branches on top. More snow on top of that.

Jack looked to the sky. "I'm a Louisiana boy. I have no idea what snow clouds look like."

Dieter looked up and allowed a slight smile. "Like that. Now get back in the wheelbarrow, Jacques."

He climbed in on top of the dead man, still warm and smelling of rancid sweat and tobacco. He covered his nose and mouth to keep from being sick. Just a few branches on top, and Dieter took off running, obviously not caring how rough the ride was. Kurt's footfalls sounded ahead of them.

Jack curled into the tightest ball he could as the wheelbarrow bumped down the dirt path toward the farmhouse. He clenched his jaw with each jolt to keep from crying out. "How much farther?"

"Shh. We're almost there." That was Kurt.

The wheelbarrow took a turn to the left and stopped. Jack heard the pop and groan of a frozen wooden door opening. A barn door perhaps? The wheelbarrow lifted again, and Jack felt himself being wheeled into some type of enclosure. He could smell hay and animals. Chickens clucked and goats bleated. A cow bellowed. It reminded him of the barn on his parents' farm in Louisiana. Barns all smelled the same—friend or foe. *Just get me out of here!*

"Kurt, set the wheelbarrow down and fetch your father."

Jack heard Kurt running away from them.

"Psst, Dieter. Get me out of here."

Dieter came alongside the wheelbarrow. "Let's give it a few minutes to make sure it's all clear. Elsa's put the clothes out for you."

"Not a chance. I've got to get out of here." Jack pushed a twig away from his face, spitting out grit. He didn't wait for Dieter to unload the branches. With his good arm, he threw them to the side. The body of the soldier was beginning to grow cool. He burst out of the wheelbarrow, stumbling onto the floor of the barn, retching once he fell to his knees.

Dieter helped him to his feet and led him to a hay bale. The barn door opened and a short, plump woman wearing a heavy black woolen shawl and a matching kerchief entered. Kurt and Elsa followed behind her. The woman bent over Jack and held a lantern in front of his face. Cornflower blue eyes, the same color as Elsa's, peered at him, and the bare hint of a smile accentuated laugh lines around her mouth. He'd never seen a kinder face.

"This is my mother, Frau Hoffmann." Dieter smiled and patted her on the arm.

Jack started to stand but she motioned for him to remain on the bale of hay. She walked to the wheelbarrow and stood over it. "*Mein Gott.*" She touched the body then withdrew her hand quickly. Stepping away, she took a deep breath.

A tall, slender man with a gray woolen cap and jacket opened the barn door. Striding to the wheelbarrow, the man surveyed the situation quickly. He mumbled something to Kurt in German and walked toward the animal stalls. Removing a shovel from a peg on the wall, he placed it in the wheelbarrow before lifting it and starting toward the door.

Kurt ran ahead of him and opened the door for his father but turned his head to Jack. "We're going to throw the body into a ditch," he said in French. "It runs across the back of our property. We'll cover it with snow. The ground is too hard to bury him."

Kurt's father pushed the wheelbarrow out the door with a nod. "We won't be long."

The woman examined Jack's eye and said something in a calm, soothing tone. Jack didn't know what the German words meant, but her tone conveyed all he needed to trust her.

Dieter smiled. "Mutter, French please."

"Of course, forgive me." She put her hands on her ample hips. "We do have a bit of a problem here, don't we? Let's get him in civilian clothes." She peered at him. "With that blond hair and blue eyes, you could be a cousin of ours. Hmm, yes. That will be our story if we are confronted. You are a visiting cousin—from France." She pointed toward the barn entrance. "Elsa, keep a lookout for visitors."

The little girl bobbed her head, took her seat on a bench beside the door, and peeked through a knothole in one of the slats.

Dieter went toward the back into a stall and emerged with a fully dressed scarecrow. "Here's your new wardrobe, Jack. Hope the clothes are a reasonable fit."

Jack smiled and nodded. "Very clever." He fumbled with his flak jacket. "I'm afraid I'm going to need some help. We'll probably have to cut this off. I don't think I can get it over my arm."

Dieter took Jack's knife and started cutting. Jack tilted his head toward the children's mother. "Frau Hoffmann. Thank you for your kindness."

"Young man, do you have any sort of pain killer with you?" The compassion in her voice matched the kindness of her countenance.

"Morphine. In the first aid kit in my pack." He handed it to her.

She opened the kit, took out a small yellow box, and examined the Syrette. "Are you in excruciating pain? Pain you absolutely cannot stand? There's only one dose."

"I can handle it. Let's save it."

Dieter handed his mother the sling, which she refolded and held as she talked. "I would suggest you take the maximum dose of aspirin tonight and then inject the morphine in the morning to carry you over until we get you medical help. We'll connect with the French Résistance on the other side of the river. There is an evacuation hospital in Saint-—the 51st—which is not far. You'll be safe then."

"When will we go?" Jack grabbed his arm as Dieter cut the sleeve off of the jacket.

"Right before dawn. The guards are not very alert at the checkpoint in the early morning hours."

Pain like he'd never experienced before—deep, bone-throbbing pain—shot through his body.

Dieter stopped, holding the knife in midair. "Did I hurt you? I'm sorry."

"That's all right. Can't be helped." He turned toward Frau Hoffmann. "What about my eye? Can you tell anything? I can't open it."

The children's mother prodded around the eye area gently, shaking her head. "I can't really tell with that gauze on it. All I can probably do is clean it up a bit, but I'd need more light." She placed his broken arm back in the sling and tied it tight against his ribs. "We're going to take you into the house after you change your clothes. Can you walk, monsieur?"

"Yes, I think so."

"It would be good if you could walk into the house normally, without assistance. Anybody watching might be suspicious if they see us helping someone who appeared wounded." She moved to the door and motioned for her daughter. "Come with me, Elsa. Dieter and Lieutenant…"

"Blauvelt. Jack Blauvelt."

"A good French name. Dieter and Lieutenant Blauvelt will come after he changes his clothes."

Dieter slid the barn door open and pointed outside as a grin slid across his face. "It's beginning to snow."

Frau Hoffmann took Elsa by the hand and headed back to the house. The scarecrow's clothing, although old and tattered, was clean and fit well enough, and at least was warm. Dieter carried Jack's pack as they marched the short path from the barn to the back door of the typical German cottage, complete with Bavarian paintings on the scalloped eaves. The windows were closed and shuttered. Bubbling soup on the stove gave off a warm, aromatic greeting. Jack suddenly felt famished.

Frau Hoffmann stood at the stove stirring a pot of steaming vegetables. "Not much meat, I'm afraid, but plenty of potatoes and turnips." She indicated a straight-backed chair at the end of a long kitchen table. Another woman, about the same age as Frau Hoffmann, but more petite and with blond hair poking out from her kerchief, wiped her hands on her apron and placed blue and white bowls on the table.

"This is Kurt's mother, Frau Schneider. She and her family are sharing their home with us these days."

Jack stepped forward with his cap in his hand, holding his arm. "Pleased to meet you, Frau Schneider."

The woman simply looked at him and gave him a slight nod.

Jack sat down just as Kurt and his father came in, stomping snow onto a mud rug. Jack pushed himself up, stepped forward, and offered his good hand to Kurt's father. "Thank you for your hospitality, monsieur. I'm most grateful."

The man shook his hand and nodded. His expression seemed a bit stern, but his eyes projected kindness.

Kurt hung his coat on a wooden peg beside his father's. "I see your new wardrobe fits." He motioned for Jack to sit. "Please."

Jack nodded. "Did you...is the soldier...?"

Kurt sat next to his father at the other end of the table. "It's taken care of—for now anyway. When the spring thaw comes, we'll bury him properly."

The rest of the family took their places around the table and crossed themselves as they bowed their heads for the blessing. Catholics. As they said their "amens" and crossed themselves again, Jack looked around the room for a cross. Above the fireplace there was a small one, and another above the door. "I'm Catholic too. That makes me feel like I'm with my family."

Frau Hoffmann got up. "I forgot the butter."

An underlying tension hung in the air. Dieter, Kurt, and his father conversed a few moments in German, then the boy turned to Jack.

"He understands French but doesn't speak it that well. He offers his greetings."

The older man nodded again, and the corners of his mouth turned up slightly. His smile changed the countenance of his face. His eyes, also blue, pierced Jack's. He motioned for Jack to eat as he passed a large, round loaf of bread down to him.

Wonder how my father would react in these same circumstances? He would be brave, just like Herr Hoffmann, I'm sure of it. Jack thought of his sisters and mother as well. *We are blessed in America. So very blessed. And Gracie. I couldn't bear for her to have to endure these living conditions, never knowing what the next day might bring—hunger or invasion or bombings.* The bombings suddenly became very personalized as he sat at the Schneider's dinner table, looking into each face. A family just like his own. He nudged a potato through the broth with his spoon. He wasn't hungry anymore, but he couldn't waste this family's hospitality. He forced himself to finish.

Dieter and Kurt ate quickly. Herr Schneider stood and went to his easy chair in front of the radio. He turned and said something to Dieter.

The boy translated. "He's trying to see if there are any reports of a downed plane near here."

"My navigator bailed out right before me. Any sightings of another American airman?"

Herr Hoffmann shook his head. *"Nein."*

Frau Hoffman placed a bowl of hot water on the table. "Dieter, move that green chair closer over here where the light is better."

He scooted an overstuffed upholstered chair to the table under the overhead light. Jack eased into the comfortable chair.

"Just rest your head on the back of the chair. Try to relax." She removed Jack's gauze patch and began to wash around his eye. Her hands were cool and gentle, and she smelled of lemon soap. He drifted in and out of consciousness, seeing Frau Hoffmann's face swim in front of his. He remembered her shaking her head.

A loud bang on the door startled the family. Elsa ran to the window and peered outside. She wheeled around, her eyes wide with fright. "It… it's soldiers!"

Twenty~One

Jack's heart leapt as he stood and reached for his pistol.

Frau Hoffmann thrust the bowl toward her oldest son. "Dieter, take the bowl of water and Lieutenant Blauvelt up to the attic. Quickly." She scooted the chair back in its proper place.

"My pack." Jack indicated where he'd left it in the chair.

Frau Hoffmann picked up her knitting from a basket beside the chair and sat down, shoving the pack into the bottom of the knitting basket. She covered the pack in the basket with a blanket.

Pointing to the table, she spoke low and soft. "Elsa, gather up all the soup bowls." Her knitting needles began to click-clack as she put a skein of yarn in her lap. Herr Schneider went to the door.

Dieter led Jack to a narrow stairwell and shoved the bowl of water underneath the stairwell. The stairs led to a tiny extra bedroom, stuffy and hot in its tiny size. "This is our room." Two beds took up nearly one wall. A small table with two chairs sat at the end of the beds. In the corner, a wood stove glowed.

Dieter spat out a whisper. "Take off your boots."

Jack sat on a step as Dieter helped him remove his boots. They ascended the second step of steep stairs to a dark attic.

"Won't the attic be the first place they look?" He followed Dieter into the dim interior.

"Maybe, but you're going to be in a secret compartment behind a bookcase. You'll have to be very still." He pointed to the corner of the room with a sloping ceiling. A small bookcase rested behind a rod holding out-of-season clothing. "Hurry." He thrust the clothing aside and pulled the small bookcase out. A three-foot opening appeared, just big enough for a person to crouch in.

Jack stuffed himself in a miniscule hiding place for the second time that day. Had it only been a few hours since he'd bailed out of his plane?

Dieter handed him his boots. "Stay absolutely still until we come for you." Dieter shut the bookcase door and left quickly.

Jack leaned his head back against the wall and closed his eyes. He could hear voices from the room, but they were too muffled to understand. How long would he be confined to the cramped space? His arm and eye continued to throb.

Dieter descended the stairs in his stocking feet. He eased into the large family room as Herr Schneider ushered the contingent of German soldiers into the house. Kurt remained in his place at the table. Elsa went to her mother's side at the chair and sat down on the floor beside her.

Dieter stood behind the chair and smiled as his mother peered up at him.

"Is there a problem?" Herr Schneider puffed on his pipe.

The sergeant in charge stepped forward and looked around at the family. "You may say so. One of our soldiers is missing. Corporal Hirsch."

Kurt looked up from his soup bowl. "I know him. We saw him as we were gathering cedar branches in the woods this afternoon. He waved to us."

"What time was that?"

Dieter stuck his hands into his pockets. "Oh, a couple of hours ago. Right before dark. He seemed fine then. However, we did get strafed by an American fighter plane. Maybe he got hit. Have you searched the road?"

The German soldier cursed the American air forces. "The Americans are shooting and bombing everything in sight. It's too dark to look for him now. You don't mind if we have a look around here, do you?"

"Of course not, Sergeant." Frau Schneider got several bowls from the cabinet. "Would your men care for a bowl of soup this cold wintry night?"

The sergeant closed his eyes and inhaled. "It sure smells good, but I guess we'd better not. I'll just poke around here a bit."

"Of course." She stacked the soup bowls all together in a sink full of soapy water.

The soldier drew his rifle, walked past the table and the green chair. The knitting needles clicked faster as the soldier approached her. He looked at the yarn and touched the skein. "My mother knits—in the evenings, before the fire, just like you are doing. What are you making?"

"Mufflers, blankets, socks—anything our men can use of the battle fronts."

The soldier nodded and walked toward the bedrooms. He paused at the stairs. "What's upstairs?"

"An extra bedroom." Herr Schneider puffed on his pipe. "For the Hoffmanns. And the attic."

Frau Hoffmann set her knitting needles down. "My husband, who is on the eastern front, arranged with the Schneiders for us to come here and stay. When the Americans and British started bombing Stuttgart, we came to more relative safety here."

The sergeant swore again and started up the stairs. "It's too dark. Where's the light switch?"

"The light's burned out. Rationing, you know. I can get you a lantern, if you like." Frau Schneider started toward the pantry.

"I can assure you Corporal Hirsch is not here." Herr Schneider addressed all four of the soldiers. "He and my son, Kurt, have made friends, and if he were here, Kurt would know." He motioned toward the table. "At least let my wife wrap some warm bread and butter for you."

The soldier paused on the stairs. "Well, I suppose that would be acceptable."

Kurt got up from the table. "You don't suppose he's deserted, do you?"

"Kurt!" Frau Schneider paused in preparing the bread for the soldiers and frowned at her son.

"Well, he'd told me how tired he was of the war and how easy it would be to just walk away."

Herr Schneider cleared his throat. "Simply the musings of a weary soldier, son. I'm sure he'll show up soon."

The soldier frowned. "He'd better, or a court martial awaits him."

Or a cold, snowy grave. Dieter exhaled a sigh of relief as the soldiers left with a basket of warm bread and the assurance from the Schneider family that if they saw Corporal Hirsch, they would certainly let the unit know.

Herr Schneider closed the door on the increasing snowfall outside. He put his finger to his mouth. "Shh. Elsa, help dry the dishes. Good thinking, Gretchen, to stack all of the soup bowls together so they couldn't count them. Let's wait awhile before we let Jack out. That was too close a call to botch it up now."

Someone shook him awake. "Jacques, Jacques. Wake up. We must go now."

Jacques? Who was calling him Jacques? Then he recalled where he was. Dieter had showed him to his own bed after releasing him from the cramped cubbyhole in the attic. He sat up and looked around. Dieter stood with a flashlight at the side of the small bed while Elsa slept in the other one. Frau Hoffmann was not in the room.

Jack touched his eye. A sturdy patch covered the injury. "Where did you sleep?"

"Downstairs. I made a pallet in front of the fireplace. Not too bad."

Jack tried to stand, but the room spun.

"Take it easy. Can you stand up?" Dieter clicked on a small bedside lamp.

"Yeah, but I'm pretty woozy." He sat on the edge of the bed until the room stopped spinning. "I guess I got hit in the head harder than I realized. I think I'm okay now. What's the plan?"

"We'll take the sleigh to a bridge down from the checkpoint. The car would be too noisy. We've alerted one of our team on the French side that you will be crossing over. They will pick you up and take you to the hospital."

"That sounds dangerous…I mean, for you. What will you say you are doing if you are stopped? I don't want you to put yourself and your family at risk."

"We are already at risk. After last night…" Dieter grinned. "We're still gathering evergreen boughs for Christmas decorations. We should have plenty by the time this little adventure is completed."

Jack stood and gripped Dieter's arm. "Help me understand something."

Dieter's expression turned serious, and his face reflected the invisible scars of war. What had that young man seen, experienced, endured?

"Why are you, Germans, willing to endanger yourselves to help your enemy escape—especially one who has been bombing your cities? I'd prepared myself to be shot if I came down inside Germany."

Dieter scooted Jack's boots toward him. "Here, you need to hurry." Jack had slept in his clothes. Dieter picked up the heavy woolen coat, cap, and scarf from a nearby chair and laid them on the bed. "Gloves are in the pockets." He bent to help Jack lace his boots, his head ducked as he worked. "Not all Germans agree with Hitler and his propaganda. Not all Germans are Nazis." He stood and removed Jack's jacket from a peg beside the door. The young man helped Jack put the jacket on around his bandaged arm. He stepped back and spoke through lips set tight. "We want our country back."

"How did you escape being drafted?"

"Too young." He scoffed. "And I'm hoping the war will come to an end before they realize I've grown up. My older brother was not as lucky."

Jack sighed. "I'm so sorry. How can I ever thank you?"

"You have family?"

"Yes, a wife. We married right before I left." He was surprised at the lump that gripped his throat. And…" He swallowed hard. "And we are expecting a baby soon."

Dieter looked directly into Jack's eyes. "Just get home safely. That's the best way to thank us." The two young men walked into the small living room where Herr Schneider awaited them. Jack walked toward him with his hand extended. "Monsieur, I'm so grateful for your help."

The older man nodded and put his woolen cap on as he shook Jack's hand. "*Ja. Oui.*" He opened the front door and motioned for Jack to get on the sleigh. It wasn't exactly what Jack had pictured. It was simply a small cart on runners instead of wheels, pulled by two cows. Much better than a sleigh. It wouldn't draw much attention.

"Cows?" Jack placed his cap on his head.

Dieter laughed. "All the horses are gone. We use 'cow power.'"

Frau Schneider handed them a thermos and a lunch pail. If he decoded her German correctly, it was coffee and some kind of strudel.

Jack accepted with a smile and a nod. "Thank you. It must be very difficult, to have your home invaded like this. She's a good woman."

Frau Hoffmann smiled as she translated for her friend, then turned back to Jack. "Here's more aspirin." She patted him on the arm. "Please be safe, monsieur."

"Oui, madame. I'm sure gonna try." He touched his eye. "Thank you."

"Unfortunately, I wasn't very successful there. There are pieces of metal that need to be removed right away. It was beyond my ability. Hopefully we've been able to stave off any infection." She spoke in German to Herr Schneider.

He made a reply and headed for the sleigh.

She turned to Jack once more. "Take the morphine right before you get picked up by the French Résistance. You should get across the bridge before it takes effect. The French will take it from there."

He nodded and tipped his hat. "Oui, madame." Elsa and Kurt entered the room in the scuffle. Jack shook the young man's hand. "You had me scared for a minute there with your soldier 'friend.'"

Kurt snickered.

Jack knelt down and tugged on one of Elsa's pigtails and smiled. "Thanks for the new clothes."

She giggled and ducked her head.

Dieter put his hand on Jack's shoulder. "We must hurry. The sun will be coming up soon."

Herr Schneider ushered them out the door into the brittle cold of predawn.

Only the crunch of the snow underneath the runners of the sleigh broke the early morning stillness as the cows plodded along. The three men sat on the driver's perch in silence. Jack's life depended on these two strangers sitting with him, driving a sleigh through the darkness of an early German morning, when halfway around the globe his beloved Gracie awaited the arrival of their baby. Alone.

An ache only slightly less intense than the one from his injuries. He didn't know how much longer he could stand the pain. He needed to get into France.

They pulled up into the shelter of the trees. "There's the bridge." Dieter pointed to a small, one-lane rock bridge. "The soldiers are supposed to patrol here, but they rarely do. It's too small for anything except bicycles and horses." He swung down from the cart and helped Jack onto the ground. "The only tricky part now is…well, you're going to have to walk across the bridge by yourself."

Jack's knees weakened. "Okay." He nodded and took a deep breath. "Okay."

"Can you manage it?" Small puffs of condensation floated on the air as Dieter talked.

"Sure, sure I can. I guess I'm going to have to, eh?"

Dieter nodded. "Keep your cap pulled down. Some of our team are right on the other side of the bridge. All you have to do is get to them. They'll take care of you from there. I would suggest you inject the morphine now."

Jack opened the box, took out the Syrette, and pulled up his shirt. He stuck the needle into his abdomen and injected the welcome painkiller. He handed Dieter a safety pin from the box. "Pin the empty syringe onto my shirt, please."

Dieter cocked his head. "Why?"

"If I pass out, the medical personnel will know I've already taken the morphine."

Dieter fumbled with his gloves and pinned the syringe on Jack's shirt, where it would be covered by his jacket.

Jack held out his hand to Dieter. "Well, here I go. I'll never forget you, young friend."

Dieter grabbed Jack's hand, and they pulled each other into a smothering hug. "Nor I, you." He slapped Jack on the back—gently. "Now, go." It had started to snow again.

"A promise—I will contact you after the war if I make it."

"Go, hurry."

Jack walked toward the bridge and didn't look back.

As he got closer, he realized it was nothing more than a one-lane bridge over a narrow part of the river. Trees lined the banks. He looked both ways and stepped onto the bridge. No footprints. No one had been over it since it snowed during the night. The snowfall had steadily increased since they left the farm and stacked softly atop the rock wall on each side. Beautiful, pure, clean snow. He kept his head down and watched his feet kick the white stuff in front of him. His toes were getting cold. Just keep going—one step at a time. Almost halfway. He could see headlights ahead on the other side.

"*Halt!*"

From Jack's left he saw the telltale curve of a German soldier's helmet as a man holding a rifle ran through the snow toward the bridge. Only one soldier. Surely he could outrun him. A gust of wind whipped a small dervish of snow around Jack. It was impossible for him to see the advancing soldier—or for the soldier to see him. He took off.

"Hurry! You've almost made it!"

He stumbled toward the yelling coming from the other end of the bridge. A figure ran in front of the headlights toward him, picked him up and threw him over his shoulders and ran, slipping and sliding into France.

Twenty~Two

Christmas Eve, 1944

Naomi walked to the window, lifted the curtain, and sighed. She'd finally gotten the girls back to sleep. "Still snowing." She sat again in the big rocking chair beside the fireplace. "Hopefully those two won't get up again until morning."

Gracie lowered her feet from the stool and scooted forward on the couch. Naomi couldn't help noticing how puffy and swollen her ankles were. "Cynthia, tell me about your sister who was kidnapped. Did they never find out anything about her?"

Naomi waited for Cynthia to answer. What would she say?

Cynthia got another sugar cookie from the plate on the coffee table. "Mom needs to tell you about that, what happened and everything." She quirked her mouth and laughed. "I wasn't born yet, you know."

"I…I just thought maybe you knew the story."

Quenton sat in a recliner across from her and nestled a wooden bowl of mixed nuts in his lap. He cracked them with a metal nutcracker and plucked the meat out of the shells with a pick, plopping one in his mouth for every morsel he put in a bowl.

"That's annoying, Daddy." Cynthia frowned at him.

He grinned at his daughter. "I'll save the hazelnuts for you."

"It's still annoying, but I suppose I can overlook all the cracking for a handful of hazelnuts."

From his perch on the hearth, Robby pointed to the bowl. "I like the Brazil nuts."

Cynthia screwed up her nose. "Good, because none of us like them. You can get rid of them for us." She looked at Gracie. "What about you, Gracie? Which ones do you like?"

Gracie shrugged. "Oh, I like them all. We live where pecans grow, so I'm partial to them."

"Mom likes the pecans too, for cooking. She puts Dad to work cracking them every evening during the fall to use in the holiday baking." Cynthia took the hazelnuts her dad handed her and crunched down on one. "Umm. So good." She looked at Naomi. "Well, Mom? Are you going to answer Gracie's question?"

Naomi darted a quick look at her husband. Quenton cleared his throat and brushed bits of broken shells from his lap. He avoided her eyes.

Gracie shifted her weight. "I'm sorry. I don't mean to pry." She clasped her hands over her abdomen. "I just never knew about…I mean…" She looked down. "I'm sorry." Her voice quivered.

Quenton set the wooden bowl of nuts on the hearth and waited for Naomi to respond. When she didn't, he interjected, "It's a difficult subject to discuss, Gracie, but especially on Christmas Eve. That's when it happened. And it was a night much like this one." His voice, low and soft, barely discernible, held a note of warning.

Naomi put up her hand. "It's okay, Q. I'll tell her about it. Maybe if we talked about it, it would finally be in the past."

Robby, who had been sitting quietly beside Cynthia, spoke up. "Yeah, I'd like to hear this too. I've never known exactly what happened. I knew you'd had a daughter kidnapped, but I never knew the details." He rubbed his thighs nervously with the palms of his hands. "I didn't want to be nosy."

"I understand, Robby. It happened several years before you all took over the restaurant."

Naomi rocked in her chair and stared at the picture on the mantel. "In a way, it seems like it happened yesterday, and in other ways, it seems so long ago." She rubbed her forehead. "It was Christmas of 1926. The inn was a boardinghouse then. My parents were the proprietors, and every year on Christmas Eve they had a party for their boarders, much like the dinner we'll be having tomorrow evening. But theirs was a much more elegant affair.

"All the ladies wore evening gowns. The men wore tuxes or suits. My mother would set the table in her finest silver and china, and she always hired extra help for the evening to serve a five-course meal. We had come down from Denver the week before to spend the Christmas holidays with my parents."

"My family has a traditional Christmas Eve dinner too. They're probably having a party right now," Gracie said. Then she shook her head. "I'm sorry, please go on."

"Yes, well, our Julia was about nine months old. We had her picture made here in the Springs with the stocking that my mother had handmade for her. The photograph was to be a Christmas gift for my parents." Naomi's eyes reddened as she stared at the photo. "I've been so grateful that we had that done before Christmas, after what happened. Pictures are all we have left of her."

Gracie motioned with her hand toward the mantle and the stocking that glittered in the firelight. "Is that the same stocking?"

Naomi nodded. "That Christmas Eve was exactly like tonight. A blizzard swirling around the inn, and the electricity out, but that didn't dim the party atmosphere. Candles and lanterns lit up the dining room, creating quite a festive atmosphere. The dinner continued as planned." She walked to the fireplace and warmed her hands then turned her back to the flames, facing Quenton. "We were staying in the turret room. My mother had made me a beautiful purple dress…" Her voice trailed off.

Quenton got up and set the bowl of nuts on the hearth. He put his arm around her shoulders. "You don't have to go into this if you don't want to."

Gracie nodded. "Of course, if it's too painful…"

Naomi patted her husband's arm. "I'm fine. It's strange, but I feel compelled to talk about it tonight. I want to." She cleared her throat. "We left Julia asleep in the room so we could go downstairs and have dinner. When we returned, she was gone. We never found her." Naomi stared ahead into space. "That's it. That's what happened."

Cynthia stood and glanced back and forth between her parents. She folded her arms across her chest. "No, that can't be all that happened. There's got to be more to it. You've never told us the details. What did you do to find her? Did you call the police? Who all was in the house? What suspects were there?" She took a step toward them, around Robby and the coffee table. "Please tell me. I want to know everything that happened. I have a right to know."

Quenton shook his head. "What difference does it make now? We had a daughter who was taken from us, and we never found her. It's over. We need to move on."

"But Dad, I want to know what happened."

Naomi took a deep breath. "She's right, Q. She has a right to know. Maybe if we talked about it, I wouldn't have the…the flashbacks that hound me. Maybe they would stop."

"What flashbacks? What are you talking about, Mom?"

"Sit back down, everybody, and I'll tell you all we know." Naomi returned to the rocking chair and closed her eyes. "I can see it all so clearly in my mind. Sometimes I have a flashback to that night…and I'm there. I mean, I'm actually there. I can hear the singing. I can smell the onion soup and the smoke from the fireplace. I can see the faces of the people around the table." She opened her eyes.

"Mom, who was there that night besides you and Dad, and Grandma and Grandpa? Do you remember?"

"Yes, every single person. The Thomases…you know they've been coming here for years at Christmas. A newly married couple. Then there was the couple from Texas who lived here while their house was being built, and friends of theirs from Houston, an attorney and his wife."

"Somebody in the house had to have taken the baby." Cynthia was sitting on the edge of the couch. "It had to be an inside job."

Quenton leaned forward with his elbows on his knees, shaking his head. "The police checked out every possibility. The most likely suspect was a young woman who had been hired as extra help to serve dinner that evening. She disappeared as dinner was being served. We called her Cookie, but we doubt that was her real name. The police could find no trace of her. Just no trace left of Julia or Cookie. Disappeared into the storm. The only things missing were the baby's diaper bag and one of the photographs of her that had been lying on the dresser."

"Footprints? A car?"

"Look outside, Cynthia. Do you think footprints would last very long in a storm like this?"

Quenton stood and stuck his hands in his pockets. "I tell you, we followed every possible lead. All dead ends. We hounded the detectives until they were sick unto death of us. They never found a trace. The case is unsolved, cold."

Naomi picked up the photograph. "The one ray of hope we've clung to all these years is the fact that the police never found a body." She touched her chest. "I believe she's still alive, and we will be reunited one day."

Quenton cupped her elbow. "Are you ready to go to bed?"

She shook her head. "Not yet. You can't go to bed yet—we have Santa Claus to put out for the little girls."

His mouth was a firm, straight line. "Cynthia can do it. Gracie and Robby will help her."

Her brows raised. "You're not going to stay up and help me put out Santa Claus gifts for Myrna and Elise?"

"I'm really tired, honey. There's not anything I need to assemble, is there?"

She wrapped her arms around her middle. It wasn't exhaustion that made him want to leave. She knew him too well to think it was. "No. They both have dolls and cradles that Dad made for them."

Quenton pulled off his tie that he had loosened earlier. "You can stay here and rehash all of this if you want to. I'm going to bed." He picked up the dish of nutshells and looked at Cynthia. "That's really all there is to tell, sweet pea."

Quenton disappeared into the dark kitchen. He turned up the wick in a lantern and made his way down the hall toward their bedroom, the light shimmering around him in a small circle. The hall plunged into darkness once again as the bedroom door slammed shut.

TWENTY~THREE

December 23, 1944
San Antonio, Texas

Esperanza ripped the tape from the box labeled CHRISTMAS LIGHTS. Jorge rummaged around in the corner of the attic, grumbling under his breath.

He looked over his shoulder as she rolled the sticky stuff into a ball. "Did you find them?"

Frowning, she hurled a clipped answer back at him. "I found the outside lights. Why are these boxes not in order?" She set the box of colored bulbs aside and continued searching. "I need the Christmas tree lights."

"Why in the world did you wait until just a few days before Christmas to put up a Christmas tree?"

"You know perfectly well why. Gracie's not here. It doesn't feel like Christmas."

"We still have Serafina and Jorge Jr. Aren't they worth having a Christmas celebration for?" He snorted. "You've got to come out of this malaise you've been in since Gracie left. She'll come around eventually and return home. But right now, she's angry and wounded."

He set a large box down in front of her. "See if they're in here. It just says 'Christmas.' It's not very heavy." He cut the tape, took a handkerchief out of his pocket, and wiped his forehead. "It sure doesn't feel like Christmas."

Esperanza rifled through the contents, shaking her head. "Ornaments. Tree skirt." She glanced toward the back wall of the attic. "Let me look over there."

Several boxes sat askew under the circular window. The tops of two boxes had been ripped open. Whoever had opened them had folded the cardboard closed again but neglected to re-tape them.

"Someone has been up here looking for something."

"Any Christmas ones?" Jorge lifted the box containing the ornaments. "Do you want me to take this downstairs?"

She sat on a small footstool that had been Gracie's and nodded, staring at the two opened boxes. She waved her hand at her husband, dismissing him to carry the box downstairs. As his footsteps faded down the steep attic stairs, an alarm sounded in her subconscious like the clanging of their clock in the early morning beside their bed. Distant, yet close at hand.

But grope as she might, she couldn't turn it off. It grew louder and louder until the logic of what was happening slowly took over, and panic set in. The blood drained from her face, leaving her lightheaded. She could no longer reject the rationale of what plainly lay before her. The boxes of Gracie's records and mementos had been opened. The secrets, hidden for so many years, had been set free like the malevolence from Pandora's box. She tore into the boxes like a mad woman, screaming and cursing, strewing papers and toys and baby paraphernalia from one corner of the attic to the other.

Jorge bounded up the stairs and grabbed her by the wrists. "Esperanza! Calm down! What in the world...?"

She flung herself at her husband and beat her fists against his chest. She threw her head back and wailed. "Gracie's things are all gone. She knows. She knows." Her shoulders heaved as Jorge gathered the grieving woman and eased onto the floor with her.

"Of course, she knows, *mi bonita*. There, there. She's still our daughter." He held her head against his chest as she wept. "You must give up this obsession with Gracie. It doesn't matter that she knows she's adopted. There's no shame in that."

Gulping for air, Esperanza lifted her tearful eyes to look at her husband's kind face. "You don't understand. It's not that she knows she was adopted, it's how we got her."

"What do you mean?" He handed Esperanza his handkerchief. Several moments of silence passed as he searched her face. His usually bright eyes darkened into a scowl. "Esperanza? Answer me. What do you mean? We got her through your brother. Charlie had a client who needed to adopt out an orphan child, whose parents had been killed in a car accident." He took his wife by her shoulders. "Didn't we?" He shook her like the rag dolls that lay on the dusty floor of the attic. "Didn't we? Answer me, Esperanza."

She hung her head and covered her face with her hands. She shook her head and tried to speak, but her throat closed on her words. Finally, she took a deep breath and wiped her eyes. "I...I never wanted you to know. Ch...Charlie said I should tell you, but I didn't want to burden you with it. There was no need—"

"No need for what?" Jorge stood, leaving her crumpled on the floor. He paced in front of her. "I'm not liking the direction this is headed. Tell me, Esperanza. Now. Whatever it is, I need to know."

Images of the beautiful, frightened child Charlie brought to them that night raced through her mind. The hazel green eyes that stared at her. The fair skin and auburn hair, so unlike their coloring. The child screamed and cried "Mama" for weeks after they brought her home. Nothing soothed her. Esperanza told Jorge it was because of the trauma of losing her parents. All Charlie had given them with her was a blue and red diaper bag with a sleeper and diapers. And a photograph of the child with a Christmas stocking draped across her lap and the name *Julia* stitched across the cuff.

Jorge had looked at the photo and remarked, "Well, I guess her name is Julia."

Esperanza shook her head. "No, I want to name her Graciela Esperanza Gonzales, and I want to teach her Spanish."

Eventually the child settled into calling her Mama and Jorge, Papa. She was just beginning to walk, and soon they had to put all the breakables in the house up on high shelves, or the child would dash them to the floor and watch to see if they would punish her. She was tall and lean for her age. Active and curious. It was all Esperanza could do to keep up with her, but she loved having a little girl.

She dressed the child in the finest dresses, bright hair ribbons, and black patent Mary Janes. Everyday playwear was cute sundresses with matching hair bows and shoes. Esperanza brushed Graciela's hair two hundred strokes every night, keeping it shiny and clean. A nanny was hired to hover over the child during the day. In fact, several nannies were hired before Esperanza found one good enough for her Gracie.

Jorge stopped his pacing and turned toward his wife. "Esperanza, talk to me."

She pushed herself off the floor and dusted off an old deacon's bench with the handkerchief before she slumped down on it. She hated that bench. It was so lacking in personality. It didn't fit their Spanish décor, but a friend had given the piece to them as a wedding gift, and she didn't know what to do with it. So it had sat in the attic all these years gathering dust.

Now she sat on that despised bench on the precipice of having to reveal dreaded information to her husband. What irony. She felt as if she were sitting on a hot seat. Alternately wadding the handkerchief into a ball then pulling it back and forth in her hands, she wiped her nose with it.

Jorge sat beside her, with his arm draped on the back of the bench, waiting for her to speak. He drummed the wood with his fingers.

She stared past him as a long minute passed with no sound but her sniffling. "I don't know where to begin."

"Start wherever you need to, but just start. You have some explaining to do."

She sniffled in gasps. "I…I can't say really how it started, but Charlie knew how much we wanted a child. He knew we'd investigated adoption but had been turned down because of my health issues. After the fourth miscarriage…" She paused and blew her nose. "After that…he…he mentioned to me one evening that he could get us a child to adopt if we were willing to spend a lot of money to get it done. I told him money was not a problem. I told him to go ahead with the process."

She stood and walked to the window. "I didn't know there would be anything illegal about it. I just thought Charlie had connections where he knew about situations where…where maybe a single young woman needed to adopt out a baby and didn't want to go through the usual channels. I was shocked when he brought us a child nearly a year old, but I fell in love with her from the beginning and thought of her as our own immediately. I didn't question the circumstances…at first."

"At first?"

"Yes, at first." She stared into space as if she were seeing the scene unfold in front of her. "The months went by, and I was busy trying to learn how to be a mother. Then miracle of miracles, I got pregnant with Serafina, and then Jorge Jr. came along. I was overwhelmed with the busyness of a household brimming with three children. Before I knew it, years had gone by. But always, always in the back of my mind, was the nagging question of where Gracie had really come from.

"One day shortly before Christmas, I took Gracie to Houston to see Charlie and Carmen and do some shopping. She was five years old."

Jorge nodded. "I remember you going on that trip."

"We'd had her four years by then. She'd lived with us and become a Gonzales. She was ours. I left her with Carmen that day, so I could do Santa Claus shopping without her. While downtown, I stopped by Charlie's office to ask questions that had plagued me since we'd brought her home. We'd never gotten a legal birth certificate for her. What exactly was the situation surrounding her adoption? I wondered if he had taken care of everything legally as far as having her was concerned. And what of her biological parents? Were they really dead? Had she been taken from an abusive situation? Was her mother alone and unable to care for her? I simply needed to know more about our daughter." She folded her hands together and turned to face her husband. "I wished later I'd not insisted he tell me. Ignorance would have been better. I've had to live all these years with this on my conscience."

"What, Esperanza?" Jorge's voice grew soft. Enveloping her in his arms, he turned her face toward him. "You can tell me. It's all right. Whatever it is, we'll deal with it. We'll get through it."

She took a deep breath. "She…Gracie…Julia…was kidnapped, taken from her parents from a boardinghouse in Colorado Springs…on Christmas Eve in 1926."

TWENTY~FOUR

They sat enveloped in each other's arms, Esperanza sniffling, wiping her tears away, and Jorge in stunned silence. She took a deep breath and pushed away from her husband as she had pushed away the years that had gone before, living with the knowledge that shattered parents somewhere in the country mourned their child as she celebrated hers.

Self-doubt had never left her, but she plunged it into the depths of her heart and buried it. But like pesky weeds, they would sprout if watered by a word, or a thought, or an article about a kidnapped child. With grim determination, she trampled the doubt under the black soil of lies. She would stare at the newspaper pictures of a distraught mother with bowed head and a tight-lipped father begging for the child to be returned, images that burrowed into her brain in shades of black and white newsprint.

She'd wondered about the birth mother—was she young? Was she pretty? She had to be, Esperanza surmised, looking at her beautiful Gracie. How could she stand to ever lose her? Like the birth mother had... No, she wouldn't think about that. Surely God wouldn't have brought Gracie to them if he hadn't wanted her to be their daughter, would He? There must be some reason they'd been given the child. Her brother would not give her details. And honestly, she didn't want to know.

She looked into her husband's dark eyes, his thick eyebrows furrowed into a deep frown. She held the handkerchief wadded in her fist next to her chin, chewing on her lip. "What are we to do now? What *can* we do?" A sob clutched her throat. "Do...do you hate me?"

Jorge stroked his moustache and shook his head. "This is too much to take in." He stood, took two steps away, and then stalked back to her. He repeated the pacing process. "Why did you keep this from me all these years? Why didn't you tell me?"

"I...I was afraid. Afraid you'd make me t-take her b...back." A sob interrupted the unimaginable statement that refused to be spoken. "After all these years, we've lost her anyway." She stood and went into Jorge's open arms. She dissolved into tears. "We...we've lost her."

His voice was firm and steady. "Whether we've lost her or not, we must do what is right. We've committed a terrible wrong—innocently, to be sure—but a wrong nevertheless." He held her close, rubbing a hand over her back. But there was no wavering in his words. "We must do what we can to right it."

Christmas Eve, 1944
Colorado Springs, Colorado

Gracie struggled to her feet. "I think perhaps we'd better go." Robby took her elbow to assist her. She grabbed hold of the arm of the sofa and chuckled. "I don't seem to have very good balance these days."

"That's perfectly normal." Naomi motioned for her to sit and walked to the window once more. "You all don't need to try to get across the street in this blizzard. I can barely see the streetlights or the edge of the road."

Gracie plopped back down on the cushion. "You're probably right. I've heard stories of ranchers in the Wild West who would be found frozen just outside the door of their cabin, having become disoriented in a blizzard. I didn't understand how that could possibly happen—that is, until I experienced my first snowstorm here a few weeks ago."

Robby laughed. "Yeah, we couldn't get Gracie away from the door during that storm. She kept opening it and going out into the snow, until it started drifting so bad we could hardly get the door open."

Naomi came back to the fireplace. "Talk about drifts, it's piling up pretty good out there now. I haven't heard a snow plow come by. We're going to be snowed in if they don't get the roads graded soon."

Outlined by the glow from the fire, Cynthia stood by Julia's stocking on the mantel and traced the name on the cuff. "So, Mom…what happened after you discovered Julia was missing? Do you remember?"

"Like it had happened tonight. So many times I've relived it. Seen it again, experienced it again as I did that night."

Cynthia sat on the hearth in front of her mother. Several more moments passed with only the crackling of the fire. Robby walked to the copper tub, pulled out two more logs, and put them on the fire. He poked around in the coals, and when he was satisfied with the flame, sat down beside Cynthia on the hearth. Nobody spoke as the seconds ticked by.

The steel band around Gracie's abdomen tightened again. She held her breath and squirmed to find a more comfortable position without calling attention to herself. This time the pain lasted longer, and her back hurt something fierce. Could she be in labor? She glanced over at the window.

In this storm? The steely fingers finally released her, and she relaxed. She realized she'd been scrunching up her toes.

"Do you think I'm crazy?" Naomi reached her hand toward Cynthia. "Seeing things like that?"

The girl's eyes grew wide as she started to get up then sat back down. She clutched her hands in front of her in a fist. "No, I don't think you're crazy. Maybe God is trying to give you some sort of clue."

"I don't know. It's been so long—seventeen years. Julia is a grown young woman by now...out there...somewhere." The rocking chair creaked as Naomi sat down and set it moving.

Cynthia toyed with the belt of her robe. "You think she's still alive?"

Naomi nodded in rhythm with the rocking chair. "I know she is."

"How can you know? After all this time?"

Naomi stopped rocking and tapped her chest. "I know in here, in my heart. My mother's heart knows she is still alive. Ever since that night, my life has simply been a collection of puzzle pieces. Some of them wonderful pieces, like you and Myrna and Elise. But puzzle pieces, nonetheless. Nothing seems to fit right—and won't fit right until we find Julia. I hope one day she will come looking for me, for us, for her real family."

Gracie's heart thudded. *They want Julia to come looking for them. They want me to...*

Scooting forward, Cynthia rested her elbows on her knees. "Did you call the police? What did the rest of the guests do? Did they leave?"

Naomi slowly shook her head. "No one left. They couldn't, the storm was so bad. And of course we called the police, but it took them so long to get here, through the snow... Everyone was afraid to venture out except that 'Cookie' person. And she had my baby," Naomi whispered as her lip quivered. She took a deep breath. "Someone had to have picked her up. It had to have been prearranged. The police investigated everyone who was there that night but didn't come up with a single lead. Any tracks were covered by the blizzard by the time they got here. She simply vanished into the snowstorm."

Gracie couldn't take her eyes off the mother and daughter sitting across from her by the hearth, the firelight glinting off Cynthia's auburn hair. She curled a lock of her own hair around her finger. She'd let it grow since Jack left. It was getting really long.

Cynthia's profile stood silhouetted against the glow of the fire. Gracie stared at Cynthia—her nose slender, and slightly upturned at the end. And her chin, rather long and strong. Just like her own. She rubbed the tip of her nose with her fingers. Just like Cynthia's.

Gracie swallowed the dry, cottony lump in her throat. Naomi's face swam before her. This was her mother, her birth mother, in front of her. This was the woman who had carried her for nine months and suffered the pangs of childbirth to bring her into the world. Then she was ripped from her in a single moment.

Gracie placed her hand on her abdomen protectively. She couldn't imagine the horror of enduring such heartache, such emptiness. How had Naomi made it through all these years? She imagined herself surging forward and embracing the woman, shouting, "I'm your daughter! I'm here! I've found you!" But she sat frozen to the couch, unable to speak.

The woman who had raised her was an imposter. The woman who had sheltered her, fed her, clothed her, brushed her hair, taught her manners, and taken her to school was a deceiver. But perhaps her parents didn't know the circumstances of how she came to them. What if they had stumbled across some black-market adoption ring that snatched babies and adopted them out for money, hiding the real truth of those children? Questions raced through Gracie's mind.

"What…what…" The words stuck in her throat like a piece of meat swallowed hastily. She cleared her throat. "What would you do if she—your daughter—found you? What if she just showed up one day and said, 'Hello, I'm your long-lost daughter?'" She looked at Cynthia. "How would you feel, Cynthia, if you suddenly had another sister?"

Naomi and Cynthia turned toward Gracie. The girl said, "Gee, Gracie, I've never thought about that. I mean, I've thought how neat it would be to find Julia, but in my mind she's still a baby. She'd be grown by now, though, wouldn't she? About your age, probably." Cynthia giggled. "I'd be thrilled to find her. Wouldn't you, Mom? Wouldn't that be fun?"

The corners of Naomi's lips lifted in a slight smile. "I've thought about it constantly through the years, at each stage of her life—as a toddler, and a precious three- and four-year-old, and then elementary aged. I could picture pigtails and hair bows. It appeared she was going to be tall and have hair red like her father's—like yours, Cynthia. Then as a teenager in saddle shoes and a pony tail." She hesitated. "I spent hundreds of sleepless nights worrying about her. Was she safe? Was she cold? Was she being taken care of? Was she loved and cherished? Or was she…gone?"

Gracie glanced at her black-and-white saddle oxfords sitting next to the couch.

Naomi stared into the fire. "I used to pray that we'd find her. I prayed a lot in the beginning, begging God to find her for us, to bring her back to us. But He never answered. I gave up praying."

"You gave up…praying?" Gracie's eyes grew wide. She wanted to cross herself but, embarrassed, she refrained. "Why?"

"I prayed, and she didn't come back." Naomi shrugged. "Lupe used to lecture me about that. She'd say, 'Mrs. Lockhart, you must never give up praying. You never know when or how the Good Lord will answer. Remember Joseph in the Bible. He was ripped from his father's arms for years and thrown in prison, but God reunited them. Never give up.' But that was in the Bible. This is real life…and if there is a God, He has chosen not to answer our prayers to return our daughter." She glanced at Robby. "Your mother is a godly woman, Robby. I don't mean to disparage that. I simply don't have that kind of faith."

A log popped, sending a spray of sparks against the fireplace screen.

Naomi let out a long breath. "Sometimes I almost let myself believe that someday we'd find her… Almost. But it hurt too much to have our hopes dashed time after time. It became much easier to accept that God was deaf, or uncaring, or…or both." Her chin trembled ever so slightly. "Yes, I stopped praying for her, but I never stopped loving her."

Robby cleared his throat. "How did you even search for her after that night?"

"We did everything we could possibly do. We hounded the police, hired detectives, even went chasing state to state ourselves, but all attempts led to dead ends. She just was gone into the swirling blizzard." Naomi stood, setting the chair rocking, and straightened her scarf. "Enough talk about the past. Let's get Santa Claus put out for the little girls."

Gracie opened her mouth to speak then clenched her teeth as a wringing of her insides began deep within her and spread throughout her entire body, forcing a moan. All eyes turned toward her as a gush of water trickled over the edge of the couch, down her legs, and pooled around her feet.

Twenty~Five

Christmas Eve Morning, 1944

San Antonio, Texas

I know where Gracie is." Esperanza set her coffee cup on the table as the smell of bacon filled the brightly lit kitchen. Early morning sunshine poured through the louvered shutters, highlighting the yellow-and-white tiled counter tops.

Rosa flipped a pancake in the skillet and lifted another onto the stack on the back burner. She put a pitcher of melted butter and heated syrup on the table, along with two cobalt blue glasses of orange juice.

Jorge ignored Esperanza's statement. Instead of answering, he looked up from his paper and smiled at the maid. "Rosa, how long have you been with us?"

"Seems like all of my life, Señor Gonzales. Since before you got Gracie." She set the plate in front of Esperanza. "Be careful, señora. The plate is very hot."

"Yes, I will. Thank you." Esperanza frowned at Jorge.

He gave a slight shake of his head. "That's a long time. You've been a loyal employee." He set the paper aside. "You may go about your other chores.

171

Señora Gonzales and I have some private matters to discuss. Thank you for the pancakes." He inhaled. "They smell wonderful."

"*Sí*, señor." She turned off the burner, set the mixing bowl in the sink, leaving the skillet on the stove. "I need to get the silver out for the dinner party tonight. I polished most of it this week but need to finish."

Esperanza threw back her head and groaned as Rosa bustled through the swinging door. "I do not want to play the gracious hostess tonight."

Jorge motioned to the plate of pancakes. "Pass those down this way. I'm hungry." He helped himself to three of the platter-sized cakes and poured butter and syrup over the stack, topping it off with four pieces of bacon.

"Well, your appetite certainly hasn't been affected by our present circumstances."

"You know I always eat under stress."

"And I do not." She cut a pancake in half and mixed some butter and syrup on her plate. She dabbled a piece of the hot cake in the mixture and took a bite. "Everything tastes like sawdust to me." She put her fork down and wiped her mouth. "Did you hear me say that I know where Gracie is?"

Silence overtook the room despite the clink of Jorge's knife and fork against the china plate. He ate his breakfast slowly. "Is there more coffee?" He held up his cup.

Esperanza pushed back from the table and got the coffeepot from the stove. She poured her husband a cup of the steaming hot liquid and sat back down. "Are you not going to answer me?"

He wiped his mouth with his napkin and pushed back from the table. Folding the newspaper commanded his attention as he slowly and carefully returned the morning rag to its original shape. The second hand of the clock on the kitchen wall tick-tocked through the heavy silence. Finally, he looked at his wife. "Very well, where do you think Gracie is?"

She folded her napkin and placed it beside her plate. "The only clue would be the signature of the photographer on that picture of her. It was in the diaper bag. I knew I probably should have gotten rid of it, but it was so cute, I just couldn't do it." Shaking her head, she mumbled softly. "That's where she's gone. Jack's been sent overseas, and she went in search of her... her real par..." The sentence hung suspended in the morning sunshine, like dust particles dancing in the sun, floating in the air, never landing.

"Esperanza, we are her parents. We raised her, loved her, educated her, clothed and fed her. Nothing can ever change that, but she does have a right to know who she is. We mustn't begrudge her that. And I believe we need to help her if we can."

"I want to talk to Charlie and find out everything he knows. He would only give me the bare bones, and although I was curious, I let the sleeping dog lie, so to speak. But now we need to know. And, Jorge." She leaned forward and slapped the table top. "I will find our daughter."

His crooked grin that always pricked her heart tugged at the edge of his mouth. "I know when you get a burr under your saddle you're going to hang on until you get it out." He patted her hand. "*Mi bonita,* this is not the end of the world, nor the end of our relationship with our daughter. I'm convinced she will come back home when she has worked through her hurt and anger. We will find her together."

"And how long is that going to be?" Her mouth quivered. "I can't stand to simply sit around and do nothing. I need to find her and bring her home."

Jorge sat straighter. "You think you could get her to come home? Not right now. She's a grown, married woman and will come home when she's ready. She needs time. And we need to give her some space." He stood, walked to the sink, and rinsed off his plate.

"Leave that. Rosa will get it."

Jorge turned from the sink, punctuating the air with his fork. "I know it is probably fruitless to even say this, but I want you to lay this aside until after Christmas. Concentrate on the holidays for our other children and family. Enjoy our annual Christmas Eve party. Charlie and Carmen will be in this afternoon. We can talk to Charlie about what we need to do—but *after* Christmas." He waited for his wife's response. "Esperanza?"

She grumbled and tapped her long red nails on the table top.

"Promise me."

"I won't promise to wait until after Christmas, but I will wait until after the party tonight."

Jorge sighed and tossed his fork into the sink. "I suppose I'll have to be happy with that." He walked and kissed her on the top of her head, where her braids were swirled into a neat coronet. "Junior and I need to finish the luminarias along the front walk."

"What about the driveway?"

"Already done, my dear." He picked up another piece of bacon and left Esperanza sitting alone at the kitchen table.

Prominent San Antonio citizens came and went that evening for the Gonzales' traditional Christmas Eve buffet. José, his son, and Jorge Jr. acted as valets, parking cars around the property as guests arrived. A crisp, chilly breeze swirled around the luminarias rattling the sacks. The house sparkled with the Christmas lights Jorge and Esperanza had uncovered during the upsetting episode in the attic. Put up at the last minute and seemingly emitting the joy of the season amid the twinkling lights, that joy did not reside in the hearts of the hosts of the gala event. But Esperanza knew the guests would see nothing but hospitality at her home.

A large silver ladle rested in creamy eggnog within an ornate silver punch bowl at the end of the beautifully appointed table. Serafina stood behind it, manning the ladle. As a child, Serafina loved dressing up for their Christmas buffet and ladling up the eggnog into the matching silver cups. Now it was a bother, of course—she would rather have been out with her friends. She looked radiant in a red and green plaid taffeta skirt and red sweater. A bright red headband kept her hair out of her face and complemented her dark hair and olive skin. She reached into her pocket and pulled out the small white lipstick case, turning her back for a moment to freshen her pouty red lips. Esperanza frowned but refrained from barking at her daughter.

Random inquiries from their guests about their children, especially about Gracie, were quickly answered with an awkward but socially proper dismissal. "They are all doing well. Would you care for some more wassail, or wine perhaps?"

In spite of rationing, Rosa kept the tables and sideboards full of ham, turkey, potatoes— both sweet and white—Jell-O salads, and their traditional tamales she had labored over for days. The luminarias flickered down as the evening waned and eventually snuffed themselves out in the sand that anchored the paper sacks.

Esperanza caught hold of Charlie's sleeve as they told the last of their guests good-bye and Serafina and Jorge Jr. had gone upstairs. "Jorge and I need to talk to you."

Her brother had developed quite a paunch as he'd aged. *Probably from drinking too much beer.* Esperanza noticed he'd drunk his fill of eggnog and wine throughout the evening.

He looked at her with reddened eyes. "Tonight?" He patted his belly. "I'm full and ready to get to bed, dear sister." He gave her a sideways hug.

"Tonight." She motioned toward the parlor. "Get your drink and come sit down."

"Very well. Does this include Carmen?"

"Yes, the four of us need to talk." She called to Jorge, who was closing the front door. She nodded her head toward the room. "We are going to the parlor."

Jorge pulled his tie loose and sighed. "Yes, I'm coming, dear. Be right there." He walked to the liquor cabinet and pulled out a bottle of Scotch. "I think I'm going to need this." He poured a shot. "Charlie?"

"Believe I will, thank you."

Jorge sat in his leather recliner across from Charlie and Carmen, who were settling into the plush couch. Carmen took one of the tasseled end pillows and put it behind her back. "I love your new couch, Esperanza. The colors are beautiful—all these burgundies, wines, and gold. Chic."

"Yes, thank you." Esperanza paced in front of her brother and sister-in-law. Jorge set his drink on a heavy side table. Esperanza shoved a coaster under his glass. She cleared her throat.

Charlie took another swig of his drink.

Carmen looked at Esperanza then at her husband. "What's going on? Is something wrong? Has something happened to someone in the family?" She scooted forward to the edge of the sofa. "You've heard from Gracie?"

"No, but Gracie is the subject of this little gathering."

Charlie gulped down the remainder of his drink.

Esperanza took his glass away from him. "You've had quite enough for tonight, little brother. I need you coherent." She set it on a coaster on the coffee table and stood in front of him, her hands on her hips. "I need you to tell me everything you know about Gracie's family of origin."

Charlie shifted in his seat, and pulled on his collar. "You know everything I know, Esperanza. Her father had been killed, and her mother was—"

Esperanza held up her hand. "Cut the bull, Charlie. I don't want the front story we've told everybody all these years. Jorge knows now."

Carmen cut her eyes at her husband. "You told me that Esperanza and Jorge knew everything."

"Well, Esperanza did, but apparently she never told Jorge, I guess—until recently."

Jorge swilled his drink around in his glass and stared at it as if doing so would conjure up some magic solution. Then he leaned forward with his elbows on his knees, the recliner creaking. He squinted his eyes at his brother-in-law. "Esperanza never told me. All these years, she never told me the dark secret the two of you harbored. That our Gracie had been torn from the arms of loving parents. Kidnapped—criminally kidnapped."

Charlie jumped to his feet. "Now wait just a minute—"

"No, you wait. Sit back down."

Charlie looked at his wife and complied.

Jorge continued. "I've waited seventeen years. Gracie's birth parents have waited seventeen years. What has been in darkness all this time needs to come to light, and we need to try to make this right…if there's any way we can."

Esperanza plopped down in a side chair and stared at her husband. Such a burst of authoritative demand was unlike him.

"Start talking, Charlie. I want to hear every detail. I want to hear every excuse, every reason, every rationalization that led you to decide to snatch a child from her parents. I know how much money it cost. We paid you thousands of dollars for the adoption." Jorge thumped his chest. "We paid you! Did you pocket all of our money yourself? Or did you have henchmen you had to pay who helped you pull off this—this 'adoption'?" He jabbed his finger in Charlie's face. "Adoption? Ha! That's a laugh. No wonder we could never get a birth certificate out of you. There wasn't one. What kind of man compromises his integrity to do such a thing?"

Twenty~Six

Colorado Springs, Colorado

Oh. Oh, dear." Gracie stood and looked down at the moisture dribbling down her leg. "I'm so sorry." She looked frantically around the room at Naomi, Cynthia, and Robby. "I need a towel, or… or…something."

Naomi chuckled and stood. "Come with me, honey. Your water just broke." She put her arm around Gracie's shoulders. "Looks like you are going to have a Christmas baby. You will be going into labor shortly, if you haven't already. Is your stomach cramping?"

Gracie nodded. "Yes, like a tightening that takes my breath away, but I didn't know for sure what it was." She backed out of the slippers Cynthia had given her as the liquid oozed into them. "Ew, it won't stop. I can't stop it."

Cynthia, who had run to the bathroom for a towel, returned and held it out to Gracie. Gracie looked at the towel, then at Naomi, her eyes wide and filling with tears. "What do I do? I…I'm scared."

"I understand, but there's no reason to be. Women have been having babies for centuries." She retied her headscarf and reached for her hand. "Let's get you cleaned up first. Robby, this couch folds out into a bed. Would you do that while I get something for Gracie to put on? Cynthia, get some more towels and clean sheets out of the laundry room. Put the sheets on the sofa bed and the towels on top of them." Naomi led Gracie down the hall to the bathroom. "Take off your clothes, and I'll get you a nightgown."

A candle on the back of the commode flickered. The green and white linoleum pattern merged together before Gracie's eyes, and her legs trembled beneath her as she felt the steely fingers once again taking control of her body, squeezing, squeezing, squeezing. *This must be what they call a contraction…good terminology. I feel like my insides are being squeezed out of me.* She clutched the edge of the sink and took a deep breath. Another gush of water ran down her legs.

"Here, hang onto me until it passes." Naomi continued to hold Gracie around the shoulders with one arm and held out the other. Gracie grabbed hold of the arm of the woman she now believed held her when she was first born. The woman who had endured the pain of childbirth to bring her into the world was once again holding her. Gracie was sure of it. This was her birth mother. Gracie's legs turned to jelly and refused to hold her up. She let go of Naomi's arm and sat on top of the toilet seat, trying to wipe up the water that continued to trickle from her body.

Naomi rubbed her arm where Gracie had left nail prints.

"Oh, I'm sorry! Guess I didn't realize how hard I was squeezing." She touched Naomi's arm.

"Oh, honey, please don't worry about that. No harm done, no harm at all. Stay right here and I'll get you a gown. Then we'll get you onto that sofa bed."

"Don't we need to get to the hospital or call the doctor?"

Naomi's eyes brimmed with compassion as she stood halfway between the bathroom door and the hallway. "I think we will be fortunate if we can get Robby's mother over here from across the street to help, much less the doctor. The phones are out. There's no way we could get to the base hospital in this snowstorm."

Gracie's eyes widened. "Can we do this by ourselves?"

"Absolutely." Naomi patted Gracie's arm. "Don't worry. Nature will take its course. You'll be fine." She called over her shoulder. "Be right back."

Gracie's heart banged in her chest. All the old wives' tales she'd heard said labor pains were like your menstrual cramps, but she'd never felt anything like this pain before. Would they get worse? She knew they probably would but couldn't imagine how they could get much worse than this. Maybe she was already in hard labor? She didn't know much about the birthing process. Her mother had never talked to her about it. She needed her mother with her.

She had her mother...she *had* her mother with her. The only problem was her mother had no idea she was attending the birth of her own grandchild. Should she tell Naomi the truth? No, not now. Not a good time.

Naomi reappeared with a red plaid flannel nightgown. "Take everything off and put this on."

The soft glow from the candle gathered the two women in a cocoon of timelessness as Gracie watched Naomi unbutton the gown. The simple execution of that maneuver seemed to move in the molasses of slow motion. How many times had this woman tugged a gown over her head as a baby? She closed her eyes and tried desperately to remember anything, just anything. But she couldn't.

She opened her eyes. "Take off ... everything?"

"Everything. Underwear will only get in the way. And forget modesty. That goes by the wayside when you're having a baby." The older woman smiled. "I remember when I was having Julia, our first baby, I was so shocked at how difficult labor was and…" She chuckled. "Well, you don't need to hear about that."

"No, please. I'm very interested. Oh…oh… OHHHH." Another contraction interrupted her.

"Hang on, honey, until it passes. Don't hold your breath. Breathe."

The contraction was shorter but more intense than the previous ones. Gracie stepped out of her skirt and pulled her sweater off as soon as the contraction receded then struggled with her undergarments. Naomi helped her and slid the gown over her head. Gracie shoved her panties aside on the floor and wiped her legs with the towel. She looked at the towel in the dim light then brought it closer to her eyes, alarmed. "Naomi, I'm bleeding."

"That's normal. Nothing to be concerned about. Mingled with the fluid from the bag of water, it will look like a lot more blood than it really is." She patted the young girl's hand. "Don't you worry. Everything will be fine." They walked slowly down the hallway back into the living room. Robby was coaxing the fire to burn higher, and Cynthia was bent over the sofa bed, putting towels on top of the sheets.

She beamed at Gracie. "All ready for you."

Gracie sat carefully on the made-up bed, shaking her head. "I'm sorry. This is not how I planned this."

Naomi put her hands on her shoulders and gave them a slight squeeze. "Don't you know babies never come according to our plans?" Pointing to Cynthia, she laughed. "This one was two weeks early. Julia was ten days late. You just never know." She fluffed the pillow Cynthia had put on the bed. "Lie down and try to relax, if you can. You're going to need your strength."

Robby stood by the fireplace and shuffled his feet. Naomi nodded at him. "Do you think you can get across the street and make it back with your mother? We're going to need her."

He walked to the side door, opened it, and looked out. The snow filtering out of the sky had lessened as if on cue. "I can see the streetlamp in front of the restaurant. As long as I can see that, I can make it."

"I'll put a lantern in the front office window so you'll have a beacon to guide you back. It will be a while before this baby is born, being the first one and all, but you'd probably better go on now while you can. Come with me to the office," Naomi said, "and go out that way. You can head directly across the street from there."

The two walked into the front office. Robby put on his snow boots and pulled his flashlight out of the pocket of his parka. "I'll be back as quickly as I can with Mama."

"Be careful on the steps leading down to the road. They're so steep and get awfully slick."

"Don't I know it? I've slipped many a time on them."

"Just don't let your mother fall on them coming back."

"We'll be careful." He tugged his toboggan down over his ears. "Is Gracie going to be okay?"

"Oh, sure. It will get a little intense for a bit, but she'll be fine. Childbirth is as natural as anything—just a bit more painful than probably anything else on the face of the earth. But once she holds that baby in her arms, all the pain will be forgotten." Naomi waved him toward the door. "Now go on and get back as quickly as you can."

The young man pulled the hood of his parka over his head and opened the door. The wind had died down, but drifts of white covered the porch. He grabbed the shovel standing beside the front door and swung it back and forth as he held the flashlight under his arm and moved across the wooden floor down the steps. He leaned the shovel against the railing at the bottom step.

Naomi watched the light as he crossed the road and disappeared in the falling snow. She whispered, her breath blowing puffs of frost into the night air, "Hurry back, son. We're going to need your mother tonight."

"Mama! Mama, come quick!" Cynthia's screams accelerated in pitch. "Hurry, Mama! Something's happening!"

Twenty~Seven

I'm waiting, Charlie. What kind of man does something like that?" Jorge's usual smile had turned down into a controlled grimace. Esperanza held her breath, waiting for her brother to answer.

"Aw, Jorge." Charlie leaned forward with his elbows on his knees and put his head in his hands. He sighed and ran his fingers through his thinning hair. "I didn't think—"

"That's one thing I would agree with you about. You didn't think." Jorge stepped closer to Charlie until he was hovering over him, each sentence louder and more threatening. "Why would you have done anything that stupid?"

Charlie looked up at Jorge through bloodshot eyes. "I knew how much Esperanza wanted a child. Watching her grieve time after time, miscarriage after miscarriage, broke my heart. It's not like I was running a black-market adoption ring—selling babies for profit." He buried his face again in his hands. "I had helped some other couples with adoptions…" He hesitated and looked up. "All perfectly legal."

Jorge rubbed his chin and turned away from his brother-in-law. "You'll excuse me if I don't believe you."

"I'm not surprised you're skeptical. But the adoptions I brokered were legal. Well, all except maybe the one right before Gracie's."

"I don't care about any of the other adoptions, legal or otherwise, you had anything to do with before Gracie. What I want to hear is…what made you decide to kidnap her?"

"Convenience. The right circumstances." He pointed his finger at Jorge. "And I told you I didn't want any money for bringing her to you."

"But you certainly took it."

"Sure I did, after you insisted and wouldn't take no for an answer. And I had…I had expenses…"

"You mean you had to pay off the scumbags who helped you."

Charlie stood, took off his jacket, and hitched up his pants. He doubled up his fist and held it in Jorge's face. The two men stared at each other, posturing, neither one backing down.

Esperanza jumped from her chair. "Oh, for goodness sake. Don't be ridiculous, you two old geezers." She tugged on Jorge's sleeve and gently pushed Charlie back. "Exchanging fisticuffs is not going to solve anything."

Jorge blustered and shook her hand away. "No, but it would sure make me feel better."

Charlie stuffed back into place his shirt that had worked itself out of the waistband of his trousers. "Hit me or do whatever you want to do, but I was trying to help my sister. The opportunity came along and I took it. The child was there, left alone. We could get her out of state quickly as we were leaving the next morning. Our friends knew a young woman of questionable scruples who had connections and would help us. It was wrong. I admit it now. But at the time it seemed the right thing to do." His face flushed red, his bulbous nose almost glowing. He pulled a handkerchief out of his back pocket and wiped his face then blew his nose.

Carmen sniffled and reached for Charlie's hand. "I told you, Charlie. I told you we shouldn't have done that. It wasn't right."

Jorge turned his attention to Charlie's wife. "And you. He had to have your support to pull this off. The trip on the train back from Colorado Springs. Did you take care of Gracie all the way back? Someone had to."

Charlie sat back down. "We hired a girl to take care of the baby on the trip."

Jorge waited. "I am appalled, stunned, exasperated. Angry!" He gritted his teeth, and looked to the ceiling as if looking for someone or something to answer him. "No, furious would be a better word. Furious at the fact that you played God with this child's life, and now there are two heartbroken families without their daughter. I don't know what I need to do, but I'm going to do something."

From the foyer, the bright, colored bulbs on the Christmas tree they'd just decorated the night before contrasted starkly with the mood in the parlor.

Esperanza put her hands on her hips. "You may not know what you are going to do, but I know what *I'm* doing. As soon as we can get our things together, we are going to Colorado Springs to find our daughter. That's got to be where she is. She obviously found the photograph. It's missing, and it had the photographer's name on it. We'll start there." She turned to her brother. "I've never asked you any details about this before, but I'm asking you now. I want to know the name of the place where you were staying, where you were when you took Gracie. If it's still there, I want to talk to the proprietors. Maybe they have kept up with the parents. Maybe Gracie has been there looking for clues."

Charlie reached for Carmen and pulled her up beside him. "The proprietors at the time were the child's grandparents. It was a boardinghouse where we were visiting friends of ours who were living there while their house was finished." He gathered his jacket in his other hand.

Esperanza gasped. "Perhaps they are still there." She went into the foyer and got a pencil and pad from the phone table. "What was the name of the boardinghouse? I'm going to look them up."

Charlie shook his head. "They were an older couple then. Even if they were still alive, they would certainly not be up to running a boardinghouse. And I don't even know if the place is still there." Charlie pulled Carmen toward the stairs. "It was called the Golden Aspen Inn, but who knows now? Anyway, it's too late to try to find out anything. I'm going to bed."

He looked at her and Jorge, and his face drooped with fatigue…and years of guilt. "I'm so sorry. I was afraid for you, Esperanza. Afraid you'd be like Tia Maria—so blue after losing a baby that she took her own life. I didn't want to see you succumb to that kind of thing. So I convinced myself I was doing a good thing, but deep down…" Head shaking, he didn't meet her gaze. "Please forgive me, sis." His voice was so soft Esperanza could hardly hear him.

He and Carmen disappeared up the stairs.

Esperanza drew in a long breath. How could he have thought she would be like their aunt? She'd been down after the miscarriages, yes. Of course. But she'd always been stronger than that.

As she would be now. She went to the phone table in the foyer and sat down. Hands steady, she picked up the receiver and stuck her long red nail into the orb designated "Operator."

"Esperanza, it's too late—"

"Shush, Jorge. It's an hour earlier in Colorado. I'm just going to see if there's a boardinghouse by that name still located there anymore."

"May I help you, please?" The tinny voice exuded confidence.

GOLDEN KEYES PARSONS

"Yes, I hope so. I need the number of the Golden Aspen Inn in Colorado Springs, Colorado."

"One moment, please." Clicking and other tinny voices chattered in the background as Esperanza waited, tapping the pencil on the pad, making little black marks.

"Ma'am?"

"Yes, I'm here."

"I found a listing for a Golden Aspen Inn under 'Hotels and Lodging.'"

"Could I have the number…and address as well, if you have it?"

Esperanza scribbled both on the pad. She brushed a tear from her eye as she looked up at her husband. "It's still there. It's got to be the same place." She picked up the receiver again. "I'm going to call right now."

"Nobody will be answering their phones this late, especially on Christmas Eve. Wait until morning."

"No, I'm going to try to reach somebody right now. What if they have a vacancy, and we can actually stay there?" She held the receiver out so Jorge could hear the annoying *br-r-ring, br-r-ring*.

Jorge sighed and shoved his hands in his pockets. "What about Serafina and Junior? We can't just leave them here at Christmastime."

Esperanza covered the mouthpiece of the black phone. "We'll tell them we'd planned a surprise trip to the mountains for Christmas. They'll be excited."

It kept on ringing. *Seven. Eight. Nine…*

Twenty~Eight

Naomi hurried back through the door separating the office from their apartment, to the drama taking place in their living room. Cynthia met her and grabbed her arm, pulling Naomi toward the couch. "Hurry, Mom. Something's happening."

Naomi took a deep breath and emitted a nervous chuckle. "That's a fact, Cynthia. Something definitely is happening. We're having a baby." She willed herself to stay calm, but her insides were a quivering mess. She'd fall apart later. Right now, she needed to recall her long-ago attained nurse's training and attend to the emergency at hand. She blew out through her pursed mouth.

"B…but, look." Cynthia pointed down at Gracie, who was in the middle of a contraction with blood spurting onto the towels Naomi had laid out on the sheet. "Look at all that blood. I'm scared." The girl picked up the last towel from the stack on the hearth. "Is she going to be all right?"

A moan escaped from Gracie's throat, wrung from the depths of her body. "Is…is it supposed to hurt this much? Oh…oh no. I don't know if I can do this." She tossed her head from side to side and bit down on the pillowcase. "Jack, where are you? I need you here with me. Jack!"

Naomi sat down beside Gracie and wiped her forehead with a damp cloth, wondering if the girl was losing too much blood. She tried to keep her hands from trembling and looked at her daughter. "I think she's fine."

The contraction passed, and Gracie relaxed. She exhaled and tried to raise herself off the couch. "I'm sorry. I'm messing up your sofa. I'm so sorry."

"You lie back down, young lady. Don't you worry one moment about that. We're taking care of it. A sofa can always be cleaned."

A sharp ring in the office startled mother and daughter. They stared at each other with eyes wide.

"The phones! They must be back up."

The lights flickered on. Naomi pulled the bloody towel out from under Gracie. "Go get as many towels as you can carry from the laundry room. I'll answer the call. It's probably Lupe." She handed the soiled towels to her daughter and shooed her with her hand. "Quickly now."

She ran into the office and grabbed the phone. "Hello? Hello? Golden Aspen Inn. May I help you?"

An older woman's voice came through heavy static on the other end. "I'm sorry to bother you so late, but our family has decided at the last minute to make a trip to Colorado Springs and plan to arrive on the twenty-sixth. Do you have any vacancies?"

Naomi held the receiver in front of her and stared at it. *Are you kidding me? Calling for reservations on Christmas Eve at eleven o'clock at night?* The stupidity of tourists amazed her. She cleared her throat. "I'm so sorry. We are full. Christmas is our busiest season."

"We don't have a very good connection. Did you say you're full?"

"That's correct, no vacancies."

"Is this the Golden Aspen Inn that used to be a boardinghouse?"

"Y…yes it is. Have you been here before?"

191

"No, but my brother has and…had such good things to say about it that we wanted to stay there."

Crackling broke into the connection. Naomi shouted into the mouthpiece. "Hello? Are you there?" The static lessened. "Are you still there?"

"Yes, yes, I'm here. So you are still in operation?"

"Yes, but the Golden Aspen is no longer a boardinghouse. When we took it over from my parents a few years ago, we turned it into an inn with rooms for rent. However, we have no vacancies until after the new year." Naomi let out an exasperated huff. "Listen, we're having a bit of an emergency, and I need to see if I can get through to the hospital."

The phone line went dead. "Hello? Hello?" Naomi clicked several times, but with no response on the other end, replaced the receiver. *Guess not. Hope they find something.* She lifted the phone again. Perhaps they could get through to the hospital now. No dial tone—the lines must have gone down again.

Well, she didn't have time to worry about that. She turned her attention to the more immediate task at hand—delivering Gracie's baby.

Esperanza shook the receiver then put it back to her ear. "Hello? Hello? Oh, please come back. Hello?" She clicked the receiver bar, up and down, up and down. "Hello?"

Jorge stepped to the phone table and held it down with his finger. "It's no use, Esperanza. They must be having a power outage. You probably were lucky to reach them at all."

"It's them, Jorge. Gracie's parents now run that inn."

"How do you know that?"

"Putting two and two together from what Charlie told us. Gracie's parents were visiting their parents, who ran the boardinghouse, that Christmas Eve. The woman told me on the phone that they'd taken over the inn from her parents several years ago. I was talking to Gracie's mother." Esperanza laid her hand on her cheek. "What luck. All we have to do is go to Colorado Springs and find the Golden Aspen Inn, and we'll find Gracie."

"You don't know that. You don't know that Gracie is there."

"Not for sure, but I'd be willing to bet my right arm if she's not there now, she has been, and they might know where she is." She patted the phone. "Whatever the case may be, we are headed for Colorado tomorrow. If she's not there, we'll simply have a nice vacation."

"Tomorrow? They have vacancies?"

Esperanza avoided his eyes. "Well, not exactly. She said they were full until the new year. If we catch a train tomorrow, we won't even get there until the twenty-sixth."

Jorge shook his head and sighed. "What do you plan to do if she is there?"

"Bring her home, of course."

"Gracie will come home when she is ready. We cannot force her."

"She'll come home when I say so—and I say so...now."

Jorge grasped his wife by the shoulders. "Esperanza, Gracie is an adult. She's not your little girl anymore. She is a married woman. You cannot make her do anything."

Esperanza shook her husband's hands from her shoulders and stepped back. "She wasn't married in the church—we can simply have the marriage annulled and bring her home."

"Grab her away from her real parents again?"

She huffed. "We are her real parents. We raised her. She is ours."

Jorge loosened his tie. "I'm going to bed. There's no reasoning with you when you get your mind set on something, no matter how illogical it may be."

She turned out the Christmas tree lights and followed her husband up the stairs. "I know I'm right. You'll see. We'll find our Gracie in Colorado Springs."

T~WENTY~NINE

The trip across the road took longer than Robby would have dreamed. Shielding his face with his muffler, he'd inched his way down the slick, steep wooden steps leading down the terraced hill in front of the inn. The ice was so thick on top of the railing that it provided no traction. The snow-laden branches of the huge blue spruce in front of the inn drooped toward the ground like weary arms.

Behind him, the lantern Naomi had placed in the office window sent a muted glow into his periphery. He kept the restaurant's lights straight ahead of him. Once off the steps, he put his shoulder into the wind and walked as fast as he dared toward the restaurant. His eyes watered, blurring the lights in front of him. Gasping to breathe in the swirling wind and snow, he inched toward the restaurant.

He remembered every story he'd ever heard about people being found frozen to death just outside the door of their house because they became disoriented. But he made it and burst into the restaurant, the banging of the door against the wall announcing his entrance.

Lupe came through the serape curtains separating the kitchen from the small dining area, wiping her hands on a dish towel. "Oh, Roberto. I was getting so worried. This storm is…" She looked behind her son. "Where's Gracie?"

Robby stomped his feet on the mat just inside the door and shook the snow from his boots. The peppery aroma of chili and cumin filled the restaurant. Although Lupe would fix turkey and dressing for Christmas dinner, they'd had enchiladas and tamales for Christmas Eve as long as Robby could remember. "Mama, she's having the baby. She's in labor. Naomi needs you right away."

"Oh my." She hurried back to the curtain and yelled into the kitchen. "Ernest, Gracie's in labor. I'm going over to the inn."

Robby's father, a tall, slender, handsome man with his dark longish hair that curled around his neck, poked his head through the curtain. "What? I thought she wasn't due for another two weeks."

"You ought to know by now babies come when they are good and ready, and obviously, Gracie's baby is ready tonight." She made the sign of the cross and kissed the crucifix she wore around her neck. "A Christmas baby. The same night our Lord was born."

Robby stood with the snow on his parka melting and dripping on the floor. "Hurry, Mama."

Lupe nodded and turned to the stairs. "Gracie will need her things. I'll run upstairs and get her bag. She said it was packed and ready, by her bed."

Robby sighed and shook his head. "I'll take care of that. You get your coat and boots on." He ran past his mother, tracking wet footprints across the floor and up the stairs—but he figured his mother would forgive it, given the circumstances.

Robby opened the door to the apartment his family rented to Gracie and flipped on the overhead light. The train case did indeed lay beside the bed. As he grabbed it, he spied a small gray diaper bag with red trim hanging on the bedstead. He set the train case down and looked inside. Diapers, a receiving blanket, and footed pajamas were stuffed into the bag, along with baby powder and baby oil. He picked up both bags, turned out the light, and ran down the stairs.

He pulled the hood of his parka over his head as he hit the bottom of the stairs. "C'mon, Mama. Hurry!"

Lupe sat in a chair lacing up her boots. She tied a plaid wool scarf around her head, tugging on her gloves as she stood up. "I'll carry that." She took the diaper bag out of Robby's hand and draped it over her shoulder. "Let's go."

Ernest stood at the door, a worried frown creased his brow. "I don't know, Lupe. Maybe I should go with you. That snow is really swirling around out there." He tugged at the tie on his apron.

"No. You need to stay here and finish cleaning up. Come over later if you want to, but I don't want to come home to a mess in the morning. And it probably will be morning. Babies take their time, so don't get worried."

Ernest laughed and retied the apron strings. "Thought I could get out of cleanup for once. And don't I know about babies taking their time? After six of our own?" He turned to Robby. "Son, keep your eyes on the light over at the inn. And don't let go of your mother."

"No sir, I won't." The case in one hand and his mother's arm in his other, Robby started out of the door Ernest held open for them. The sign above swung wildly, its hinges creaking with each swing.

Lupe stepped out behind her son. "Woo-hoo! That took my breath away." She held her muffler over her mouth and nose and followed closely behind Robby as he pulled her along. The lantern in the window at the inn came and went out of sight as the two fought against the wind. The blowing snow bit at Robby's cheeks. *Wish I'd gotten my goggles.*

His head snapped to the side. The drone of a plow broke through the soft ch-ch-ch-ch of the snow. Lights of the lumbering machine came toward them slowly but steadily, bouncing up and down with each bump in the road. He could see the plow, but he knew the driver couldn't see them, bearing down upon them faster than Robby could imagine a vehicle could move in this snow.

"Mama! Hurry!" He jerked her arm, sending her feet out from under her and her arms spinning like a windmill as she struggled for her balance. The diaper bag flew into the air as she fell onto the icy road. Robby tried to help her up but fell to his knees. The scraping of the plow and the pulsing of the engine grew louder. Robby threw the train case onto the sidewalk, picked up his mother, and carried her to the edge of the road before the snow plow whirred by.

"Mama, are you okay?" He set her on her feet and moved her scarf out of her face.

She sputtered and brushed the snow off her skirt. "I don't think they even saw us. We could have been killed."

Robby took her by the elbow. "But we weren't." He stooped to pick up the train case. "Come on. We need to get inside."

"The diaper bag. I don't have it. I dropped it when I fell." She began to paw through the snowdrift formed by the plow.

"Don't worry about that now. I'll come out in the morning and find it. There couldn't be anything too important in there—just diapers and stuff."

"You're right. We have a baby to deliver."

The bell jangled above the office door. Naomi rushed out to the foyer as

Lupe and Robby shed their coats and mufflers, hanging them on the hall tree and stamped the snow off their boots.

"Oh, Lupe, I'm so glad you are here. I'm not sure I know what we need to do. I wasn't a labor and delivery nurse."

Lupe chuckled as she and Robby pulled their boots off and left them on the mat beside the door. "You've had three babies yourself. You ought to have some idea." She fell in beside Naomi as they padded toward the living room in their stocking feet. Robby headed straight for Cynthia, who was sitting on the hearth staring at Gracie.

"Yes, well, actually…I… I've had four babies…you know…"

"Of course, dear one. I'm sorry." Lupe patted her hand. "Very insensitive of me."

Naomi gave her neighbor a half-smile. "No problem."

Lupe moved quickly to the couch, sat down beside Gracie, and kissed her cheek. "How're you doing, sweet thing?"

"I'm so glad you are here, but I didn't intend it to happen like this. I've ruined everybody's Christmas Eve."

"Ruined it? *Gracita,* you are making this the most memorable Christmas Eve of our lives. Don't you worry one moment about that. And one thing is universally true about babies getting born. They don't hurry up or wait for anybody. They come when God's ready."

Naomi picked up a clean towel from the stack on the hearth and stood behind Lupe. *The most memorable Christmas Eve of my life was seventeen years ago, and was the worst night of my life.* The thought flitted in and out of her mind as she continued preparing for what was to come.

"Gracie seems to be progressing awfully fast for a first baby." She spoke in low tones to Lupe, while Cynthia said something to Gracie. "I think maybe she's been in labor all evening but didn't say anything to us. Either she didn't know or was just embarrassed. Then all of a sudden her water broke, and the contractions started coming harder and faster." She looked at the young girl on the couch. "And she seems to be bleeding a lot. See what you think."

Lupe nodded without looking at Naomi and took Gracie's hand. "I want you to squeeze my hand in correlation with how painful the next contraction is. When you get toward the end, your grip should nearly be breaking the bones in my fingers. In fact, you probably won't be able to hold onto my hand then."

Gracie blinked and nodded. They sat in silence until the next contraction started. Gracie started squeezing. Lupe looked at her watch, squinting. "It's too dark. I can't see the minute hand on my watch. Do you have a clock with a minute hand?"

Cynthia stood from where she'd been sitting on the hearth. "How about a wind-up kitchen timer?"

"That'll be perfect."

Cynthia returned quickly with the timer and set it on the coffee table.

"Set it for two minutes."

Gracie squeezed harder and harder then let go as the contraction subsided. The timer had thirty seconds left on it.

"Hmm, a little over a minute long. Now set the timer for ten minutes, and let's see how close together the contractions are."

The four onlookers stared at the timer as it ticked along, with Gracie closing her eyes, trying to rest between contractions. Only four minutes had passed before she began to squeeze Lupe's hand again. "Oh, okay then. Less than five minutes. Have they been pretty regular in the last hour or so?"

Gracie seemed not to hear her. "I...I feel like I need to push." She leaned her head back and let out an almost inhuman moan.

"Not yet. I know you're hurting, but it's too early. We need to wait until the pains are only a minute or less apart." Lupe stroked the back of Gracie's hand. "Getting pretty bad, huh?"

Gracie tried to lean up on one elbow, but wobbling on the weak limb, she fell back on the pillow. "You…you mean it's going to get worse?"

Naomi leaned over and brushed Gracie's hair, now damp with sweat, out of her face. "I'm afraid so." She stood and stretched her back. "But you can do it. The pain becomes nothing but a shadowy memory when you catch sight of that cuddly bundle of joy. When you hold that firstborn baby in your arms, it's all worth it. There's never another moment like it…in your whole life."

Robby rocked back and forth with his hands clenched together. "Is it always this bad?"

Cynthia shrugged. "I've never seen a baby being born. Mama had Myrna and Elise in the hospital. I never saw them until my parents brought them home." She sprang to her feet and approached Naomi. "Mama, should we wake Daddy?"

Naomi looked at the clock on the wall. Eleven. "Oh, I don't think so. There's nothing he can do, and, honestly, he'd just be in the way." She motioned toward the kitchen. "Why don't you and Robby go make some popcorn? You can clear the cups and plates off of the coffee table and wash them. Then sit at the kitchen table and wait." She leaned in and whispered, "Robby doesn't need to be in here."

"But I want to watch."

"You can do that from the kitchen, and when the baby's about to be born, I'll call you, but I think Gracie would be embarrassed to have Robby in the room. There's no modesty when a baby comes into the world."

Cynthia nodded. "All right, but I don't want to miss anything. Gracie promised me I could be with her when the time came."

"You won't miss a thing. Once the baby's head is visible, I'll call you, and you can see it all."

"Promise?"

Naomi drew an X over her heart. "Cross my heart, and hope to die...."

Cynthia finished it. "Stick a needle in my eye. Okay, I'll be right here at the table." She stacked the plates and mugs and headed for the kitchen. "C'mon, Robby, let's make some popcorn."

A low sustained groan, wrung from Gracie's throat, progressed to a muffled scream, and stopped Cynthia in her tracks.

"Jeepers!" She shooed Robby into the kitchen as a full-blown scream exploded into the night air.

THIRTY

Saint-Dié, France

White everywhere. White sheets hanging from iron pipes encircling his bed. White uniforms walking in and out of his room. White jackets. Jack opened his eyes—or more accurately, his right eye. The left one refused to respond. He lifted his right hand and touched his face. Bandages. He tried to sit up, but jabbing pain in his left shoulder pulled him back into the crinkling comfort of white sheets. He closed his left eye and went back to sleep. *Gracie. Had to get back to Gracie.* Her face floated in and out of his dreams. Then he heard her scream.

He gasped for air. His heart hammered against his chest, and he tried again to open his eyes. It was dark in the room now, except for a dim light over his bed. White sheets no longer surrounded him. He looked to his right, where a solider in the bed next to him let out a snort.

Thirsty. He was so thirsty. A cup with a straw sat on his nightstand. He reached for it, and knocked it over. The clatter seemed to go on forever, out the door, and down the hall. The other man turned over and resumed his nighttime serenade.

A white uniform floated to his bedside. It had a face, a nice smiling face. Was it an angel? Was he dead?

"Lieutenant Blauvelt? Are you awake?"

"I…I'm sorry. I'm so thirsty. Could I…"

"Of course, I'll get you a fresh cup."

He looked at her feet. Not an angel. No wings, but feet and legs sheathed in white.

He must have drifted off to sleep again. The next thing he knew, the vision in white was helping him to sit up and eased a straw to his lips. He drank, pulling time and again on the straw. The water tasted delicious.

"Whoa, there, sir. You'll be upchucking that if you drink too fast." She set the glass back on the nightstand.

"Tastes so good. Where am I? I heard my wife scream. Am I dead?"

The woman laughed. "If you are, then I am too. And I assure you that I am very much alive." She fluffed his pillows and rearranged them. "You were dreaming. You're in the 51st Evacuation Hospital in Saint-Dié, France. Been here about two weeks now."

He'd made it. But everything between the bridge and those white sheets was a blur. He turned his head to the right—rows of beds with sleeping, snoring, bandaged men. Then he swiveled to the left with some effort. "Arggh." A searing blade of pain stabbed down his left side. He fell back into the mattress.

"Take it easy, soldier. Ribs are still tender, eh? You had a pretty bad break there. You'll be going to the States to recuperate as soon as you are able to travel." She tucked the corners of his blanket into the edges of the bed. "The war is over for you, young man."

"My flight crew? Are they here as well?"

She stuck a thermometer in his mouth. "You seem to be more alert than you've been."

He laid back, crossed his arm over his eyes, and waited for her to remove the glass instrument. "My…my eye. What about my eye?"

"The doctor will be by in the morning to talk to you about that." She held his wrist and stared at her watch.

"But my crew. Where are they?"

The nurse stood at the end of Jack's bed and picked up the clipboard to make her report. She looked at Jack and shook her head. "I'm so sorry, Lieutenant. You were the only survivor."

He closed his eye, blew out a breath, and lay down, covering his face with his arms once again. "Would you mind turning off that light?"

"Sure." The nurse hung the clipboard on the foot and walked to the head of the bed, leaned over and shut off the light. Her perfume, a soft floral scent, followed her as she bustled around the bed.

"What day is it?"

She patted his shoulder. "It's December twenty-fifth." She smiled. "Merry Christmas, Lieutenant. You woke up just in time for the holiday."

He looked around then and noticed a small Christmas tree with meager lights on it near the door. Gracie. He'd not been able to get letters out to her for a couple of weeks before his flight, and now he'd lost two weeks while he was unconscious in the hospital. She was probably frantic. "My wife. She'll be worried. We're expecting a baby any day now."

"Congratulations. And you are headed home to your family. Is this your first baby?"

"Yes, we married right before I left. I need to get a letter to her…right away. Can you help me do that?"

"Mm-hm." She walked to the nightstand and threw the straw in a trash can next to his bed. "Tell you what. I'll bring paper and a pencil when I bring your breakfast in a little bit. And more water as well. In the meantime, you try to rest. Deal?"

He nodded and closed his eyes. The nurse left, the shuffle of her feet fading as she walked down the aisle between the beds, checking on patients as she passed. She *was* an angel, of sorts. The kind that took care of people, like Michael on his plane. As he drifted off to the misty world between sleep and wakefulness he wondered what this angel's name was. He would ask her when she came back.

"Angela."

"What?"

"You asked me my name."

He forced his eye open. "I'm sorry. I must have drifted off again. I thought I was dreaming." He grinned at her and struggled to sit up. "Angela. So you *are* an angel."

"Hardly." She helped him up, set the breakfast tray on the bed, and removed the cover. "Stewed prunes, hot mush with milk and sugar, toast, and hot chocolate. Not a bad breakfast…if you like prunes, that is. And a pitcher of fresh water." She wore her strawberry blonde hair in a short page boy, pulled back from her face by her nurse's cap. A sprinkle of freckles lay across the bridge of her nose, which wrinkled as she smiled. She was pretty in a clean, natural sort of way. Looked like a farm girl. "Even if you don't like prunes, I would advise you eat them, unless…" She tilted her head and raised her eyebrows.

Jack cleared his throat. "I like them all right." He moved the dishes around. "But I wonder if I could have some coffee? Sure would like some coffee."

"I'll check. You don't remember, but you refused the coffee we've tried to give you. In fact, you spit it all over me."

"Sorry." A grin tugged at the corner of his mouth. "I really am. If I was eating and conscious enough to refuse coffee, why don't I remember anything?"

She flicked her wrist. "Trauma, medications. It's common. And don't worry about it. It's not the worst thing I've ever had spit on me."

"Sure is strange to have lost two weeks and not know what I did." He chuckled. "I probably refused the coffee because it wasn't strong enough. I'm from Louisiana, you know. Love strong, chicory coffee."

Angela poured milk and sugar into the hot mush, stirring it briskly. She handed Jack the spoon. "Go ahead and start eating. I'll get you some coffee. They might not brew it as strong as you like, but I'll bring some extra instant to add to it. Not as good as you get back home, I'm sure, but maybe you can tolerate it." She reached into her pocket. "Here's some paper and a pencil. You can start to work on that letter to your wife. I'll be back in a moment." She turned to leave.

"Wait a minute. How's the war going? What's happening on the front?"

She paused. "I'll be right back." She hurried through a side door across the aisle from his bed.

Men up and down the ward were waking up, stretching, coughing, and moaning. The young soldier in the bed to his right turned toward him and muttered a hoarse, "Good morning, Lieutenant."

"Oh, uh, good morning."

"You're awake, are you now?" He leaned toward Jack, his dark brown eyebrows uplifted. "Are you...really awake, conscious?"

"Yeah, I think so." Jack took a bite of the prune and cocked his head.

"Not too bad. Not bad at all." He took another bite. Pointing at the young soldier with his spoon, he asked, "Do you know what's going on at the front?"

A food cart clattered down the aisle between the beds and stopped at the foot of the soldier's bed. The young man sat up as an orderly placed a bed tray over his legs. He lifted the food cover. "Looks like the same as yours." He chuckled. "I really do like stewed prunes. Never ate them at home, but after K rations, most anything tastes good." He took the lid off the cocoa and sipped the hot liquid gingerly.

"Wonder why the nurse brought mine separately from yours." Jack took a bite of the soggy toast and then downed several spoonfuls of mush. "It's not home cooking, but I'm hungry and it tastes good."

The soldier snorted at Jack. "You've been getting special treatment from Nurse Angela for two weeks. You're her special assignment, from what I understand." He slurped more hot chocolate then stuck out his hand across the small distance between their beds. "Bill Murphy. Captain, Army Air Forces, 361st Fighter Group."

The two shook hands. "Excuse me, sir. You look so young to be…well, uh… Jack Blauvelt, 1st Lieutenant, 303rd Bomb Group." He grabbed his left shoulder as he leaned back into his bed.

"To be a captain?" Bill smiled. "Combat makes for speedy promotions, you know, especially among pilots. We seem to be fairly expendable."

"So the 361st. You fly the Mustang?"

"Yep, sure do. Can't wait to get back out there either." Bill grinned. "I know what you do, Lieutenant. You've been bombing targets in here for two weeks."

"Sorry. I guess I've been out of my head a bit, huh?" Jack shook his head. "You guys saved our bacon up there. Until the Mustangs came into service, the German Butcher Birds were eating our lunch. Lost too many good men."

"All in a day's work."

"Yeah, I hear ya." Jack looked at the sling keeping his arm captive across his chest. "Wonder when I can get out of here."

"Not until they think you can travel. I'm due to go back to my unit in a couple of days."

"Where are you from, Captain?"

"Abilene. Texas, that is, not Kansas."

An older nurse with light brown hair springing out from under her nurse's cap in no particular arrangement approached, followed by an orderly carrying a basin and pitcher.

She peered over the rim of round gold-rimmed glasses perched on the end of her nose. "Good morning, men."

Her raspy voice both surprised and unnerved Jack as she removed his tray and threw his sheet back, exposing him more than he wished to be. He grasped for his gown with his good hand as the soldiers in the other beds chorused, "Morning, Nurse Whiskey."

The nurse rolled her eyes at Jack's grasping. "I've seen lots more than you've got there, Lieutenant. All modesty aside here. It's bath time."

THIRTY~ONE

I …I'm not quite finished. Nurse Angela is bringing me some coffee."

Nurse Whiskey smirked. "Oh, so you really are awake now, Lieutenant? Tell me, when your Nurse Angela brings you coffee, are you going to throw your cup at her again?"

"I threw a cup at her?"

"Almost hit her in the head." She looked at Bill's tray. "How about you? Finished?"

"Not quite. We've been talking." Bill tipped the bowl of mush and hurriedly scraped out the last of his cereal.

"Hurry it up then, Captain. You're next." The metal hooks rattled as she hurled the white curtain along the rod between their beds. "We'll just have time to get you bathed and shaved, Lieutenant Blauvelt." She motioned to the orderly to set the water basin on the stand and remove the breakfast tray.

Jack lunged for the toast.

"Lean forward, so I can untie your gown."

He complied and blushed in spite of himself as she let the gown fall around his waist. She quickly and expertly bathed his chest and back then tied a clean gown around his neck. She handed him a rag. "Finish the job yourself, sir, and be quick about it."

"Yes, ma'am." Jack stuffed the last bite of toast into his mouth, took the rag with his unfettered hand, and did as the authoritative nurse ordered. She strode to a metal cabinet at the end of the ward and removed a stack of clean sheets. He wondered how long it had been since he'd had a bath.

He put the rag back in the basin of water as she returned. "All done."

Nurse Whiskey set the sheets on a chair beside the bed. She wrung out the rag and wiped down his legs and feet. "Can you stand?"

"I think so." He swung his legs over to the edge next to the chair where she pointed.

"Wait, let me help you. You're weaker than you think. Don't need you falling on us." She put her shoulder under the pit of his arm and helped him to the chair. His legs trembled underneath him. She was right. He couldn't believe how weak he felt. Once he was safely on the chair, the nurse changed his sheets efficiently and helped him back into bed. She opened the drawer of the nightstand and pulled out a shaving mug.

She fluffed up the pillows. "Just relax, close your eyes, and let me get this done. You look pretty scruffy." He relaxed as much as he could as she worked the razor around the bandages, squinting his one good eye open now and then. She gave him a quick, if less than gentle shave, then flung open the curtain. Bill turned toward her and grinned.

She pointed to him. "You. Are you finished now?"

"Yes, ma'am." Bill handed the cantankerous nurse the tray, and she took it in one hand. "I'll be back in a moment to take care of you." He gave her a mock salute as she turned on her heel and left, scurrying down the aisle to the next victim.

"Oo-eee. I don't think I want to get on her bad side." Jack felt his closely shaven cheek. "I could use some aftershave lotion."

"There's some in the nightstand. Here, I'll get it for you." Bill dug around in the drawer and found a small bottle of white lotion. "Doesn't smell all that good, but it helps the nicks and scrapes." He opened it and poured some in Jack's hand.

"Did I really almost hit Angela with a coffee cup?"

"Only once. Brunhilda there made it sound like it was a regular occurrence. You were in so much pain and out of your head. You weren't responsible."

"I suppose it's a good thing I don't remember." He stroked the bandage on his head. "It's itchy. Must be healing." He sat up again on the edge of his bed and turned toward his new buddy. "So, what's going on at the front? Do you know?"

Bill returned the bottle of lotion to the drawer and pulled the hospital gown around him to cover his backside. He paced between their two beds, his hospital scuffs making a shh-shh noise on the hard linoleum floor. A slight limp betrayed his brave front.

He stopped in front of Jack. "It's not good. Hitler launched an attack in the Ardennes and skunked us. From the air, I could see our tanks retreating. Couldn't believe it. At first I just thought they'd gotten turned around and lost their way. But no, they were retreating sure 'nuff." He paused and looked through the window at the snow-covered rooftop outside their ward. "It's snowing again. We not only have to fight Hitler, we have to fight the weather as well." He leaned against the crumbling molding around the window. "That tyrant is trying to capture Antwerp Harbor. Don't know if he has succeeded or not."

Jack pointed to Bill's leg. "Are you fixed up enough now to fly again?"

"Almost. I just took a piece of shrapnel through the lower part of my leg. Missed my Achilles tendon by a hair. That alone wouldn't have put me in here. I was able to land the plane all right, but I stumbled and fell getting out of the plane and busted my head. Got a concussion. They just decided to give me a few days rest and observe me to see if I was okay. Good thing I still had my helmet on." He laughed and spun his finger in circles around his head. "They just needed to see if I was cuckoo."

Jack smiled. "Man, our troops never retreat. Why now?"

"The Fuehrer surprised us. Smart. He may be evil, but he's sly. Sly as a fox. He knew we were over confident and never dreamed he would attack us there. They came in at night, through those dense woods, in all that snow…" He chewed on a hangnail on his thumb. "That fresh snow falling outside our room. Looks so beautiful, untouched and innocent. Yet behind the veil of its protection, those slimy Nazis moved toward our line. It's still going on. Many of the wounded here are from the advance of the Germans." He paused and sat down on the edge of his bed and leaned toward Jack. "Do you believe in evil, Lieutenant?"

"Funny you should ask. My wife and I discussed that before I was shipped overseas." Jack stared at the captain across the aisle from him.

Bill's eyebrows furrowed into a frown, bringing his heavy eyebrows nearly together. "I didn't…not really. Not until I got in this war. Oh, yeah, I believed in bad guys, you know, robbers and such. They have evil motives. But I'm talking about something more than that. I'm talking about something that has a life of its own. Something that is immoral, dark, sleazy, perverted, devilish…inherently wicked."

"Do you mean do I believe in the devil?"

"Yeah, I guess so. What would make a man like Hitler do what he is doing if there's not a force of evil behind it?"

Jack sighed and lay back down. "I think you're probably right. What we've been through has been bad enough already, but there've been rumors… I can hardly believe them. I find it hard to even talk about it." He propped himself up on his elbow and looked over at Bill. "Have you heard any rumors about camps where…where people are being…"

"Exterminated?"

"Yeah. Surely not. Surely it's just rumor."

"I've heard the chatter. I can assure you it's not rumor. I've not only heard about the concentration camps, I've seen them. I've flown over them. Seen the smoke stacks going. Seen the trains unloading boxcars of Jews." He motioned toward the sparse Christmas tree and scoffed. "Look at that Christmas tree and the baby in the manger." Bill pointed to a small crèche nestled under the branches of the spindly tree. "Doesn't fit, with what we've seen and been dealing with, does it? I've been thinking since I've been overseas, shooting down enemy planes, knowing people are dying, hearing the horrid rumors of people being gassed—if there is a God, why would he allow this kind of evil?" He hit his thigh with his fist. "How can we put up our Christmas trees and sing our pretty little Christmas carols when we're fighting this kind of horror?" He smiled. "Sorry, didn't mean to get so philosophical."

"No, not at all. I've been wondering about the same things."

The two men fell silent for a few moments.

Jack spoke. "I suppose when you have stared evil in the face, it makes you wonder about whether the things we learned in Sunday school are true or not."

"All I can add is that I can't wait to get back to reality, get in my plane, and start pounding on those Krauts again."

"Doesn't look like I'm gonna have the chance. Get one for me while you're up there, pal."

"Sure, if I can just get out of here."

"What's this talk of getting out of here?" Angela walked between their beds. "I see Edna's been by."

"She took care of Jack and said she'd be back to take care of me." Bill winked. "But now that you're here…"

"If she said she'll be back to take care of you, she'll be back."

"Can't blame a guy for trying." Bill's mood shifted as he teased with Angela. "Do you know when the doc is going to discharge me? Not that I want to leave your charming company, but I need to get back to work."

"Well, I'm not supposed to speculate, but…" Her voice traveled an octave as she grinned at him. "If I were a betting woman, I'd put my money on tomorrow."

He did a fist pump. "That's swell. Boy, am I ready." He grabbed Angela by the shoulders and gave her a kiss on the cheek, swinging her around.

"What's all this commotion?" Nurse Whiskey walked toward them carrying a towel and soap. Nodding at Bill, she said, "You. You're well enough to go to the shower on your own. Here's a clean gown and towel. I'll change your sheets while you're gone."

A wide grin spread across Bill's angular face. He looked like he'd spent a lot of time outdoors in the sun. Jack could picture the captain in a cowboy hat riding a horse on a ranch in western Texas.

"Thank you, Edna." Angela grabbed Jack's wrist and started counting his pulse. She suppressed a giggle as the other nurse started pulling Bill's sheets off his bed.

Jack whispered to Angela. "Not exactly Merry Sunshine, is she?"

"Oh, that's a defense mechanism. Edna is crotchety sometimes, but she's a crackerjack nurse. She loves the men. I've seen her hold many a dying man in her arms, blood all over her, gently cradling his head until he's gone. I've seen her refuse to give up on men when the doctors could do no more, and she saved the soldiers' lives. I've seen her cry in the hall when she couldn't save one. I've seen her fall into her bed from the exhaustion of working double shifts and only sleep an hour before she was up again emptying bed pans. Her gruffness is a buffer against the cruelty of our everyday world here in the hospital." Angela let go of Jack's arm.

He caught her hand. "Nurse Angela, I've got to get out of here. If I can't go back to the front, I need to get home. I dreamed I heard my wife screaming. Will you help me…please?"

THIRTY~TWO

Colorado Springs, Colorado

Y ou can start pushing now, Gracie. When you feel a contraction, pull your legs up, and push down hard."

Gracie nodded and gripped Lupe's hand anew. The world around her swam.

"Naomi, watch for the baby's head to crown."

Naomi called to her daughter. "Cynthia, it's time. If you want to see this baby being born, get in here now. Bring another lantern with you."

Cynthia ran into the living room, lantern in hand. She stared at the scene. "Jeepers! I never...oh, wow."

Gracie heard their voices through a fog of pain that seemed to be turning her body wrong side out. She didn't know if this was normal or if something was wrong. As kind and compassionate as Lupe and Naomi were, she longed for her mother. A daughter needed her mother when she was having a baby, no matter what break in the relationship had occurred. She wanted Esperanza.

Naomi uttered a breathless, "I see it. I see the head."

At the same time, a tightening of Gracie's womb that she was sure she would not survive pressed her into the couch.

"Push, Gracie, push." Lupe's voice sounded far away. "Harder, harder."

Gracie pushed with all of her might. Her ears rang as she clenched her teeth together.

As the contraction passed, Lupe patted her on the shoulder. "Okay, good job, honey. Rest now until the next one." The woman wrung out a washcloth and wiped Gracie's forehead.

Gracie rested her head on the pillow, breathing hard. She didn't know how much more she could stand. She looked at Lupe and Naomi. "The next one? Is…is this normal? Is it usually this hard? How much longer? There's nothing wrong, is there?"

Lupe laughed. "Oh my, honey. You're actually progressing very well for a first baby."

Naomi sat on the edge of the couch. "When I had our first daughter, I was in labor for over twenty-four hours. When did you actually start having contractions?"

"Today serving lunch, but I thought it was nothing. The doctor said it was probably going to be after the first of the year."

Lupe chuckled again. "Well, take it from me, doctors are wrong sometimes. I've had six babies and only once did the doctor get the arrival date right."

"Oh…oh…here comes another one." Gracie grabbed Lupe's hand and squeezed it as hard as she could as the contraction progressed.

"Push, Gracie, push." Naomi resumed her position at the end of the couch.

"Aw-w-w-gh!" Yellow spots danced in front of her eyes, and she surrendered momentarily to the blackness closing in around her.

"Stay with us, Gracie. Fight through it. Here it comes. Keep pushing."

Another contraction came quickly, and Gracie pushed again.

"Here come the shoulders. Here we go, we've got a baby! We've got a baby!"

Gracie's muscles relaxed as the baby left her birth canal. She leaned up on her elbow. "Is it okay? What is it?"

Naomi shrieked as she held the baby in her arms. "The cord! The cord's wrapped around his neck. He's blue, oh dear God, he's blue." She thrust the baby toward Cynthia. "Hold him while I get this cord off."

Cynthia took the baby. "He's so slippery."

"Hang onto him." Frantic, Naomi unwrapped the cord, but the baby lay limp in Cynthia's arms, his head dangling.

"A boy? What's going on? Why isn't he crying?" Gracie's voice rose in pitch as the women worked on the child.

Naomi swatted the baby's bottom. No response. Lupe picked up a syringe they'd put beside the towels and cleaned out his mouth. Nothing but deafening silence. "Give him to me." Naomi took the infant by the ankles and began to swing him back and forth, swatting his bottom and legs as she swung him. "C'mon, c'mon, little one. Breathe." Back and forth she swung him. "Live, baby, live."

A whimper broke through the dim light, then a lusty cry. "Ah…ha." Naomi breathed a collective sigh of relief, started laughing, and then broke out in tears. As she held the baby close, she started wiping him off with a towel. "You gave us quite a scare, little one. My goodness, he…he looks like he could be one of mine."

Cynthia jumped up and down, clapping. "He's beautiful."

Lupe chuckled. "Doesn't look a thing like any of ours. What time is it?"

Naomi looked at the clock above the fireplace. "It's 12:04 a.m. You have a Christmas baby, Gracie."

Lupe clamped the cord and handed Naomi a pair of scissors. "Here, cut the cord."

"Uh. It's tough." She cut through the lifeline of the child with effort. "There."

Gracie, mingled tears of joy and relief trickling down her cheeks, held out her arms. "Give him to me."

Naomi wrapped the wrinkled little bundle in a towel and handed him over. Gracie took her new son, covering his face and head with kisses and her tears. "Oh, you're here. You're really here. You gave us quite a scare." The baby blinked and stared at his mother.

Naomi stood over her. "What are you going to call him, Gracie?"

"Jack. Jack Jr." The baby started rooting to nurse. She looked at the two women. "What do I do?"

"Let him nurse. There's a fluid in your breasts that will nourish him until your milk comes in. Or until we can get formula, if that's what you're planning to use. Do you have any bottles?"

Gracie nodded. "In my room there's a diaper bag. I have a couple of small ones in there."

"Uh-oh." Robby was standing at the door from the kitchen. "I'll go try to find it."

Lupe shook her head. "No, son. Let's wait until tomorrow. It's too dark out there and with it still snowing, you'll never find it."

Gracie looked at Lupe and Robby. "What are you talking about?"

Lupe explained what had happened earlier with the snow plow. "It's buried out there somewhere, but we know where it is…kinda." She smiled.

"Don't worry, we'll find it, and if we don't, we'll just buy more bottles and diapers."

"Oh." Gracie frowned. It was the picture, not the bottles and diapers, she was worried about.

"I'll find it. I promise I will." Robby shoved his hands in his pockets. "I saw exactly where it landed. It'll be fine until I can get out there."

"Of course." The baby continued to whimper and root for her breast.

"Back into the other room, son." Lupe pointed to the kitchen. "This is women's work."

The young man complied as his mother and Naomi worked to clean up the blood. Gracie let the baby nurse until he fell asleep. "What about diapers for the night?"

"I think I have a few old cloth diapers stashed away. And I have some diaper pins in the laundry room as well."

Gracie nodded and laid Jack Jr. beside her. She was exhausted. She ran her finger along his jawline. "Are you going to look like me or your father? Your little bit of fuzz doesn't look blond yet…maybe it'll be auburn, like mine." She smoothed with her hand the soft damp fuzz on top of the baby's head. *Your father. Jack, where are you? Why haven't I heard from you?*

In the deepest recesses of her heart, she wondered if he was lying wounded on a field somewhere in France or Germany, and nobody had found him. But she wouldn't let the thoughts come to the surface. Maybe he was in a hospital somewhere, hurt and unable to contact her. But wouldn't the hospital have written her? If he had been killed, surely she would have heard from the State Department. Where was he?

He has a son. Does he know he has a son?

The lights flickered, then came on. The Christmas tree began to twinkle as if to say, "Welcome to our world, Jack Jr." The radio on the library table behind the couch crackled to life in the middle of playing a recording of "The Messiah." *For unto us a Child is born. Unto us, a Son is given.*

A son is given. Gracie had been given a son. She couldn't stop looking at him. What a miracle a newborn child was. Despite that she was raised Catholic, she had never thought much about how the Virgin Mary must have felt the night Jesus was born. The horrible conditions of being in a stable, giving birth on a bed of straw with dirty animals; the pain of childbirth; the loneliness of being without her family. At least Joseph was with her. Gracie unwrapped the clean towel from around the infant and touched his tiny fingers and toes.

Naomi and Cynthia brought diapers, along with pins. And a blue baby blanket for Gracie to wrap around him. "This was one of Julia's blankets I saved. It was in a trunk with other blankets and linens." She held it up to her face and smelled it. "It may be a bit musty, but it just seemed fitting that since little Jack was born on the anniversary of her disappearance…" Her voice trailed off.

The baby woke up briefly as they diapered him, his tiny arms and legs jerking in the air, but then went back to sleep. They all stared at the child. "Naomi, do you ever tire of looking at your own children?"

"Never. Even when they get to be grown. They are still beautiful to you." She took Cynthia's hand and kissed it. "Your children are your most precious possession. I fear we don't treasure them like we should until… until something happens."

"Like what happened to your oldest daughter?" Looking at her son, Gracie pictured Naomi gazing at her firstborn, Gracie herself, with the same awe and intense love she was experiencing for Jack. She was astounded at the overwhelming love she already had for this child. She didn't believe she could survive the heartbreak of losing him.

"Yes, like what happened to our Julia."

Cynthia let go of her mother's hand and stepped back, but Naomi pulled her into an embrace. "It makes you love and cherish the ones you have left all the more."

Gracie took a deep breath. She was ready to reveal her identity. "I…I have something I—"

Cynthia jumped. "Jeepers. We still have Santa Claus to set out for the girls. I'll go get the presents from the laundry room."

"Oh, dear. I almost forgot about that." Naomi looked at Gracie. "What were you saying, dear?"

"Oh, nothing. It can wait. Go take care of your family. I'm fine." She smiled and tucked her revelation away for the time being.

Gracie could hear Lupe clattering dishes in the kitchen sink.

"Just leave those," Naomi said. "I'll get them later."

"You have open house to get ready for," Lupe protested. "Let me help you. The restaurant is closed."

Naomi looked outside, and Gracie followed her gaze. The snow had ceased, and the streetlights were back on. Her hostess sighed. "With all that's going on…I'll be honest, I could use the help. Why don't you go on back home now that the snow has stopped, get some sleep, and come back around noon? Everything is already made. I just have to heat a couple of things up."

"I can do that. Do you want us to see if we can find the diaper bag?"

"Let me send Cynthia with you. She can get it and bring it back for Gracie."

Robby, Cynthia, and Lupe went into the brittle, crystalline night air. Stars glittered from horizon to horizon, the snow clouds having moved on. Robby had his mother hanging tight to his right arm, and Cynthia held onto his left.

His mother stopped, looking upward. "Nothing more beautiful than a Colorado night sky after a snowstorm."

Robby mumbled under his breath, "Let's get across the road before we stop and admire the scenery. But first we need to find that diaper bag."

Lupe swatted at him. "Don't be such a humbug."

Cynthia giggled. "You two are funny. Now about where do you think you dropped it?"

"I think it was just below where the steps start." Lupe pointed. "We were almost across the road when the snow plow came by. When I fell, it went flying."

Robby let go of his two charges and kicked some snow around below the bottom step.

"I think it was more to the left, son, under the streetlamp." Lupe pointed.

Cynthia went to help Robby look, pushing snow aside as she went. "There it is. I see it. There, the strap is sticking out." She bent down and pulled the bag out of the snowdrift. "It looks fine. I'll take it right in to Gracie. We'll see you tomorrow." She waved good-bye to Robby and Lupe as they inched across the road. "Merry Christmas!"

"And Merry Christmas to you," Robby called with a grin.

Gracie caught the diaper bag Cynthia tossed to her, covering it with her blanket while her friend rushed into the kitchen, saying something about the nuts and oranges for the stockings. Naomi walked into the room with a cradle and doll each for Myrna and Elise and set them under the tree.

When she straightened, she was rubbing at her back. "Cynthia, would you finish the stockings? I'm through in here. I'm going to bed."

"Sure, Mom. See you in the morning."

Naomi went down the hall to her bedroom.

Gracie pulled the diaper bag out from under the comforter and set it on the floor beside the couch. She removed a diaper, diaper pins, a pair of rubber pants and the sleeper and laid them on the coffee table. She didn't remember ever being this tired in her entire life. Closing her eyes, she drifted off to sleep.

Cynthia finished putting oranges and nuts in the stockings, including Julia's. She picked up the diaper bag to set on the coffee table beside the sleeper. As she did, an envelope tumbled out, spilling a photograph on the floor. She picked it up and stared at a picture of a baby—a picture that looked very familiar. Stunned, she looked between that photo and the one of Julia on the mantle—identical.

Thirty~Three

Saint-Dié, France

Jack looked at the clock as Angela brought his coffee, with instant Nescafé to make it stronger. It was only eight o'clock.

Gracie was heavy on his heart. It would be about midnight in Colorado. She'd be sound asleep this Christmas Eve night. The baby wasn't due for another week or so. Maybe he'd get home in time?

Angela stirred a teaspoon of the Nescafé into his coffee. "Okay, Lieutenant. See if that's strong enough."

He sipped the brew. "Almost."

"You want more?"

"Just about half a teaspoon more of the Nescafé." She followed his instructions. He smiled as he swallowed. "Well, it's not Louisiana coffee, but it's much better than that hot water you've been serving me."

"I thought you couldn't remember anything."

"I can't. Or I couldn't. Except the coffee. Maybe my memory is coming back?"

"Do you remember throwing the mug at me?" Angela laughed.

"Not yet, but I apologize even if I never remember it." He took another sip as Angela wrote something on his chart.

"What are you writing?"

"Just that it seems you may be getting some of your memory back. That's a good thing."

Jack sat up as she fluffed his pillows behind his head. "I've got to get home. Please, can you help me, Angela?"

"That's all up to the doctor, what transport is available, and if you can travel." She patted his arm and turned to go. "But I will put in a good word for you. Doctor Taylor will be in shortly." She recorded another note on the chart, hung it on the end of the bed, and left.

Bill Murphy, whistling his way down the aisle, turned into his bed and plopped down. "And how are you this Christmas morning, Lieutenant Blauvelt?"

"I'm better now that I finally got a good cup of coffee."

"Nurse Angela took care of you, eh?"

Jack finished his coffee and set the cup on the nightstand. "Yes, as far as she could, but I need to get out of here and get home to my wife. If I can't get back in an airplane bombing Krauts, I want to get home."

"What does the doc say?"

"Don't know yet. He'll be by later this morning. I'm gonna see if he'll send me to Fitzsimmons Hospital in Denver. My wife is in Colorado Springs."

"I'll bet he will be open to that. Fitzsimmons is a huge receiving center for military casualties."

Jack got out of bed by himself and walked up and down the aisle throughout the morning, his strength returning each time he launched out. With Bill close by his side, he walked to the bathroom. His depth perception was off as he was seeing with only one eye, hitting doorjambs with his shoulder.

Bill stood by as he got back into bed. "Doing good, Lieutenant."

"I'll walk onto the tarmac under my own power. No wheelchair or gurney for me."

"Is that right, Lieutenant?" A tall, slender man, dark haired with graying temples and wearing horn-rimmed glasses, walked up to Jack's bed. He held out his hand. "I'm Dr. Taylor." In addition to the medical caduceus, Dr. Taylor wore Lieutenant Colonel bars. Jack didn't know whether to salute or shake his hand, but since the doctor had held out his hand, he responded in kind. "Nurse Angela tells me that you are conscious, rational, and that your memory is returning."

"Yes, sir. I'm feeling much better. Would really like to either get out of here and back to the front or get back to my wife stateside."

Dr. Taylor took his stethoscope from around his neck and pressed it to Jack's chest. He moved to his back and listened. "Take a deep breath, please."

Jack complied.

The doctor patted Jack's leg. "Sounds good. I was a little concerned your lungs were going to start filling with fluid as long as you were out of it. But they sound fine." He handed Jack a small cup with several pills along with a glass of water. "Take these."

Jack downed them all at once.

The doctor started unwinding the bandage from around Jack's head and eye. "Uh-huh. Looks pretty good." He turned around as Angela approached with a metal basin and fresh bandages. "Clean this up, nurse, and I think we can let him wear a patch over his eye instead of the bandages."

"Yes, sir." Angela smiled. "That's good news. I'll get a patch."

The doctor removed the sling and started cutting off the bandages from his left arm and shoulder. "We have the trauma of the injured shoulder, plus the compound fracture on the upper arm, and the broken bones in the hand. So how does the shoulder feel? Can you lift your arm?"

Jack lifted his arm, but his shoulder still hurt. He took a deep breath and looked at the doctor, who was busy inspecting the arm.

"Hmm, I know it's painful, but it's mending well. We had to do surgery on the hand—the bones were absolutely shattered, but I think with time and therapy it will be back in good working order. Now the eye is another matter. You will probably wear a patch the rest of your life, or perhaps a glass eye. I'm afraid that eyeball is beyond repair, but I can't really tell here in the field. I need to send you stateside to get the kind of care you're going to need."

"So I'll not regain sight in that eye?"

"Not in my opinion."

He took a moment to let that sink in…but it didn't, really. And he couldn't think about the eye—he could only think about Gracie. "I wanted to talk to you about where you'll be sending me. Would Fitzsimmons in Denver be an option?"

"Very much so. I'll put in an order for you to be transported in a month or so."

"A month? I was hoping to go right away. My wife is in Colorado Springs expecting our first baby any day now, and—"

"Out of the question." The doctor sat down in the chair. "Travel on board a ship is going to be very difficult for you with one eye and one arm. And a pretty severe concussion came with that blow to your eye and head. Blackouts are still a possibility."

"How about flying? I could be in Denver in eight hours."

"The air transports are full for weeks. Hundreds of patients are waiting to go home. Not very many are lucky enough to get a plane to return to the States." He got up and walked to the end of Jack's bed. "Build up your strength by walking the halls. You'll be home before you know it." He wrote orders on the chart, signed it, and left. "I'll check on you tomorrow." He turned to Angela. "I gave him the pain medication already. You can go ahead and dress the wound."

Jack grabbed Angela's arm. "Help me. Help me get out of here."

She shook her head. "There's nothing I can do."

"Is Dr. Taylor the only doctor taking care of me?"

"No. They rotate."

"I think I can probably help." Bill sat on the edge of his bed. "I'm being discharged later today. I have a friend who pilots one of those transport planes." He cleared his throat. "I think I could get you on it."

"Does he fly to Denver?"

"Denver, but surely he could help get you home from there."

"Angela?" Jack looked at the nurse who'd taken care of him for the last few weeks. "Will you help?"

"Are you asking me to falsify medical records?"

"No. Just try to talk someone into hurrying them up."

"I don't think I have that kind of clout with the doctors." The corners of her lips lifted. "Believe me, I would help if I could. I think it's sweet how eager you are to get home to that wife of yours. But there's not much I can do." She straightened the sling, gathered her supplies, and left.

Jack felt something in his sling. He pulled the fabric of the sling back and a bottle of pills—pain killers—fell out in his lap. Nurse Angela might not be able to get him out...but she apparently knew he'd find a way and meant for him to be well taken care of when he was gone.

Thirty~Four

Colorado Springs, Colorado

Gracie awoke to what she thought was a kitten mewing. It was her baby crying. Her baby. She sat up with a start as her body let her know it had been through trauma. "Uhh. Golly." She put a pillow behind her back. Naomi had left the Christmas tree lights on.

Gracie lifted her tiny son and felt his diaper. Wet. She looked around for the diaper bag and found it on a chair beside the couch. She needed to go to the bathroom. How could she do that with her baby? Could she leave him asleep in the bed? But he was awake now. She'd have to wait.

She changed Jack Jr.'s diaper, put the sleeper on him, and let him nurse until he fell asleep again. The clock read 4:20 a.m. She stacked pillows around him. Surely he'd be safe while she went to the bathroom. She tried to get up but sank back into the bedding. She then grabbed hold of the arm of the couch and pushed herself up. Her legs trembled beneath her, but she made it down the hall to the bathroom by holding onto the wall. She started feeling faint and sat on the edge of the bathtub, not even bothering to close the door yet.

"Are you okay?" Naomi stuck her head in.

"I'm sorry. I didn't mean to wake you up."

"I was listening for you. I figured you'd be needing to go to the bathroom." Naomi reached under the sink and set a box beside the toilet for her. "You'll need to wear a pad for a few days for the bleeding."

"I'm going to keep on bleeding?"

"Just for a little while. Some bleed a lot and for several weeks; some women hardly bleed at all. Either way, you'll still need a pad for a while." She smiled. "Didn't your mother talk to you about these things?"

She just did. Gracie shook her head. "She didn't know."

"Your mother didn't know you were expecting?"

"Not exactly."

"What do you mean?'"

Should she tell her now?

Cynthia came to the doorway rubbing her eyes. "Is it time to get up?"

"No, Gracie had to use the bathroom."

"Okay. I'm gonna go check on the baby."

"I'll give you some privacy." Naomi closed the door and left Gracie alone.

I don't know how to tell her. "Hi, Mom. I'm your long-lost daughter who was kidnapped seventeen years ago." Maybe I should just not tell her. But I've got to say something...eventually.

She finished in the bathroom and moved slowly back down the hall into the living room. She was a little surprised that her whole bottom was sore. Cynthia sat in the rocking chair with the baby, singing to him.

Naomi stoked the fire and put more logs on it. "Did you get cold?"

"No, not at all." Gracie eased herself down onto the couch. "Was he crying?"

"No, I just wanted to hold him." Cynthia laid him on her thighs and leaned over him, peering at his face. She put her finger into his hand, and he gripped it. "Look how strong he is."

Naomi stood behind Cynthia and watched the baby stretch and yawn. Naomi yawned as well and covered her mouth. "That's catching. I think I'm going to try to sleep a couple more hours. I have a busy day with the open house and all this evening."

"You go on, Mom. I'm going to stay up with Gracie."

"Okay, sweet pea. Merry Christmas." She kissed her daughter on the head then turned and kissed Gracie on the cheek. "Try to rest if you can."

"I will." She touched her cheek where Naomi had kissed her and stared after her as she walked down the hall.

Cynthia looked at her. "You look like you've seen a ghost."

"Oh, oh no. It's just…your mother has never kissed me before. It shocked me."

Cynthia stood and put the baby back on the couch. "I have an idea. Let's put Jack Jr. in one of the cradles Grandpa made for the girls. There's a doll-sized quilt in the bottom of it, and you have a blanket."

"Do you think it would be okay?"

"Absolutely." Cynthia brought one of the cradles over beside the couch. "All ready. Let's see if these things really work."

Gracie laid her precious bundle into the cradle and rocked Jack Jr. The cradle would be perfect until she could get something else. Naomi was right. She really wasn't very well prepared.

Cynthia sat in the chair next to the couch and picked up the diaper bag. Gracie reached for it, but Cynthia pulled away from her. "I need to talk to you about something." She showed Gracie the photograph of the baby and the Christmas stocking. "Would you care to explain this?"

Thirty~Five

Saint-Dié, France

Jack awoke again, late on Christmas morning, as the nurse on duty came early to check vital signs. *Why don't they just let us sleep instead of waking us up every few minutes?* He put his arm over his forehead after the nurse finished with him and bumped into the eye patch. *Gotta get used to it.* He turned over and saw a large envelope on Bill's nightstand. His discharge papers. *Lucky. I'm gonna be another month in here then another month on a hospital ship.*

He tried to go back to sleep, but his mind was too busy trying to figure out a way to get to Gracie quicker. *I could just walk out the door. But then I'd be a deserter. Don't want that on my record. I could plead amnesia about it afterward. After all, I do have a head injury.* He dozed off and on, never returning to a deep sleep.

He heard the clatter of the food cart coming down the aisle. The orderly stopped at his bed and brought a tray to him. "Lunchtime, sir. Looks like you and your neighbor are getting out of here today."

Jack hitched his thumb in Bill's direction. "He is, but I'm stuck here for another few weeks."

"Nope. My orders say this is your last meal here too. Looks like you're headed for Fitzsimmons Hospital in Denver."

He bolted upright and looked on his nightstand. A large envelope, exactly like Bill's, lay on top. He grabbed it and tore it open. Discharge papers from the hospital...and not due to report to Fitzsimmons until January second. He looked over at Bill, who was grinning at him as the orderly delivered lunch to the captain.

Jack jumped out of bed and waved the papers. "How did this happen?" He looked at the signature of the doctor—a name he didn't recognize—and the hospital administrator, General William E. Murphy. "Murphy—wait a minute, didn't you say your last name was Murphy? You wouldn't happen to be William E. Murphy, Jr., would you?"

"Hmm, what makes you think that?" Bill uncovered his lunch tray and made a face at whatever was on it.

"How did you do this? How did you make this happen? Did Angela have anything to do with this?"

"Ask me no questions, I'll tell you no lies. Let's just say I have friends in high places." The captain took a bite. "Hurry and eat, and let's get out of here. I have a jeep coming for us."

"I need a uniform. Mine probably was ruined." A fleeting memory of a young boy cutting his jacket off flashed through his head. "I left it in Germany at a farm...I think...those details are blurry too."

"Not a problem. They'll bring you one. I'll tell them when we go to the shower to fetch one. Look in your drawer. All of your personal effects are in there—watch, rings. I think your boots are under your bed."

They ate quickly, showered, and dressed. It felt good to be in uniform again. Jack didn't want this to be the end of his military career. He enjoyed the army, but with his injury, could he stay in? He'd find out in good time. His primary objective at this point was to get home to Gracie.

A doctor Jack didn't remember stopped by their beds. "Well, men. Ready to go, I see." He looked at their charts. He signed off on Bill's right away and shook his hand. "Good luck, Captain."

"Yes, sir."

The doctor looked at Jack's chart and peered over his glasses at him. "Hmm. Don't recognize this doctor's signature." He shoved it in front of Jack's face. "Who is that?"

"You're asking me to decipher a doctor's handwriting, sir? I have no idea." Jack laughed nervously.

"I can read General Murphy's signature, so I guess that's all that matters. We have a rotation of doctors through here constantly. Can't keep up with them all." He initialed the chart and shook Jack's hand. "Good luck to you as well, Lieutenant. Take care of yourself. Keep the area around the eye clean and dressed. Do you need a wheelchair or crutches?"

"No, sir. Thank you, sir."

Jack and Bill put their caps on and started down the long hall to the front door. He hoped no one could tell how weak his legs felt. "Halt, soldier."

Jack's heart jumped into his throat.

"Dad!" Bill turned and embraced an imposing figure of a man in uniform coming out of the glass enclosed offices to their right.

"Were you not going to tell me good-bye?"

"Of course I was, but I wanted to see if our jeep was here yet first. Dad, this is Lieutenant Jack Blauvelt. Jack, this is my father, General William Murphy."

Jack snapped his heels together, saluted, and then shook the general's outstretched hand. "Good to meet you, sir."

"I'll send someone to check on the jeep. Come into my office for a moment."

Jack wiped the palm of his good hand on his trousers. The duffle bag with his few personal items felt like it weighed a ton. They walked into the very plainly decorated office.

"Sit, men." He addressed his son. "Do you need any money?"

"No, Dad. I'm fine."

"Well, take this anyway. Where do you have to go to join your unit?"

"RAF Little Walden."

He nodded. "What about you, Lieutenant?"

"I'm being sent to Fitzsimmons Hospital in Denver for an evaluation on my eye." He touched the patch as he spoke.

"I see."

"Dad, could you write an order for Jack to get on a transport plane to Denver instead of having to board a ship? His wife is expecting a baby any day, and since he's unable to go back to the front …I just thought maybe you could help him out."

General Murphy looked at Jack from under bushy eyebrows. "I am honored to be able to assist one of our fighting men." He rang for his assistant, issued the order, and leaned back in his chair. "He'll type it up and have it back in here shortly." He steepled his fingers as he talked. "I don't have to tell you men how proud we are of the job you're doing. Your country thanks you."

Jack felt heat rise in his cheeks. "Yes, sir." He fidgeted in his chair.

"Are you nervous, Lieutenant?"

"No, sir. I mean, yes, sir. I am, honestly. I've never had a sit-down conversation with a general before."

"Would you be more comfortable standing at attention?"

"Yes, sir. Truthfully, I would."

"Don't be ridiculous. I put my pants on the same way you do."

Bill snickered. "Dad, ease up. The man's been in the hospital for two weeks."

The man chuckled. "Forgive me, son. Just having a little fun."

"Yes, sir."

The assistant came in with the general's orders for Jack's plane.

"Time for you men to be on your way." General Murphy handed his son a one hundred dollar bill. He turned to Jack and gave him the folded orders. "Good to meet you, Lieutenant." He still held his wallet. "Could you use a little cash?"

Jack's eyes widened. "Oh, no, sir. I'll be fine." The truth was he had two dollars in his wallet.

Bill took another one hundred dollars out of his father's hand. "Of course he could, Dad." The young man handed the crisp bill to Jack. "You can pay me back next time you see me."

"I don't know what to say."

"Just 'thank you' will suffice." General Murphy shook Jack's hand again. "Good to meet you, Lieutenant. Take care of yourself."

"Yes, sir. I sure do thank you, sir."

The general embraced his son. "Come back safe, son."

"I plan on doing just that, Dad. I need to get in a plane and get back to work."

"I understand. Godspeed."

The two left, got in the awaiting jeep, and took off. "Friends in high places, eh?" Jack held his arm in the sling as the jeep jostled down the bumpy road.

"Yeah, you might say that." Bill laughed and pounded Jack's back.

Jack caught a last glimpse of his friend standing on the tarmac waving good-bye as the cargo plane lumbered down the runway headed across the Atlantic for the United States of America.

THIRTY~SIX

Cynthia walked to the fireplace and held the picture next to the one on the mantel. "What does this mean? Why do you have a picture of my missing sister?"

Gracie looked down at her hands. Her nails were a mess of chipped red polish. She couldn't seem to keep them nice anymore. What did that matter now?

She took a deep breath. Her hands began to shake. "I…uh…"

"Well?"

"I…I have that picture because…because I found it in my attic in my house in San Antonio."

"Why would you have a picture of my sister in your house? Unless…"

Gracie pushed herself up, her legs threatening to give way beneath her. Would Cynthia believe her? "I believe…I'm certain…" She squared her shoulders and took a deep breath. "Cynthia, I am your sister, Julia."

Cynthia stepped back and bumped her foot into the wood box. "Wha… what?" She sat down heavily in the rocking chair. "You? You're Julia?" Laughing and crying at the same time, she sprang up and gathered Gracie in her arms. The chair rocked back and forth, hitting the hearth.

She held Gracie at arm's length and stared at her. "I thought you were

Mexican. Or Spanish. The way you fit in with Robby's family, spoke the language, knew all their foods…" She picked up a lock of Gracie's hair. "Oh, how did I miss it?" She pulled Gracie over to the mirror on the wall. Cynthia's hair hung loose around her shoulders.

Gracie took the ribbon out of hers and let it flow. "Look at us. It's so obvious we're sisters." They hugged again.

Gracie's knees buckled. "I think I need to sit down."

"Oh, I'm sorry. Here…" Cynthia helped her to the couch again. She pulled the rocking chair up to face Gracie, with the cradle in between them. "This is unbelievable. Tell me how you found out. What happened? How did you find us?"

Gracie laughed and held up her hand. "Wait, wait, wait. One question at a time." She took a deep breath. "I don't really know—how I came to be with the Gonzales family in San Antonio. All my life I was told I didn't look anything like my parents and siblings, but my mother would explain it by saying that I look like her relatives from Spain. I began to suspect I was adopted last year when my elderly grandmother slipped and said something about me being the girl my parents had adopted. She's not thinking too clearly these days."

She smiled and shook her head. In a few sentences, she explained about finding the bag in the attic, meeting Jack, being locked away, and Jack's rescue. "We eloped, and as soon as he was shipped overseas I came looking for you. I started with the photographer whose name is on that photo. He said he only remembered the photo because it was used when a baby went missing from the Golden Aspen, so I came here. Saw the restaurant and figured it would be a good fit for a job, and…well, I just settled in to figure things out—I didn't realize your family was the one I was looking for, I thought perhaps mine had just been staying here. And I got a bit distracted from my search when I realized I was having a baby." She put a hand on her stomach, now empty. "And with worrying over Jack."

"How romantic. He rescued you."

"Yes, he really did. My mother came after him with a fireplace poker."

"She sounds charming."

"I've made her sound awful, but she has been a good mother. I've had a wonderful life. My father is a doctor, and we are…well, I suppose we're wealthy. I have a younger sister and brother. My mother has just always been very possessive of me. I guess now I know why."

Cynthia got out of the rocking chair. "What do you plan to do now? Are you going to tell my parents?"

That had been the plan all along, of course, but the thought of opening her mouth and letting that truth spill out was somehow frightening. Would they even believe her? "Do you think I should?"

"Absolutely."

"When? This morning?"

"Yes. What a fabulous Christmas present." Cynthia paced from the couch to the kitchen and back again. "We'll just let everybody get up to have Santa Claus, and we'll tell them. We'll play it by ear. We'll know when it's the right time."

Gracie lay down on her side. "What time is it?"

"It's almost six o'clock. The girls will be getting up soon, I'm sure. You try to rest some, and I'm going to make some coffee. Mom and Dad will smell it and get up."

Gracie closed her eyes. The clank of coffee mugs and spoons followed Cynthia as she rummaged around in the kitchen. The pop-pop of the percolator filled the room, and the aroma of coffee drifted through the apartment. Soon Gracie heard giggles down the hall. Cynthia's little sisters must be awake—*her* little sisters.

She heard Quenton. "Wait here, girls, and let me check to see if Santa has come." His muffled footsteps told her he had on house shoes.

She opened her eyes and sat up.

He grinned at her. "I hear we had some excitement last night, and I slept through it all."

She stared at his auburn hair. He rubbed his head. "Guess my hair is a mess." He bent down to look at the baby. "Little, isn't he?"

"Yes." She couldn't quit staring at him now that she knew for sure he was her father. He was so big, strong, and masculine. And their eyes were exactly the same color.

"I smell coffee. Did Cynthia get it started?"

"Yes." Seems she couldn't say anything else. She heard more squealing and giggling.

Quenton came from the kitchen with two mugs and went back down the hall. "Wow, girls. Santa has been here."

Grandpa, wearing a burgundy robe, came into the living room also. "What do we have here?" He sat in the rocking chair, set his mug on the coffee table, and bent over the cradle. "A new life. On Christmas Day. How fitting, young lady."

Myrna and Elise, hand in hand with Naomi and Quenton, stood at the door to the living room. The ever-present headscarf did not cover Naomi's hair this morning. Her beautiful thick locks hung loose around her shoulders with a silver ribbon around her head. She looked ten years younger.

The girls jumped up and down and ran to the tree. "A cradle for our dollies!" They sat on the floor and rocked the empty cradle back and forth.

Naomi knelt at the tree with them. "Actually, there's a cradle for each of you, but someone seems to be using the other one."

Myrna inhaled sharply as she stared at Gracie's baby.

Naomi chuckled. "Let's try to be quiet. He's asleep."

The two girls tiptoed amid oohs and ahhs. Elise looked up at Naomi, her eyes wide. "Is it Baby Jesus?"

Laughter erupted all over the room. Naomi smoothed her littlest girl's hair. "Oh, honey, no. It's Gracie's baby. He decided to be born last night. Is it okay if he uses your cradle for a few days?" Both girls nodded vigorously.

"May I hold him?" Myrna sat on the couch beside Gracie.

"Sure, as long as you're sitting here by me. But let's wait until he wakes up."

"Why don't you girls finish unwrapping the rest of your gifts and look at your stockings?" Naomi unhooked them from the mantel, all except Julia's.

Oranges, nuts, apples, hair ribbons and barrettes, perfume, aftershave, and assorted small gifts were removed from the stockings and strewn over the living room floor. Naomi started gathering up the trash. "Opening gifts on Christmas morning always comes to an end too quickly."

Cynthia stood on the hearth and clapped her hands to get everyone's attention. The rattling of paper stopped. "I have an announcement. Actually, the best and biggest Christmas gift we've ever received is yet to be opened. Gracie has something for us."

"Oh, Gracie, you didn't need to get us a gift," Naomi said. "That was entirely unnecessary. Being part of delivering your baby last night was the most wonderful Christmas gift ever."

Quenton put his arm around his wife's shoulders. "And I missed it all."

Naomi smiled and chucked his chin. "You would just have been in the way."

"Hmm. Probably."

Gracie leaned forward and picked the baby up out of the cradle, nestling him in her arms. He stretched and yawned. She smiled, struggled to her feet, then walked to Quenton and Naomi. Emotions roiled in her stomach, and she took a deep breath. Swallowing the lump in her throat, she said, "Last night, Naomi, you helped me deliver my baby. Actually, due to your quick actions, you probably saved Jack Jr.'s life. I can never thank you enough."

Naomi shook her head. "My goodness. No thank you is needed."

Gracie gazed around the room at the faces of her newly-discovered family, their eyes watching her as she spoke. "If you could have your deepest wish granted…if you could have anything you wanted for Christmas, what would you ask for?"

Naomi looked up at Quenton. "What I would ask for is not in the realm of possibility."

Smiling, Cynthia ducked her head and wiped a tear away.

Gracie persisted. "But what would it be?"

"I…I would ask for our daughter who was kidnapped to be found—alive, safe, and healthy."

Tears glistened in Gracie's eyes. "Last night, it's true, you helped me deliver my son. And it was a wonderful Christmas blessing. But what you don't realize is that it was much more than that. Last night your deepest desire came true. Last night you delivered your own grandson." The young girl took a deep breath. "Naomi, I…I am Julia."

Thirty~Seven

hat? How…my grandson?" Naomi looked from Gracie to the baby to Cynthia to Quenton. "What are you saying?" She leaned back against Quenton as her knees buckled. He caught her and slid to the floor with her. She closed her eyes for a moment then shook her head and stared at Gracie.

Quenton cleared his throat. "Are…are you claiming…? What exactly are you claiming?"

"Just what I said. I believe I am your daughter, Julia."

Quenton helped Naomi to her feet. "Impossible. What proof do you have?" He sheltered her in an embrace with his arm around her shoulders.

Cynthia handed a photograph to her father. "It's not impossible. She had a copy of this picture, Dad."

Naomi stared at the photograph with him—the photograph she'd treasured all these years, identical to the one still sitting on the mantle.

Quenton huffed. "Anybody could have gotten a copy of that picture."

Cynthia stood beside Gracie. "Look at us, Daddy. Look at our hair. Look at *your* hair and her eyes. They're your hair and eyes."

Quenton shook his head and ran his hands through his hair as he always did when frustrated. "I don't know. Naomi?"

She faced Quenton and held on to his hands. "I...I don't...see how...."

"Why would she make this up? She came out here looking for her family, that photograph her only clue. And she found us." Cynthia stepped forward. "I believe her."

Myrna and Elise chimed in. "We do too."

Naomi slowly nodded, never taking her eyes off of Gracie. She pulled a hankie out of the pocket of her robe. "I...I have to admit I've had an affinity for Gracie ever since I m-met her." Her chest heaved with sobs. "I have been drawn to her." She stepped closer to Gracie and with trembling fingers touched her hair, her cheek. She touched her eyelids and traced her fingers along Gracie's jawline. Then she gently stroked the hands that held the sleeping infant. "My...my grandson?" She covered her mouth, stifling a whimper.

Gracie smiled. "I have something else that might look familiar to you." She pointed to the diaper bag on the floor beside the couch. Cynthia bent down and picked it up.

Naomi gasped. "Oh my, Quenton. That was Julia's diaper bag. It was the only thing that was taken. The picture was in the bag." Her breath quickened, and she could not tear her eyes away from Gracie. "It...it is you, isn't it?"

She pulled Gracie and the baby into a smothering embrace. Tears coursed down both their faces as they stepped back to look at each other then fell back into each other's arms.

Gracie wiped her tears with the corner of the blanket—the blanket that had been hers as a baby. "You need to know this is all new to me as well. I've only known I was adopted since March."

Naomi couldn't take it all in. Her daughter, her firstborn daughter, was standing here. Holding a baby of her own. "But you found us."

Gracie nodded. "I know you want answers about how I was taken. And

I'm sorry, but I don't have those yet. Only my parents do, and at the moment I'm estranged from them. My husband and I eloped, and my mother went ballistic. I had to run away."

Quenton paced in front of the fireplace, his face stoic. "What do you think, Grandpa?"

Gracie's eyes filled with tears. Obviously, she knew as well as Naomi did that Quenton still didn't believe her. Her chin dropped. "I'd hoped this would be a happy time. I'm so sorry if I ruined your Christmas."

Naomi's father rocked back and forth, lit his pipe, puffing and puffing on it until it caught, taking his time. He took another puff and blew the smoke into the air. The rich aroma of tobacco filled the room.

"The way I see it," he finally said, "Cynthia's right. This young woman has no reason to lie about this. We certainly have no money for her to blackmail us." He puffed again on the pipe. "Look at her and look at that baby. He looks just like Julia did when she was born. I think she's telling the truth."

Quenton stared at Gracie for what seemed to be minutes but was only seconds. His eyes slowly reddened and welled with tears. He covered his mouth with his fist then his face contorted as he opened his arms to his long-lost daughter. "Welcome home, Julia."

Something in Naomi's heart broke. Or, perhaps, mended. Knit together for the first time in seventeen long years.

The room erupted in laughter, sobs, tears of sorrow for years lost, tears of joy for years now regained. Everybody hugged everybody, and then they hugged on one another again. Grandpa turned on the radio and led an air orchestra in a rousing version of "Joy to The World!" The two younger girls jumped up and down with glee, doing a dance with each other.

Dabbing her eyes with her handkerchief, Naomi guided her new-found daughter back to the couch. "Here, Gracie—Julia. What do we call you now?

Whichever, you need to sit. After all, you just had a baby a few hours ago." She stuffed the handkerchief in the pocket of her robe and took the infant from Gracie. "Let me hold my grandson."

She held Jack Jr. close to her chest and rocked him in her arms. She looked at Quenton, her throat tight with emotion. "God didn't forget us, Q. Our prayers have been answered. I had given up, but now our child has been restored to us." She kissed the baby's cheek. "And now we have a grandson. Oh, my goodness. I'm a grandmother. Now that's going to take some getting used to."

San Antonio, Texas

"It's Christmas morning. Get up, Jorge, and go turn on the coffee." Esperanza reached to shake Jorge awake. Her hand touched only sheets. She sat up in the bed.

He was gone. She smelled the coffee. She smiled and swung her legs to the side of the bed, wriggled her feet into the red mules on the floor. She walked to her closet, pulled the red satin robe off the hook, and belted it around her still-small waist. Looking at her roots in the mirror, she tied her long black hair back with a red scarf. *No time to get to the beauty shop.* Opening the door, she started down the stairs but met Jorge on his way up with a tray, holding two mugs of coffee and a carafe.

"Umm, that smells good." She held the door open and let him into their bedroom before her. "How nice to be served coffee on Christmas morning."

He put the tray on a table between two chairs in front of the large bedroom window. "Yes, I thought that would be nice since our kids are no longer up at the crack of dawn clamoring for Santa Claus." He motioned for Esperanza to sit, poured her a cup of coffee, and added her preferred cream and sugar. Then he poured his usual—black and strong.

Her hands flitted from her hair to the coffee cup to the lapel of her robe. "I'm so excited about our trip to Colorado today." Two suitcases sat beside the closet door like sentinels waiting to be given orders. Her coffee cup clanked against the china saucer. "We need to get the kids up and tell them about our surprise trip. I can't wait to see our Gracie."

"You're convinced she's in Colorado Springs?"

"Absolutely. She went in search of...of..."

"Her parents?"

"We are her parents. We raised her." She picked up her suitcase and threw it on the bed. "Now, let's get packed."

"Sit, Esperanza."

She walked to her dresser and pulled open drawer after drawer, removing one item of clothing after another.

Jorge stood and pointed to Esperanza's chair. "I said, 'sit.' Now."

She turned and stared at her husband, her mouth open, clutching an armload of underwear to her chest. "Wha... Are you ordering me?"

"I am." Jorge took her by the elbow and escorted her to her chair. "Give me your things."

"Just put them in the suitcase." She handed the silky underthings to him.

He took the armful of clothing and returned them to the drawers, slowly. "We're not going." He took his time opening first one drawer then another, folding Esperanza's things carefully. He sat in his chair opposite his wife and leaned toward her, his elbows on his knees as he reached for her hands. She kept them clasped in her lap. He sighed and threaded his fingers together.

"What do you mean, we're not going? I already made the train reservations." She stood. "The train leaves at two o'clock. We need to get ready."

"Sit." The tone of Jorge's voice startled her, and she slowly returned to her chair, frowning at him.

"I cancelled our reservations this morning. We are not going."

"You what?" Esperanza jumped to her feet. "How dare you go against my wishes! You have never done anything like this before." She started for the door. "I'll just reinstate the reservations. We are going."

Jorge looked at his wife and shook his head. "No, I never have gone against your wishes, demands, manipulation, or bullying."

"Bullying? You cannot talk to me that way." She opened the door, but Jorge rushed to her side and closed it again.

He took Esperanza by the shoulders. "Yes, bullying. And I can, and I will, talk to you this way. I am your husband, the head of this family. I should have put my foot down many times before, but I never wanted to displease you. I do not intend to be unkind, but I am, after all of these years, speaking up. You are not going to bully us into going after Gracie, when it is just wrong. If you do, it may ruin any chance we have for a relationship with her in the future. She will call us or come home when she is ready. She's not vindictive or revengeful. She's compassionate and forgiving. She knows we love her and will reach out to us when the time is right. If you interfere now, it may drive her away forever. I will not allow it."

Esperanza shrugged out of his grip and slapped him, hard. He said nothing, simply held her gaze. Her jaw worked back and forth as she strode to the window. "You? You will not allow it?" She raised the blinds and looked out over the courtyard. The fountain lay silent in the cold December morning, dead and still. She spun back to face him. "Since when do you tell me what to do?"

Jorge cleared his throat and rubbed his cheek. He hitched up his pants. "Since today, this morning, right now." His voice rose, and he punctuated the air with his finger. "So get used to it."

She narrowed her eyes.

He took a step toward her and lowered his voice. "*Mi bonita*, I've done an injustice to our family by not doing what I felt was right. I let you cajole and persuade me against my better judgment too many times. I'm not going to allow that to happen anymore."

Tears sprang to Esperanza's eyes as she returned to her chair. "What of our Gracie? She'll be lost to us forever." She put her face in her hands and wept, her shoulders heaving. "Wha…what about Gracie? What about our Gracie?"

"She'll come home when the time is right. I'm sure of it." He patted his wife's arm. "But in the meantime, we have to deal with what we did."

"You mean what *I* did. I knew and I hid the truth."

Jorge hung his head. "Yes. Well-intentioned, but there will be a reckoning." He looked at her, and she could see a wave of profound sadness and weariness sweep over him. "If we ever hope to have Gracie back in truth and freedom, everything has to come to light. Nothing will be right until that happens." He sighed. "Don't you want to be done with the deception?"

Esperanza looked at her husband through eyelashes clumped together with tears. "I just want my Gracie back."

"She never was ours to begin with, and she will never be ours again if we don't take steps to bring this out of the darkness."

"But—"

"One day the phone will ring, and it will be Gracie. She'll want to come home, but for now, we must release her." He took her in his arms again. "Let her go, Esperanza. Let her go."

THIRTY~EIGHT

Denver, Colorado

The plane landed in Denver late Christmas afternoon. Light flurries of snow fluttered in the air. Large banks of the white stuff towered on either side of the runway. Men were being taken off the plane on stretchers, in wheelchairs, and some in coffins.

Jack desperately wanted to get to the Springs before Christmas was over—something the time difference might make possible. He hoped the highway had been plowed. What was ordinarily an hour and a half trip would probably take two or three hours in this weather.

He pulled out the hundred dollar bill—perhaps he could persuade a cabbie to take him. Surely they wouldn't charge more than a hundred dollars.

Jack hefted his duffle bag to his good shoulder and adjusted the eye patch as he made his way down the steep metal steps of the airplane. He was one of the last to get off. His depth perception skewed, he stumbled on the last step.

A medic who'd helped with the patients on the plane caught his arm to prevent him from falling. "Easy there, Lieutenant."

"Thanks. I'm not used to this eye patch yet."

They stepped onto the tarmac and hurried into the terminal in the light snowfall. The sun was slipping toward the mountainous horizon. "Look at those beautiful Rocky Mountains. Man, is it ever good to be home."

"Isn't it?" Jack held out his good hand to shake, and his duffle bag clunked from his shoulder. "Sorry about that." He untangled himself and shook the officer's hand. "Jack Blauvelt."

"Good to meet you, sir. Chet Holcomb. Welcome home."

Jack straightened his cap. "It is good to be back on American soil." He took a deep breath. "Got just a few more miles to go." The two started toward the terminal.

"Where are you headed? I have my car here. Can I give you a lift?" Lieutenant Holcomb opened the heavy glass door.

Jack walked in the direction of a pay phone. "I'm being sent to Fitzsimmons Hospital, but I don't have to report in for a few days. My wife is in Colorado Springs. I'm going to see if I can get a cab to take me."

"Wow. A cab to the Springs is going to cost you a pretty penny." Lieutenant Holcomb stopped and touched Jack on the arm. "Wait a minute. I have a buddy, a civilian government employee, who works here in the airport. A single guy, and he lives in the Springs. Maybe he's on today and would give you a ride." He looked at his watch. "It's almost five o'clock. I think he usually works until six. You may have to wait for him to get off, but I'm sure he'd welcome the company."

"He'd be working on Christmas Day?"

"Like I said, he's single—and he's Jewish, so he doesn't celebrate the same holidays. Come on. Let's see if he's in his office."

The congenial man, likely in his mid-thirties, Jack thought, maneuvered his considerable belly underneath the steering wheel of the old black Chevrolet. "Just throw your duffle bag onto the backseat."

Jack set his bag down, opened the door, then tossed his bag in. He struggled with the handle of the passenger side. The man leaned over and unlocked it for him. "Sorry, sir."

Jack slid in. "No problem. Tell me your name again. Oscar, was it?"

"Yes, sir. Oscar Levitz."

"German?"

He started the engine. It ground and then stalled. "Ole Betsy's just cold. Been sitting out here all day." He tried again with the same result. "Polish. Grandparents came over in the late '30s, brought the whole family. They were warned by the rabbis that that Hitler scumbag was dangerous. Boy, were they right." He pumped the gas pedal. "Don't worry, sir. She'll start in a minute. Just needs a little persuasion—like asking a reluctant woman to dance." He threw back his head and laughed, his belly jiggling.

On the fifth try, true to his word, the car started, and they crept out of the parking lot and through the streets of the base. "The roads should be better than they were this morning. Woo-ee! I had a slip-sliding good time trying to get to work. We had more snow at home than they had here in Denver, but I slid pretty good a couple of times. Sure was glad nothing was coming the other way." He pulled out onto the highway and gunned the motor, tires spinning, but they gained traction and made the turn. "Here we go."

The road had been scraped and sanded. Oscar was able to maintain a steady pace and gradually upped their speed. It grew darker and icier the farther south they drove.

After about twenty minutes of silence, but for the road noises, Oscar said, "Some of them stayed."

Jack pulled out of his memories of the war and turned to Oscar. "Pardon me?"

"Some of our relatives, my mother's brother and family, didn't come with us. They stayed. They thought we were being alarmists." He lit a cigarette. "Do you mind?"

"Go ahead." Jack's conversation with Bill echoed in his mind. *I've seen the smoke stacks. Seen the barbed wire.* "Where did you and your family live?"

"Warsaw." Silence—heavy and suffocating, even in the cold. Some of the worst of the rumors concerned the Warsaw ghetto. Oscar shook his head. "Haven't heard from my uncle's family for months. My mother is frantic about them."

"I'm sorry."

Oscar turned to look at Jack. "Do you know anything? Have you heard the rumors? Are they really…?"

"Watch out!" A car's headlights came toward them out of nowhere. Oscar veered to miss the vehicle, and Old Betsy fishtailed. Flashes of spinning in the air as the bomber went down exploded in Jack's mind.

He grabbed hold of the dashboard as the car lurched out of control. Branches of pine trees slapped against the windows. Finally the car came to rest in a snowdrift up against the trunk of a large pine tree. *God, please. Not another pine tree. Not this close to getting back to Gracie. After all those bombing missions, don't let me be killed in a crazy car accident on the way to my wife.*

The lighted cigarette landed on the seat beside Jack's leg. Oscar picked it up, stuck it back in his mouth, and brushed the spot where it had landed. "You okay, sir?"

"I…I think so. What about you?" Jack pointed to blood tricking down the side of the man's head.

Oscar touched his temple. "Just a scratch." He took out a handkerchief and dabbed the blood. "Well, let's see if we can get Old Betsy out of here." He revved the engine, put it into gear, and tried to drive it out, but the tires simply spun on the snow.

Up on the highway a truck stopped then backed up. A rough-looking mountain man with a scruffy sandy-colored beard and a red plaid flannel shirt stepped out of the cab. "You folks okay?" A piece of mistletoe was stuck in the side of his cap. He chewed on a cigar even as he spoke.

Oscar pushed open the door. "Yeah, I think so. Where'd you come from?"

"Just passing by. Saw headlights down here. Figured you might need some help."

"You got that right. You're here just in the nick of time. Got an important passenger who needs to get to his wife in the Springs tonight. We could use some help getting out of here. You got a chain or a rope?"

Jack's door was pressed against the tree, impossible to open. He peered up at the truck. The mountain man lumbered toward them, holding a heavy chain.

He looked into the car. Taking his cigar out of his mouth, he spat on the snow. "Are you hurt, sir? I mean, I can tell you are wounded, but did this little escapade further injure you?"

"I don't think so. I just need to get to the Springs tonight."

"Not to worry—Lieutenant, is it? We'll have you out of here in no time at all." He stuck the cigar back in his mouth and talked around it. "I just got home a couple of months ago myself. I know how eager you are to get to your woman. Hang on." He hooked the chain onto the front of the car, then trudged up the side of the ditch to his truck. He pulled them out in a few minutes.

Jack got out of the car once it was back on the highway. Jack dug in his pocket for the hundred dollar bill. "Can we pay you? This is all I have, but it's worth it to me—what you did for us tonight." He shook the man's hand. The truck driver's palm was soft, not calloused and rough like a mountain man's.

The stranger adjusted his cap and laughed. "Put your money back in your pocket, sir. This is what I do."

Oscar walked up to them, pulled off his right glove, and shook the man's hand too. "We are grateful for your help."

The man gathered his chain and threw it into the bed of the truck. Climbing into the cab, he grinned and waved. "No problem. Love your families well when you get home. Merry Christmas." He started the engine and left them in a flurry of snow. The sign on the truck's door read MICHAEL'S GUARDIAN SERVICE.

The two men got back into Old Betsy and let the car warm up. Jack still had his cash in his hand. As he stuffed it in his pocket, it felt different. He looked. He now had two of the hundred dollar bills. "Wha… Where did this come from?" He swiveled around in his seat and looked behind them. "That man. He put another hundred dollar bill into my hand. Why would he do that?"

Oscar chuckled. "I dunno. Christmas gift, I guess."

"But why?" Jack folded the bills together and stuck them into his pocket. He wrapped his good arm around the sling to hold it steady. "Did you notice anything about his hands?"

"Yeah. He wasn't wearing gloves. Everybody wears gloves in this part of the country in the winter time, especially when they do work like that."

"Exactly. And his hands were soft, not like a laborer's." He looked out the rear window again. "Wait a minute." He got out of the car, walked to its rear, and stared down the highway.

Oscar remained in the car and lit another cigarette.

Jack slid back in his seat and looked at Oscar. "No tire tracks."

Oscar's eyebrows lifted, and his hands shook as he stuck the key in the ignition and started the car. "Ya don't say?"

Thirty~Nine

Jack stood in front of the Tres Hermanos restaurant as Oscar sped off, leaving a cloud of snow in his wake. He too refused to let Jack pay him. The CLOSED sign was hanging in the window, but Jack assured Oscar that Gracie lived in an apartment above the restaurant, so someone would answer the door. He knocked again, but no one seemed to be inside. He banged as hard as he could. No response.

He looked down the street, but everything appeared to be closed, except the inn across the street. All the lights were on over there. Gracie had mentioned doing some housekeeping and laundry for them from time to time. Maybe she was there, or perhaps they might know where she was.

He looked at his watch. Nearly nine o'clock. He picked up his duffle bag and crossed the slick road. No traffic. Everyone was home with their families. *Soon I will be too.* His heart pounded at the thought of seeing Gracie. Light flurries of snow danced in the air. With his good hand, he held onto the railing beside the steps while he climbed up the steep hill to the inn. He had to stop a couple of times to catch his breath. The altitude difference was getting to him.

He opened the door to the office of the inn and heard laughter and talking. It appeared a group of people had gathered in a dining room off to the left.

Nobody came to the desk.

They must not have heard the bell. He hit the bell on the counter a second time. Still nobody. He didn't know what to do. He didn't want to crash a private party.

Slowly he walked toward the dining room, where several people were seated at a long table. An attractive middle-aged woman sat at one end, a red-headed man at the other end. Around the table an older couple, two little girls, a young couple, an elderly gentleman. And then he saw Gracie, her auburn hair curling softly around her shoulders and tied with a green bow. She was sitting beside the woman at the end of the table.

He stepped into the shimmering light of the room. Everyone turned toward him. Gracie gasped and struggled to her feet. She hesitated for a moment then moved toward him crying.

"Jack! Oh, Jack! You're home." She covered his face with kisses. Her hair smelled the same. He gathered her to his chest with his good arm and kissed her long and hard. He didn't want to let her go, but she pulled back and looked at him. "You're hurt. Jack, you're injured." She touched the eye patch and his arm, then the eye patch again. "Are you going to be okay? What happened? Oh, it doesn't matter. You're home. You're back. That's all that matters." She kissed him again. She wobbled a bit and held onto his good arm. "Come here. I need to sit down. And there's someone I want to introduce you to."

She tugged him toward a cradle near her chair. A *cradle*? Had she had the baby early? A million questions surged into his mind, but he bit them all back.

She smiled at those gathered around the table as she sat down in her chair. The woman sitting next to Gracie's place at the table had risen, and the red-headed man came up behind her. Three girls who must be the couple's daughters—two young and one who looked to be around Gracie's age—came to their side, watching Jack and Gracie.

She laughed. "Actually, there are several people I want to introduce you to, but this little one first."

Gracie picked the baby up from the cradle. He whimpered and blinked his eyes open, then stuck his fist in his mouth and began to fuss.

Gracie smiled at him. "This is our son, Jack Blauvelt Jr." She chuckled. "I think I might call him JJ."

Jack's eyes grew wide as he took in the perfect little one—so unbelievably tiny. "Our baby?" He kissed the top of the baby's head as tears gathered in his eyes. "Our son. I can't believe it. When was he born?"

"Today. He was born right after midnight."

"Are you all right?" He took Gracie's hand.

"I'm fine. But what about you? Your eye?"

"We don't know yet, but I'm sure it'll be okay. I've been sent to Fitzsimmons and will have to report in a few days, but for now, our little family can be together."

"There's something else I need to tell you." She smiled. "Our little family isn't so little anymore."

Jack cocked his head. "What do you mean?"

"Come back into the apartment with me." She signaled the woman sitting at the head of the table.

Jack tried to remember anything Gracie had mentioned about her in her letters. The innkeeper, he assumed—Mrs. Lockhart. Gracie had mentioned working for her, liking her. He hadn't realized they were close, but there was familiarity in their every glance.

Mrs. Lockhart spoke to the crowd. "Please stay as long as you like. We have a little family business to take care of."

A short woman with a Hispanic accent spoke up. "It's getting late. I think we'd best call it a night as well and get this cleaned up." She waved her hand. "You all go on. Ernest and Robby and I will take care of all of this." She began to clear the dishes.

An elderly gentleman took the hand of the woman sitting next to him. "I agree. It's been a long day, and I for one am ready to retire." He started singing in his booming bass voice, "We wish you a Merry Christmas," as he and his wife started up the stairs. The rest of the group dispersed to their respective rooms. Several shook Jack's hand. "Welcome home, sir."

"Thank you for your service."

Slaps on the back.

The two youngest girls who stood by Gracie ran giggling into their apartment. The other stepped forward and said, "I'm Cynthia. Nice to meet you, Jack." She giggled as well and ran into the apartment.

"What's with all the giggling?" Jack walked with Gracie and JJ behind the Lockharts, into the living room of their apartment.

Gracie pointed to the mantel. "Look."

Jack looked at a lovely fireplace with a crackling fire and a mantel filled with colorful stockings. A beautiful Christmas scene, but what did Gracie want him to see? Jack scanned the mantel further, searching for something of significance to his wife.

There. The picture. The same one Gracie had of a laughing baby, sitting above the Christmas stocking that was in the photo.

Gracie, extended her arm toward the couple beaming back at her—the woman wiping tears from her cheeks, the man whose eyes were filling with moisture; Cynthia biting her lip to keep from breaking down; the younger girls sniffling…and still giggling.

"Jack, I would like to introduce you to the Lockharts. These are my parents and my sisters. I have found my family."

EPILOGUE

Naomi lifted the curtain and looked up at the streetlamp on the corner. Snow continued to fall, forming a gauzy veil around the haloed light. Unlike the preceding evening, the electricity remained on this late Christmas night. She picked up a few cups in the living room and carried them to the kitchen. A smile played across her face, and she couldn't seem to wipe it away. Not that she wanted to. She had not been this happy since the day Julia was born.

Lupe had washed and put away the dishes from the dinner. All Naomi had to do was rinse out the cups and let them drain. She didn't want the night to end. Quenton had put Myrna and Elise to bed, then he had retired. He was probably snoring away by now. She heard Cynthia finishing up in the bathroom. Her daughter had given Gracie, Jack, and the baby her room for tonight and would sleep with Myrna and Elise. Tomorrow the young couple in the turret room would check out, and Naomi planned to put the newest additions to her family there until Jack had to check in at Fitzsimmons Hospital next week. Seemed fitting.

Humming "Deck the Halls" along with the radio, she puttered around the kitchen, straightening this and that. "'Tis the season to be jolly..." The Christmas season had not seemed jolly to her in many years. Now that would change. She reached for her apron hanging on a hook beside the Hoosier cabinet and tied it around her waist. A can of Old Dutch Cleanser sat on the cabinet, so she decided to go ahead and scour the sink. After wiping it down, she dried her hands, untied the apron, and hung it back up.

Quenton came into the kitchen. "I'm hungry."

"I thought you were asleep."

"I tried, but too much excitement tonight, I guess." He opened the pantry door and pushed things around on the shelves. "Any cookies left?"

"To your left in a tin." She reached in front of him and handed him the container.

Quenton pried open the tin, took out three cookies, and returned it to the pantry shelf. He opened the icebox door and got out a bottle of milk. "No better snack than cookies and milk." He sat at the kitchen table and munched on the goodies.

Naomi sat across from him and stroked his hand. "I still can't believe it, Q. Our Julia is back. I just want to stare at her." She smiled. "She looks so much like you. I don't how we didn't spot it right away."

"And we have a grandson. A boy in the family. I won't know how to deal with a boy." He drained the last of his milk, shoved the chair back with a screech, and put the glass in the sink. "But I'm eager to learn." He held out his hand and grinned at her. That grin still melted her heart. "Tomorrow will be another busy day—and an emotional one, if Gracie calls her adopted parents, like she said she wants to do. We'll have more answers then. But for now, let's go to bed."

Naomi took his hand and turned out the kitchen light as they left the room. They walked into the darkened living room toward the fireplace. Naomi stepped to Julia's stocking and caressed the velvety nap. The beaded

Christmas tree on the toe of the stocking sparkled in the gentle glow of the fire and the Christmas tree lights. The icicles seemed to shimmer in the dim light. She fingered the name *Julia* on the cuff. "I guess we'll need to put *Gracie* on here now. I like that name, don't you?"

"I do. It fits her—Grace. She is full of grace."

"I suppose I'll have to break down and learn how to make the stockings. We'll need one for Jack and one for JJ. And now I can add items of interest to Julia's—Gracie's." She stood back and surveyed the mantel with all of the stockings hanging in perfect order. "The mantel's going to get crowded eventually with grandchildren and all."

Quenton stood and dusted his hands as the fire blazed. "We'll figure it out." He put his arm around her shoulders and kissed her on top of her head. "Ready to call it a night?"

She nodded. "Go on. I'll get the lights and be there shortly." She turned out the lamp and stopped at the fireplace as Quenton went down the hall to their bedroom. The carved figures of the nativity scene sat in relative darkness—the kneeling shepherds, the random animals, a protective Joseph, Mary with her hands clasped in prayer, and Baby Jesus with a permanent halo around his all-too-adult face. Beautiful, inert, impotent—packed away every year in its proper box after the holidays, only to be brought out for display the next Christmas. Sudden tears blurred her vision of the silent scene as crystal clarity came to her spiritual sight.

Oh, God! This is what I have done to you. I have put you on the shelf all these years and packed you away into my little box of expectations. When you didn't answer my prayers like…like I thought they should be answered, I set you aside, convinced you were either uncaring or unable to act, like these stagnant figures.

She picked up the Baby Jesus, and waves of emotion swept over her. *But this is real, isn't it? You are real. You're not simply a carved figure of some artist's imagination. You reached down to humankind in the form of a baby on that Christmas night long ago. You sent your son. You knew the pain of losing your child too.*

Her head swam as the pieces of the puzzle snapped into place. Suddenly Christmas made sense, the words to the Christmas carols blossomed with life, the Christmas story became more than just a story. The truth of Christmas pierced her heart with the very presence of God.

Joy to the world! The Lord is come. Let earth receive her king. Let every heart prepare him room... It was as if scales fell from her eyes. *I never prepared room in my heart for Him.*

She clutched the Baby Jesus figurine to her breast as tears slid down her cheeks. *God, I'm so sorry, I'm sorry, I'm sorry. Please forgive me.* She sat on the hearth, still gripping the Christ Child in her hand. *Thank you for returning our Gracie to us, but I'm so sorry for doubting your love for us. I should have trusted you no matter the outcome or how long it took. I don't understand your ways, but I'm going to trust you from now on.*

How long she sat there she had no idea. The fire had gone out. Only a few embers remained. The room was cold.

"Naomi, are you all right?" Quenton stood shivering in the doorway. "Come on to bed. It's cold out here."

She pushed herself from the hearth. "I've never been more all right in my entire life. I'm coming." She returned the Baby Jesus figurine to the manger scene. Quenton turned out the Christmas tree lights and took Naomi into his arms.

She snuggled close to him. "God gave us the best gift we've ever received this year—our child. And I think I'm beginning to understand that the Christ Child is the greatest gift of all."

Quenton chuckled, lifted her chin, and kissed her. "Yes, we received the best gift of all this Christmas. And, by the way—Merry Christmas, Grandma."

Golden Keyes Parsons authored eleven books, including a slew of historical novels as well as two non-fiction works. She and her husband, Blaine, retired from the pastorate and moved to Waco, Texas. Golden is survived by her husband of 55 years, her three children, and eight grandchildren.

Learn more about her books and ministry at
www.GoldenKeyesParsons.com

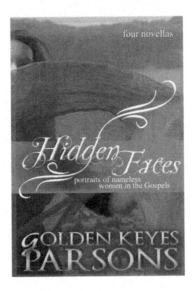

Four novellas based on the lives of the unnamed women in the Gospels, including:

Trapped: *The Adulturous Woman*

Alone: *The Woman at the Well*

Broken: *The Woman Who Anointed Jesus' Feet*

Hopeless: *The Woman with the Issue of Blood*

CPSIA information can be obtained
at www.ICGtesting.com
Printed in the USA
BVOW03s0457061117
499644BV00001BA/42/P